Always Faithful and True

Always Faithful and True

"In danger I called on the Lord; the Lord answered me and set me free. Psalm 118:5"

By
Janet DiFabio

Starwolf Communications LLC, New Jersey

Always Faithful and True
©copyright 2011, 2015, 2019 Janet DiFabio
Third Edition. ©copyright 2022 Janet DiFabio

All Scripture quotations are taken from The New American Bible. NAB ©copyright 1987 World Bible Publishers, Inc. All Rights Reserved.

Cover and interior design by Janet Kath. Licensed images used with permission from DepositPhotos.com. Fonts and images used in this fiction are used with permission from Microsoft.

ISBN: 978-0-578-45394-1
Library of Congress Control Number: 2019932100

Published by Starwolf Communications, LLC
Ingram Spark & KDP Distribution

Dedication

For my children:

"Everything is possible to one who has faith."
Mark 9:23

Acknowledgements

To my loving and caring husband Mike, my heartfelt thanks for your patience while I worked endlessly on these revisions. Your encouragement when I became frustrated is much appreciated.

To my two teenage daughters, the countless times you entertained your younger siblings when I was in writing mode will not be forgotten. Also, the extra help you gave doing household chores made my day. Thank you.

To my little ones, thank you for getting along so well and sharing your toys with each other.

Special thanks to my critique partner and friend, Monica, for editing, revising, and reading my manuscript more times than any one person should have to. There are no words to express my gratitude for your hard work and valuable time.

To my cousin, Officer Christopher, thank you for educating me on criminal law.

To all my colleagues at DTS, thank you for inspiring me to pursue my endeavor to write.

To my readers, I appreciate all your honest feedback. I value your opinions and your comments. Thank you.

Most of all, thank you, Almighty God, for your strength, guidance, and infinite love.

Chapter 1

What if? The question swirled in Gianna's head. What if today's weather was twenty degrees cooler and less humid?

She sat apprehensively in her white cap and gown wedged between two classmates in the sweltering heat. She was sure the city smog added to her discomfort, but she wasn't going to let a little stickiness in the air spoil this joyous occasion in May. For at last, she was graduating with honors from a prestigious New York university.

"Gianna Rose Stefano!"

Loud and clear, her name echoed through the speakers that surrounded the football field.

Her heart raced. She grabbed her classmate's arm and exchanged jubilant smiles, then eagerly bounced to her feet. She carefully walked across the stage to accept her degree. When she sat back down, a serene sensation came over her as she thought about her achievement.

She finally had her Master's in Education. Her state certification was all behind her now, and she was officially a teacher. This was her chance to show her parents that she was responsible and independent.

When the ceremony concluded, she actively searched the crowd to reunite with her parents. *Oh, being five-feet-three isn't going to cut it if I want to find Mom and Dad anytime soon.* She had to blame both her parents for being short. Her father was only five-feet-seven, and her mother was just a smidge taller than her, standing five-feet-four.

After she squeezed through mobs of sweaty people, she spotted them. "Mom! Dad!" she hollered. She welcomed her parents with open arms.

"Ah, there's my bella ragazza!" Dad said. He enveloped her in his massive arms and gave her a kiss. "Congrats!"

She smiled at the thought of her father still calling her *bella ragazza*, which meant *beautiful girl* in Italian. He had given her that nickname the day she was born.

"Ciao, Daddy. You look well."

Gianna took a good long look at her father. His deep brown hair seemed a little grayer since she saw him last. He was only fifty-two but was still just as handsome as ever, and the gray in his hair gave him a more distinguished look. He had such a gentle smile for a hardworking, robust man. She could tell by his strong embrace that he was still putting in long hours on his 100-acre cattle ranch in Sheridan, Montana.

"Congratulations, honey! We're so proud of you," Mom said. Her brown eyes welled up with tears of joy.

"We missed you so much and can't wait to move you back home. Your room is still waiting for you."

Gianna could hear in her mother's voice *just* how much she was missed. Before she left for college, she and her mother did everything together from cooking to sewing to shopping. She shared her deepest secrets, her biggest dreams, and her darkest fears with her mother.

However, since Gianna had been away at college, her mother was left to contend with her father and her four brothers. The thought of her having to manage a house of five needy males made Gianna want to cringe, but it was obvious that she handled the task well. She looked incredible for just turning fifty. There wasn't even a hint of gray in her natural golden-brown hair. She still had it cut in a tousled bob, which framed her petite face, just as she wore it six years ago when Gianna left for college.

"I missed you both very much!" Gianna said. She really wanted to say that she couldn't wait to come back home for the summer, but she decided against it.

She did miss her family very much but having been raised Roman Catholic in a large Italian family had its challenges. She was the second oldest of five children, and she was the only girl. Although she was protected and loved, she felt suffocated. Everyone always knew her business.

Her parents were loving, but strict, especially with her. However, she could talk to them about anything. If she was honest, her parents were fair. With that in mind, she needed to find a proper time to share her great news with them. She had landed the perfect teaching position in New York City.

"Bella, we'd like to take you to supper. Are you hungry?" Dad asked.

"I'm starved. Hey, I know of a family-style Italian restaurant in the Theatre District that's supposed to be good."

"What family-style? What restaurant knows about Italian family-style cooking?" Dad replied haughtily.

Gianna's mother quickly chimed in. "That would be fine, honey." She elbowed her husband in his side. "And, Gianna, you can show us around this fine city."

"What is she, our tour guide?" he groused.

Gianna recognized the bitter tone in her father's voice. He disliked city life ever since his parents immigrated from Italy to Jersey City. Although he was only seven at the time, he didn't adjust well to the new scenery, the people, and the English language.

"Daddy, I promise you'll have a wonderful time, but first, let me get out of this cap and gown before I roast."

Gianna and her parents grabbed a cab and headed to the hotel where they were staying for the weekend. They freshened up, went out to dinner, and then explored the Big Apple. She gushed while showing them Times Square, Rockefeller Center, and the Empire State Building.

The next morning after breakfast, Gianna and her parents returned to her college dorm to gather up the rest of her belongings and to officially checkout.

She examined the emptied room. *Wow, this is it. No more dorm life.* She sat down on her stripped bed and drifted into deep thought. *Boy, life is about to change again.* As an honor student, she was privileged to have her own private room. Now, she'd have to go back home to a full, crazy house.

"Boy, it's going to be weird moving back home again after living away for six years."

Gianna's mom laughed gently. "It's not like you haven't been home in between semesters." She sat down beside her. "Your room is just like you left it."

"I'm sure, Mom, but here I didn't have Matt bossing me around, Mark teasing me, and John and Luke pestering me all the time. I had my own dorm room. I never had a roommate and didn't have to share a bathroom with brothers or anyone else."

"Is that *all?*" Mom asked, trying not to laugh.

Gianna sighed. "Well, no. I'm not exactly a little girl anymore. I can take care of myself now. Besides, I like my privacy." She had this unpleasant taste in her mouth just thinking about losing her independence.

"You'll always be our little girl." Mom put her arm around her. "I know it will be an adjustment for you to live with a big family again, but it'll be ok. Mark will be starting college in September, and in a short six months, Matthew will be married. You know honey, you're not the only one who grew up," she said, wiping away a tear.

"Your mother's right, bella. Stop your fretting. I'll tell you one thing; it's a lot quieter in Montana than in this *crazy* city!" Dad grumbled.

"I suppose." Gianna raised her finger to her lips. *Maybe going home for just the summer will be alright.* Her spirit brightened. She leaped off the bed and said, "Ok, let's go."

Gianna's father picked up an overstuffed suitcase and held the door ajar. Her mother grabbed the laptop and a duffle bag.

"Are you *sure* you have everything, bella?"

"Yes, Daddy," she sighed. "Yesterday, I shipped the majority of my stuff home."

Before she closed the door, she glanced back at her dorm room once more. She wiped her tears. *I'm off to a new beginning.*

Chapter 2

The following morning, the weather was miserably cold and wet. The city smelled of fumes, opened drains, and hot, stale pretzels.

While Gianna waited in the hotel lobby, she noticed her mother staring out the window at the stream of black bubbles that moved swiftly down the street. Meanwhile, her father started to venture out of the lobby into the pouring rain to fight the umbrellas that filled the bustling street.

"Daddy, what're you doing?" She reached for his shoulder to stop him from going outside.

"I'm going to get the taxi for us to go to the airport."

"Daddy let me do this. You will pay too much. I will get us there, trust me," she insisted. She stepped outside the hotel and expertly hailed a cab, loaded their suitcases, and ordered the driver to Penn Station.

"Penn Station? We're going to the airport, not taking a train," he bristled.

"Daddy! We will take the train to the airport. It's faster, easier, and cheaper."

Gianna's father opened his mouth, his face stunned by his outspoken daughter. Gianna's mother elbowed him and shook her head. Once in the taxi, her father quietly stared out the window into the polluted haze.

Within fifty-five minutes, Gianna and her parents arrived at Newark Liberty International Airport.

As Gianna schlepped through the chaotic airport, she felt like a drenched rat in a maze. Flights were delayed due to severe thunderstorms. She hated feeling stranded in a noisy, crowded airport, and being painstakingly bored to boot. It was unnerving that her father was unusually quiet. After two hours, they were able to board the plane for the five-hour flight home to Sheridan, Montana.

Aboard the plane, Gianna and her parents settled in their seats, held one another's hands, and softly prayed the Lord's Prayer. Nestled between both of her parents, she tried to unwind for the long flight. She was almost asleep when her father grumbled under his breath.

"Glad I'm leaving this stinking city for good. I'll never come back. I miss my cattle and the fresh mountain air."

"What'd you say, Daddy?" She lifted her head and rubbed her sleepy eyes.

"I'm thrilled that you finally graduated, and you'll be out of that pollution-filled city and back home."

Gianna stared at the floor. With reluctance, she mumbled, "I guess I should've told you and Mom sooner. I accepted a job offer teaching in Manhattan. I'll be flying back to New York in August to get settled in."

She squinted as she peered up at her father. She noticed his face turned pale, and his eyes widened with concern. For a moment he didn't say a word, but then he thundered, "Gianna, you did what?"

Mom, who was quietly reciting a novena, looked up at her and asked, "Are you saying you took the job without our approval?"

Gianna stared at her feet. *Oh, boy. I really did it now.* Quickly and assertively, she kept her position. "Mom! Dad! I'm twenty-four years old. I worked hard to get this degree, and I need to work. You should be proud of me, not disappointed."

"We are proud of you, bella," Dad said.

"This is the school I did my student teaching in. They liked my style, especially how I interacted with the kids. This is a fantastic opportunity for me. Besides, it's hard to get the first teaching job."

"Well, I don't like it. You're supposed to come home and teach. You'll be all alone and away from your family." Her father looked at her with a lack of understanding in his eyes.

"You didn't seem too concerned the last six years," she snapped.

"That was, uh, different." Gianna's father cleared his throat. "You lived in a secure dorm, and it was only because of your scholarship offer at the university that you went to New York. It wasn't supposed to be permanent," he replied irritably.

She threw her head back against the plane seat and responded sharply, "I understand that, but I can do this. I need to do this. You can't run my life! Besides, I already accepted the position."

Gianna's father's expression was one of pained tolerance. "We'll continue this discussion at home," he said, calmly.

Mom sighed then stared out the plane window.

Gianna knew the bickering broke her mother's heart, but she couldn't let the conversation rest. She just couldn't understand why her parents objected to her moving.

Still boiling inside, Gianna snapped, "Daddy, just because *you* want to live home on the range, doesn't mean I want to!"

"That's enough, Gianna!" Mom scolded.

Gianna lowered her head and kept quiet for the rest of the flight. She regretted her comment about *living home on the range.* She knew how much the cattle ranch meant to him, and she knew he was hurting inside. She recalled his story of how he ventured from New Jersey to Montana. He had told her that he wanted more than just asphalt, concrete sidewalks, and tall buildings. He wanted the picturesque views of the mountains, green landscapes, and blue skies that reminded him of the little village of Monteferrante, Italy, where he lived as a young boy.

When Gianna's father was eighteen, he convinced his parents to move to Montana where he promised to give them a better life in their old age. On the outskirts of Sheridan, he built a small cattle ranch on a measly fifty acres. When he met and married Gianna's mother, his parents moved into a cottage nearby. Through the years,

Gianna's father bought more acreage and expanded his ranch to what it was today.

All her father ever wanted was for the family to stay together. *Now I ruined it. I upset the applecart. As soon as I get home, I'm declining the job.* She hated to see her parents, especially her father, so angry.

The plane landed. Gianna and her parents exited the gate and headed for baggage.

"Now to find Matt and Jessica," Dad said.

"I see them!" Gianna sprinted ahead of her parents. Her heart was bubbling with happiness. Just the sight of her brother and Jessica made her realize how much she missed her family.

"Gianna, welcome home," Matthew said. He grabbed her with his strong arms and twirled her around.

"So good to be home, bro."

Matthew was her older brother. At the age of twenty-nine, he still lived at home. A diesel mechanic by trade, he repaired the farm machinery on their father's ranch.

Gianna greeted Jessica with a hug. "I missed you."

Jessica Duncan, Matthew's fiancée, was her best friend since kindergarten. Jessica just graduated from college with a degree in social work.

Gianna stepped back and took a good look at the happy couple. She never realized how tiny Jessica was compared to her brother.

"Congratulations, Gianna! I'm so glad you're home," Jessica said, grabbing her hands. "You'll have to tell me all about your plans. We have so much wedding stuff to do over the summer. I'll fill you in on the details later."

"Perfect! I'm not going anywhere, at least not yet. Hey, I love your haircut," Gianna said, admiring Jessica's new hairstyle. Her strawberry blonde hair accentuated her beautiful green eyes.

Matthew grabbed an armful of luggage. "C'mon, you two can catch up on the way home."

Gianna shook her head. *Bossy Matt. Always in a rush and wanting to be in control.* "Cool your boots, Matt. We're going."

When Matthew pulled the burgundy Chevy Suburban off the highway onto a country road, Gianna was awestruck by the beautiful view that she had left behind. She'd forgotten how lush the green grass was, how blue the sky was, and how the mountains completed the backdrop. It was amazing how the evergreens looked on the mountain. They were more magnificent than the skyscrapers in the city.

The very moment they arrived home, she climbed out of the SUV, took a deep breath of the crisp mountain air, and gazed at the huge, center-hall colonial home. It had new beige vinyl siding, a big, wrap-around porch with a wooden glider swing.

As she climbed the porch steps, tears filled her eyes. *I really do miss home.* All her childhood memories were there.

Suddenly, she was jarred out of her thoughts when the front storm door flung open, and her younger brother Mark hugged her hard.

"Welcome home, sis!"

"Slow down, little brother!" She dropped her bag and returned the hug. "It's so good to see you too, Mark."

At eighteen, Mark was tall, stocky, and handsome. Although he was a few inches shorter, Mark was a mirror image of Matthew. Casual acquaintances had mistaken them for twins.

While Gianna took in the peaceful scenery, Luke and John, the twins, barreled through the front door. *Oh, well! So much for the peace and quiet.*

"Sis! How are you?" they asked simultaneously.

"Good, really good," she said.

Luke and John, thirteen years old, were intelligent but mischievous. They served as altar servers at their church. It was their mother's idea to keep them out of trouble. Except for sporting longer hair, Luke and John looked just like their big brothers. At five-feet-five, and still growing, both twins were taller than she was.

"You two haven't changed a bit," she said.

"Neither have you. You're still annoying," John said.

"Yeah, thanks for the complement, sis," Luke said.

Gianna rolled her eyes. *Whatever.*

Mark tapped Gianna's shoulder. "Never mind them. Supper's ready."

"What's for supper?" Mom asked with a look of horror painted on her face.

"I know that look, Mom. Everything's cool. We ordered a bunch of pizzas, so c'mon inside," Mark said, displaying his goofy grin.

Gianna and her family gathered around the large dining room table. As they do at every meal, they bowed their heads and said the blessing.

She enjoyed listening to all the stories she missed while she was away. She couldn't keep from laughing. The joy warmed her heart, and her cold resentment toward her father vanished.

Her father's mood seemed suddenly buoyant as well, as if their argument on the plane had never happened, but then the question hit.

"Gianna, what're your future plans?" Jessica asked.

Gianna sucked in her lower lip, then took in a deep breath. "I, uh, got a job...teaching in Manhattan."

Immediately, all eyes fixated on her, and the room went silent. *Awkward. Someone, please say something. Like congratulations! Isn't anyone happy for me?*

Finally, Gianna's father spoke. There was a thawing in his tone. "Yes, Jessica. Bella was offered a teaching job in the city. She proved herself to them and they realized what they would lose if she declined. I am proud of her success." He looked at Gianna with a smile of approval.

Gianna merely stared, surprised at his response. She glanced at her mother, and they exchanged puzzled looks.

"May I be excused from the table?" Gianna asked, while trying to suppress a yawn. "It's been a really long day and I'm exhausted."

"It has been an eventful day, honey," Mom replied. "Get some sleep, and we'll see you in the morning."

Dazed, Gianna slowly climbed the staircase to her bedroom. She couldn't believe her father's change of heart. He supported her decision to move, and he didn't try to persuade anyone to convince her to stay.

At the top of the stairs, Gianna's bedroom was the first door on the left. Fortunately, for her, being the only girl, she didn't have to share it with anyone. Matthew, on the other hand, had to share a room with Mark, and the twins shared another room. But sadly, she had to share a bathroom with them, and that was frustrating. Her parents were fortunate to have their own master suite just down the hall from hers.

There was one more bedroom in the house—on the first floor. It was a guest suite with its own private bath. Gianna had always wanted it for herself, but her mother insisted it remain a guestroom just in case her grandparents needed to move in. But Gianna couldn't understand why. Both sets of her grandparents were independent, even in their advanced age.

As she opened the door to her room, the scent of fresh cut flowers drew her in. She flipped on the light and looked around her powder blue room. A vase holding yellow spray roses, purple iris, and yellow Gerbera daisies adorned her dresser. Tied to the vase were two Mylar balloons that read *Welcome Home and Congratulations.*

Tears blurred her eyes as she tried to scope out the rest of her room. She was pleased that her mother kept the room clean and organized just like the day she had left it. Her bed looked so inviting, blanketed neatly in the floral quilt that her grandmother had made her for Christmas.

When she sat on her bed, a sense of tranquility came over her. *It'll be fun spending the summer at home.*

After a warm, relaxing shower, Gianna changed into her nightshirt and climbed into bed. She lay there drowsy, under her crisp, clean sheets. Her mind flashed exciting thoughts about her future, but at once, sleep consumed her.

Chapter 3

The delicious aroma of bacon and eggs frying in the kitchen awakened Gianna. *Mmm, I've missed Mom's cooking.* She rubbed the sleep out of her eyes and stretched her arms. She had a long, restful night. No question about it, she was home.

She remained in bed a moment longer, appreciating the cool spring breeze that blew through her window and the beautiful song that the birds chirped. *Thank you, Lord, for all your blessings.*

Gianna meandered downstairs and greeted her mother in the kitchen. "Good morning, Mom," she said with a hug.

"It sure is, honey."

Gianna's mother placed a plate of sunny side up eggs and bacon on the counter for her.

"Aw, thank you, Mom," Gianna said, hopping up on the counter stool. "Where's Daddy this morning?"

"In the barn office. He has paperwork to catch up on," Mom said, sitting beside her with a fresh cup of coffee.

"I wanted to ask you and Daddy if I could work on the ranch this summer to earn some money for my new apartment."

"I'm sure we can work something out. Your father's newly hired help, Brody, had knee surgery and won't be working at all this summer." But suddenly, Mom's tone changed. "On second thought, I rather you didn't. Herding, baling, and stacking hay is rough work."

Gianna rolled her eyes. "Oh, please. I can handle it. Besides, it's not like I don't know how to ride a horse."

Mom shook her head. "There's plenty of office work you can do."

"Ok, I'll talk to Daddy later," Gianna said with eagerness. "Right now, I'm going out with Jessica to discuss her wedding plans.

After a catch-up day out with Jessica, Gianna spoke with her father about working for the family business during the summer.

"I could sure use the help, bella," Dad said, tossing a notebook on his desk. "Maybe I can even convince you to stay."

Gianna looked at the stack of papers scattered on his desk and laughed. "Only if the pay is good."

Dad shook his head. "Go on, get out of here. Go help your mother with supper."

Gianna kissed her father. "Thanks, Daddy." As she walked out the door, she turned and said, "Don't worry, I'll make you proud."

"I'm already proud, bella," he said.

That evening, Gianna retreated to the backyard firepit with her father, relaxing and admiring all the stars in the big, endless sky, rekindling their special father-daughter time together.

"See what you're going to miss when you move back to New York, bella?"

Gianna sighed. "Yes, Daddy. I'm going to miss *you*, too." She knew he was really referring to their close relationship and not the big, open sky. "Daddy, I'm going to be fine," she reassured him. "I *know* what I'm doing."

"What? You don't even have a place to live," he grumbled. He opened his hands, palms up. "Where're you gonna' go?"

"Daddy, I'll get a hotel room until I find an apartment. It'll only be a week or two. Once I get settled, Mom will send the rest of my stuff which I'll pack before I leave." She touched his forearm. "Don't worry. I'll have a whole month to get it together before I start teaching."

"Don't a' worry! You kids think you know everything," he grumbled.

Chapter 4

The months flew by, and July was nearing an end. While Gianna was in her bedroom packing, a voice inside her head contemplated her decision to move. *It's nice being home. Maybe Daddy's right. Maybe moving to New York isn't such a hot idea. College life was easy, but now it'll be real life in the city, and with real life, comes financial obligations. Maybe I should've consulted Mom and Dad first before accepting the teaching job. Maybe if I tried, I could have found a job here in Sheridan.* She sighed. *Too many what ifs.*

She recalled her student teaching experience and how rewarding it was. Teaching was her dream, and the reality of it coming true put a smile back on her face. She nodded. *Moving is the right thing to do.*

With only a week left, Gianna wanted to make the most out of the time she had left in Montana. Today wasn't an ordinary summer day in Sheridan. The temperature was unusually warm and humid. It was ninety degrees, and only eleven o'clock in the morning. She was going swimming.

She dug through her dresser drawer and pulled out a stylish, two-piece swimsuit that still had the tags on it. She held it up against herself. Loving the artic blue color, she decided to give it a go.

She changed into the suit and stood in front of the mirror scrutinizing herself. She hated the low-cut plunge neckline because it revealed what she didn't have. However, she liked the board shorts because they covered her wide hips. She sighed. *It'll have to do.* Before heading outside, she grabbed a cover-up wrap.

Gianna had her nose buried in a book when the sound of country music grew louder. *Who in the world is in the driveway?* She cracked open the gate to the shadowbox fence and saw a late model, white pick-up truck parking near the house.

An attractive, young man with thick, chestnut brown hair stepped out of the truck. He stood six feet tall in his muscular, well-proportioned body. He was homegrown country, wearing a pair of dark, denim jeans with holes in the knees, and black cowboy boots. He wore a tight, white tank top that revealed his muscular biceps and broad chest.

The profile of his face was strong and rigid. He had long sideburns, and the shadow of his manicured beard made him even more alluring. When he turned, she noticed his ruggedly, handsome face, which looked undeniably familiar to her.

The instant he put on his sunglasses and black cowboy hat; she became weak at the knees. Although she had seen many men in the past wear a cowboy hat and sunglasses, she never noticed anyone to this detail before. There was *something* about the way he adjusted that hat just so, and *something* about those dark shades that softened his tough-guy face that jostled her hormones.

Caught up in admiration, she was startled by her brother Matthew's husky voice as it grew nearer. To avoid being caught eavesdropping, she quickly turned away from the gate. She rushed back to her chaise lounge and grabbed her wrap. She didn't want that hunk to see her in her too-revealing swimsuit.

Her heart pounded, and she had butterflies in the pit of her stomach. *Who is that?* She opened her book and tried to read, but she couldn't concentrate. Blasted with a heat rush, she fanned herself with her book instead of cooling off in the pool in fear of being noticed. As she sat quietly in her chair, she tried to listen to their conversation but couldn't hear it clearly.

When the voices faded into the distance, she dashed back to the gate again. She watched her brother and the mysterious man walk up the path to the barn. When she could no longer see them or hear their muffled voices, she was disappointed and frustrated at the emptiness she felt inside. She wanted to meet that man.

Chapter 5

The mysterious man and Matthew trekked to the barn to escape the blazing sun, dusty air, and swarming gnats. As they neared the entrance, a gentle breeze pointed out the grazing cows in the pasture. Inside the barn, Mr. Stefano worked hard mucking stalls.

Mr. Stefano peered up as he tossed a pile of soiled hay into the wheelbarrow. "Hey, *Doctor Dan Christiansen!*" He set down his metal pitchfork, pulled off his work gloves, and gave Dan a firm handshake. "Good to see you."

"Likewise, sir," Dan said.

"You showed up at the right time; gives me an excuse to take a break," Mr. Stefano said, wiping the sweat off his face with his sleeve.

"You shouldn't need me to give you an excuse to rest. A hardworking man is entitled to it," Dan replied.

Matthew grabbed a couple bottles of water out of an ice chest and handed one to each of his father and Dan. The three men parked themselves on a stack of fresh hay bales and chatted casually.

Mr. Stefano guzzled his water. "Ah, ice cold." He looked up at Dan and asked, "So, how long are you visiting Doc Joe and Evelyn?"

Dan leaned back on the hay bale and sipped his water contently. "Been here two weeks already. I'm flying back to New York on Monday."

"New York?" Mr. Stefano questioned. His face split into a wide grin. "Oh, that's right. Matt said you were living in New York now."

"Yes, sir. Last year, I finished my residency. Now I'm working in a medical practice on the upper west side of Manhattan."

"Didn't Doc Kendall ask you to come back home and join his practice?"

Dan nodded. "He did, but I felt that I would get more experience in the city."

Mr. Stefano pried, "You must be lonely without your folks living 'round you?"

"Nah, I try not to think about it." But there was a touch of sadness in his heart. "I keep myself busy at the hospital."

"Joe and Evelyn talk about you *all* the time. They were hoping you'd move back home after college," Mr. Stefano said.

Dan sighed. "I know. I miss them, too. But this is what I need to do right now."

Dan stared at the strands of hay that were scattered on the ground, allowing his mind to wander into the past.

Dr. Joseph and Evelyn Kendall were his godparents and raised him after his parents had died. They took care of him as if he were their own. He was so grateful for their love and support through the years.

When Dan snapped out of his past, he glanced up at Matthew. "Well, enough talk about me. Give me the scoop on your wedding plans. What are my best man duties?"

Matthew dug into his back pocket, pulled out his wallet, and handed him a business card. "Here, this is the tuxedo shop you can go to in New York. They'll measure you, and the rest will be handled out here."

"Sounds simple enough. Thanks, bud," Dan said, slipping the card into his jean pocket.

"Oh! There's one more thing. For my bachelor party, I want to fly to New York, so we can bar hop all night and check out the city chicks," Matthew said with a huge grin on his face.

"Hey, don't forget your old man!" With a quirky smile, Mr. Stefano flung his empty water bottle at Matthew.

Dan laughed at the idea. "Let me know when, and I'll get right on it."

Dan wasn't much for the bar scene. If Matt wanted to fly out to New York for his bachelor party, he figured scoring box tickets to a baseball game or football game would be a hit. Besides, Matthew's underaged brothers were ushers in the wedding and should be included in the plan.

Dan stood up and put on his cowboy hat. "Well, I should be going."

"It was good seeing you again, Dan," Mr. Stefano said. He hopped off the hay bale and shook his hand. "Hey, how 'bout you stay for supper? It'd be like old times."

"I'd love to, sir, but I'd best be getting back. Joe and Evelyn have a special supper waiting for me." As he started toward the barn door, he looked back and hollered, "Hey, thanks anyway."

Dan and Matthew set off down the path toward the driveway. They talked a while longer alongside his pick-up truck.

Dan stared at the ground. "Hey, uh, Matt," he stuttered. "I meant to ask you...uh, how's your sister, Gianna?" He grabbed his bandana off the front seat and wiped the beads of sweat off his forehead. "I haven't seen her since I left for college."

Matthew nodded with assurance. "Gianna's good, really good. She just graduated in May with her Masters. In fact, she's leaving us Monday and moving to New York City to teach middle school."

Dan raised his eyebrows in surprise. "Wow, New York, what a small world." He climbed into his truck and pulled on his seatbelt. He rubbed his chin and mumbled, "Eleven years ago, shoot, Gianna was just a kid then." He glanced at Matthew. "That makes her...twenty—"

"Four," Matthew responded.

Dan had known Gianna since the day she was born. Having been best friends with Matthew, he virtually lived at their house. He recalled how she used to follow him around like a lost puppy. She was a cute kid, but five years apart was a significant difference.

He scratched his beard nervously. "Doc Kendall's trying to get me to go to the church dance this Friday. Think your sister's going?"

"Yeah, she's going." Matthew smirked. "The whole family's going, and I'm bringing Jessica."

"Ok then, thanks." Dan smiled approvingly, then shifted the truck into reverse and waved goodbye.

ೞ

That evening, Gianna and her mother were preparing supper in the kitchen when Matthew strolled in. He grabbed a soda out of the refrigerator then walked over to the stove and lifted the lid off the pot.

"Mom, what's for supper?" he asked.

"Spaghetti and meatballs," Mom replied.

Gianna turned away from the counter and casually asked, "Hey, Matt, who was that guy you were talking to this afternoon in the driveway?" She folded her arms across her chest and waited impatiently for his answer.

"Dan Christiansen. Why?"

Immediately, Gianna's cheeks burned. She bit her lip, then bashfully lowered her head, and stared at the floor. "Wow, I haven't seen Danny since I was thirteen and he was, um—"

29

"Eighteen," Matt said, smirking. "Dan was asking about you. He wanted to know if you're going to the dance on Friday."

"What? Are you serious?"

"Yeah, I'm serious," he said.

Gianna shook her head. "No, you're playing with me." Unexpected warmth surged through her body. "I've always had a crush on him!" She slapped her hand over her mouth.

"Gianna!" Mom's voice rose in surprise.

"What, Mom? What's the big deal? I'm twenty-four and he's twenty-nine. I'm not a kid anymore."

She grabbed the silverware out of the drawer and left the kitchen to avoid further interrogation.

Mom followed her into the dining room. "Honey, please calm down," she said, placing her hand on Gianna's shoulder.

Gianna sensed a lecture coming on. She continued to set the table hoping to avoid her mother's speech, but she hovered over her like a vulture.

"It's been years since you've known Daniel. I'm sure he's not who you remembered him to be. People change, just as you have."

"I know that, Mom." *My stars! Why do you have to be so prim and proper?*

"Ok, honey. I just don't want to see you hurt. Now, come on. It's time to eat."

After Gianna's father gave the blessing, he served the meal. "You'll never guess who stopped by for a visit today," Dad said with enthusiasm.

"Oh? Who?" Mom said casually.

"*Doctor* Daniel Christiansen," he said proudly, then added, "I haven't seen him in years. He looked all grown-up and respectable."

Gianna nearly choked on her meatball. She turned toward Matthew and glared at him. "Doctor? You didn't mention he was a doctor."

"You didn't ask," Matthew replied.

"How could that be?" she asked. "He's friends with you, and you're no Einstein by any means!"

Luke cackled at Gianna's remark. "I guess Matt also forgot to mention that he lives in New York."

A rush of excitement flowed through her and settled into her cheeks. She quickly turned away to hide her embarrassment.

"Ok, Luke that's enough!" Mom scolded.

"What's this about?" Dad asked.

"Gianna's sweet on Dan," John snickered.

Gianna felt the sweat beading on her forehead. This was not a topic she wanted to have with her parents or with her two juvenile brothers.

Mom set her fork down and gave both Luke and John a stern look. "Enough of the childish behavior, boys. Gianna, you're excused from the table."

Gianna placed her cloth napkin on the table and left the dining room. She parked herself on the couch in the family room to cool off. *I can't believe those two! Oh, yes, I can. They are the two reasons I can't wait to move.*

Still within earshot of the kitchen and dining room, she listened while her parents lectured the twins.

"Alright, boys. Give it a rest," Dad said. "So, what if your sister likes Dan? It's none of your business. I would be pleased to have him as my future son-in-law."

Gianna's mouth fell open. *Daddy didn't just say that. Or did he?*

"Vincenzo, aren't you a bit premature talking about marriage? I just got through telling *your* daughter that he's not the same kid that we knew years ago."

"Arianna, you're right in *one* aspect. He's not a kid. Dan's a responsible, respectable, young man. If *my* daughter falls in love with him, it would be a blessing."

Gianna's hands trembled. *Did Daddy drink too much vino tonight?*

"Really, Vinnie. We don't know a thing about this respectable, responsible man, as you call him. Besides, no one says he likes her."

"Of course, he'll like her. She's *my* daughter. Arianna, doesn't it seem coincidental that *our* daughter is moving to New York and here, a close friend resurfaces, who also happens to live in New York?"

Gianna's stomach fluttered. *Daddy has a point. Could there be another reason to be in New York besides a career?* She got off the couch and crept toward the kitchen doorway to eavesdrop some more.

"Arianna, I admit I got a little excited on the plane, but Gianna is a bright, responsible, young lady," he argued. "And...sometimes a little stubborn, too."

"Just like you," her mom threw in.

Gianna heard Mom clearing the dishes from the dining room table and followed the sound of her footsteps into the kitchen. Quickly, she tiptoed back to the couch, not wanting to be caught listening.

"Vinnie, aren't you forgetting? Gianna is a dreamer, and when driven by ambition, she tends to think with her heart and not her head."

The conversation was getting interesting. Gianna tucked her hair behind her ears hoping to hear more. Her father was also in the kitchen, and his voice was loud and clear.

"Stop worrying, Arianna. Have faith," he urged. "I'm going outside on the porch for some fresh air."

Gianna went upstairs to her room and tunneled through the bottom of her closet, in search of her childhood photo albums. She scooped up the albums and carried them to her bed. As she flipped the pages, she was on memory lane. *Danny practically lived here. Our families did everything together: swimming, hiking, fishing, camping, and horseback riding.*

How did we let all these years go by without staying connected? Well, Matthew kept in touch with him. He's his best friend and his best man. Oh, my goodness! I'm Jessica's maid-of- honor. We'll be partners. How did I miss that minor detail?

Hastily, Gianna jumped off her bed, put away her memories, and logged onto the Internet. She wanted to find the perfect dress for the church dance and only had four days to find one. If Danny was really going to be there, she needed to make sure she didn't look like the tomboy she once was.

The next day, Gianna and Jessica set out on a mission to find the perfect dress for the dance. After two department stores and several dress shops later, Gianna was frustrated.

"Nothing fits right."

"Here, try this on," Jessica insisted. She handed her a periwinkle, bias-cut, chiffon dress.

Gianna tried on the dress and studied herself in the mirror. "I'm not sure about this."

"Why? You look beautiful."

"Don't you think it's...overkill?"

"No, it's perfect on you. Few people can pull off a style like that. You have the right curves in the right places," Jessica said.

Gianna twirled around, checked out her backside, and then her side view. Although she hated being dressed up, she admitted the dress complimented her figure. It was clingy in the right places but not too revealing. She pulled her hair up and tried to figure out how to style it.

She sat down on the bench and blew out her cheeks. "I don't know, Jess. Maybe I should just skip the dance."

"Why?" Jessica audaciously asked.

"Because." Gianna looked away. She'd been out from under her father's wing for six years and turned down any love interest that came her way. She glanced at Jessica, and in a weakened voice, said, "I have no experience dating."

Jessica rolled her eyes. "You crack me up. You've got to be the most unpretentious girl I know."

"Well, I focused all my time on my college studies."

"Yeah, and I'm sure Dan's just the party animal," Jessica said sarcastically. "Think about it. He put himself through med school. Do you really think he's had any time for dating?"

Gianna shrugged her shoulders then lowered her eyes. "You're lucky. You found your one true love. I wish I were getting married."

"Just wait, some lucky man will come into your life when the time is right," Jessica said with extreme optimism. "Trust me on this. Buy the dress!"

Gianna acquiesced and bought the dress. She knew she could always rely on Jessica's honesty and would never steer her wrong.

On the way home, she daydreamed about her big day. She smiled at the possibility of someday shopping for a wedding gown. She hoped Jessica would be as patient then as she was now.

Chapter 6

Friday was finally here, and it was the day of the church dance. Jessica persuaded Gianna to have a day of pampering at the health spa. When Gianna entered the salon, she became increasingly uneasy about getting a massage.

"I can't believe I let you talk me into this."

Jessica placed her hand on Gianna's shoulder. "C'mon, you deserve it, my treat to you."

Gianna nodded. "Thank you, Jess."

Once Gianna was in her peaceful treatment room, her mood instantly transformed into a relaxed state, but the massage was too calming. Her subconscious thoughts floated to the surface. *Perhaps Matt exaggerated Danny's interest in me. What if Danny doesn't show up at the dance tonight?* Negative thoughts bobbed in her head. *Ok, stop being a pessimist.* She tried to put a positive spin on her feelings, convincing herself that the massage was a well-deserved reward for her achievements.

A few hours later, Gianna was home in her bedroom feeling completely rejuvenated. She had her makeup done, her hair styled, and her nails manicured. All she needed to do now was change into her new dress.

"Gianna, honey. It's five thirty. We need to leave," Mom called from the bottom of the stairs.

"I'm coming."

Gianna quickly slipped on her chiffon dress. She took one last gaze at herself in the mirror. *Oh, I love it!* Her complexion glowed flawlessly. Her modern up-do was simple with just a few loose curls framing her face. She was amazed at how a little self-indulging lifted her spirit. She was thankful that Jessica influenced her.

She stepped into her shoes and grabbed her shawl and purse. Careful not to trip, she held onto the banister and took one step at a time. Her knees trembled as she felt the stares of her family watching her from the foyer.

"Look at my bella ragazza!" her father said, proudly.

"Oh, Daddy," Gianna said, fanning herself. Getting all dolled up was awkward enough; she didn't need him making a fuss. She gave him a hug, then realized her brother wasn't there. She pulled away and asked in a panic, "Where's Matt?"

"He left to pick up Jessica. He'll meet us there."

Butterflies fluttered in her stomach. She was hoping that Matt would have reintroduced her to Danny.

Gianna's mother grabbed her purse. "Mark, do you have your camera?"

"Yeah, Mom."

"Don't worry, Mom," Luke said. "Mark will take plenty of pictures of Gianna and Dan dancing," he snickered.

Mom shot Luke a look of disapproval but didn't reprimand him. She seemed more concerned with staying on schedule. "C'mon, John, let's go," she yelled into the kitchen.

John moseyed into the foyer with a half-eaten sandwich in his hand. With a mouthful, he asked, "Do we really have to go to this dumb ol' dance?"

"Yes, you do."

"Let's get this over with then," he grumbled, then stuffed the rest of his sandwich into his mouth.

Gianna's father pulled the Suburban into the parking lot of the Silver Star Banquet Hall and Restaurant. "This looks nice," he said.

Gianna's mother pointed out the window. "Oh, what a beautiful lake. And there's even a gazebo!" she gushed. "Matthew and Jessica could've had their wedding here."

"Arianna, the place they selected is fine. You pick the place when your daughter gets married," Dad said, wryly.

"Vincenzo, you're rushing things again," Mom replied, sounding annoyed.

Gianna sat in the third row of the SUV with her mouth zipped. She pretended she couldn't hear her parents planning her imaginary wedding. The conversation was hilarious; especially since she wasn't even sure how Danny felt about her.

Once the Stefano family settled in at their table, Gianna's parents excused themselves to the dance floor. As soon as Luke and John found their friends, they vanished. Once Mark saw a familiar face, he disappeared too, leaving her alone.

Gianna tossed her purse on the table and sat down. *Terrific. Now I'm really a nobody.* She watched nervously as other guests arrived. When Matthew and Jessica finally strolled in, she waved her hand anxiously, motioning them to join her. She sprung from her chair and rushed over to her brother.

"Is Danny here?"

"Chill, Gianna!" he said, gesturing her to relax. "He's on his way."

Jessica touched Gianna's forearm. "You look beautiful!"

"Thank you, Jess. You look lovely, too."

Matthew took Jessica's hand and started toward the dance floor. He looked back at Gianna and said, "He'll be here. He said he wanted to check you out before my wedding," he remarked facetiously.

Jessica slapped Matthew in the back of the head. "Stop teasing your sister." She looked back at Gianna and shrugged her shoulders.

As they walked away, Matthew replied as innocently as he could, "What? That's what Dan said."

Gianna sat down again, her back facing the hall entrance. She was annoyed at her brother's rude remark. *Why does he always have to needle me? What in the world does Jessica see in him?*

However, before she could ponder that question, someone tapped her shoulder. She tilted her head back. Dr. and Mrs. Kendall were standing there, holding hands. She always admired how they publicly displayed their affection for one another.

Dr. Kendall and his wife lived in a small cabin just a mile down the road from her father's ranch, which made it convenient for Danny and Matthew to hangout as kids. Since Dr. Kendall was the town's family doctor, everyone knew him.

"Hello, Doctor and Mrs. Kendall. It's so good to see you both."

"Good evening, Gianna. It's nice to see you, too," Dr. Kendall said in his affable voice.

He looked just as she remembered him. For a man in his early sixties, his white hair was just starting to thin.

"May we join you?" Mrs. Kendall asked, in a low, meek voice.

"Sure, please do."

Mrs. Kendall was the sweetest woman Gianna knew, aside from her mother. Mrs. Kendall reminded her of a slightly older version of her, but with short ash blonde hair. Like her mom, Mrs. Kendall was an excellent cook and loved to knit and sew. Gianna was certain that the pretty rose sundress that she was wearing was one of her custom-made designs.

Gianna made small talk with Dr. and Mrs. Kendall. She told them about her plans to move to New York, hoping it would strike up a conversation about Danny.

"Well, best of luck to you, my dear," Dr. Kendall said. "It's a fast-paced life living there in the city. Oh, but you already know that having gone to college there."

Mrs. Kendall chimed in. "Daniel seems happy there."

Gianna's face heated up. "By any chance, did he come here with you tonight?"

"Yes, dear. He's sitting at the bar with your brother Mark," Mrs. Kendall said. With a nod of her head and a gentle smile, she urged her to go to him.

Dr. Kendall nudged his wife and asked her for the next dance. He excused them, and they hastily left the table.

Gianna turned around in her chair and searched the bar for Danny. The moment her eyes found him, her heart began to pound. She studied him intensely. He wore a black western sport coat with leather accents, over a white dress shirt. A black tie, black jeans, and black leather boots completed his attire.

There was no doubt in her mind that he was the hunk in the driveway the other day. As a matter of fact, he was even more handsome tonight. She watched him closely as he carried on a conversation with Mark. *Why can't Mark formally introduce us?* Her nerves trembled. There was no way she was going to approach him by herself, but on the other hand, she didn't want to spend the evening alone at the table either.

C380

Dan caught a glimpse of Gianna. *Whoa! She's hot!* He was dumbfounded that the annoying little girl he used to know turned into a pretty, petite woman with silky, chestnut brown hair and big, beautiful brown eyes. Reminiscing, he remembered her dirty face, saddled on that big American Quarter horse, hair flying, riding as if demons were chasing her. *How could I let the years pass by without staying in touch with her?* The instant his eyes met hers, he knew there was more there than just friendship.

He stood to his feet. "Mark, I'll talk to you later." He grabbed his hat and walked with long strides toward Gianna.

℃℥℃

Gianna jerked her head away from the bar. *Oh, no! Danny caught me eyeing him, and now he's coming my way.* Her legs were like gelatin, but she forced herself to her feet and smiled. For a split second, she froze, but his glowing smile and open arms warmed her instantly. Before she realized it, she was twirling around in his strong embrace.

"Gianna, you look so gorgeous. How are you?"

"I'm doing well, thank you."

He smelled so good of leather and cologne that she didn't want to let go of his muscular body.

"There's a gazebo outside where it's quiet. Do you want to take a walk?" he asked, setting her down.

Unable to say no to his gorgeous blue eyes, she replied, "Sure, I'd love to."

Danny held out his arm and Gianna linked her arm through his. A shiver ran through her, a shiver that never felt so right before. There was something incredibly special about him.

"Can I get you a drink?" he asked, escorting her to the bar.

"Actually, I don't drink," she muttered, then looked away to hide her embarrassment.

"Well, that makes two of us," he said, proudly. "Besides, it's bad for the liver. Four years of medical school taught me something. So, how about a soda?"

"Really?" She laughed. "And here I thought you'd think I was some kind of goodie-two-shoes."

Danny frowned at her comment. "Gianna, we had fun hanging out as kids. If you give me a chance, I'd like to get to know you again."

"I'd like that."

"What's that, us getting to know each other, or a soda?" he asked with a flicker of humor in his voice.

"How about both?"

With a smile of approval, Danny turned and requested two sodas from the bartender.

ᘓᘔ

Dan walked her outside into the crisp, night air so they could talk where it was quiet. They sat down on a bench inside the gazebo. He gazed up at the star-lit sky and said, "It's beautiful out here, quite different from the city. So, I heard you're moving to New York."

"Word gets around fast," she said.

"It does in this small town."

Gianna nodded. "Yes, I was offered a teaching job. I'm leaving Monday."

"Congratulations! Once you're settled, we'll have to meet up," he said, hoping she wouldn't object.

"I'd like that very much."

Gianna's smile was alive and eager, and when she reached for his hand, her soft touch made his heart pound. Dan felt instant chemistry.

"I'm really glad to be here with you tonight," he said.

"So am I."

Lost in his feelings, Dan captured her brown eyes in his. He set down his glass and said, "I don't like to talk about this, but I need you to know something." He swallowed hard, pausing to gather his words.

Gianna nodded, her expression completely serious.

Dan exhaled heavily. "You were too young to remember when my parents died. I was only nine when it happened. They were coming home from celebrating their tenth wedding anniversary when a drunk driver crossed the yellow line."

His heart sunk as he recalled the horrid memory.

"Oh, Danny." Gianna clutched his hand tighter.

He rubbed the tears out of his eyes then dropped his head in grief. As he stared at the gazebo floor, he continued telling her his awful memory.

"Earlier that evening, I remember how excited I was when my parents told me I could stay up until they came home. Dr. Kendall and I were playing checkers when the state trooper knocked on the door." He took a deep breath. "When they told me alcohol was the culprit, I vowed I would never touch the stuff in honor of my parents' lives. It is amazing how one evening can change your life."

Gianna's eyes welled up with tears. "I'm so sorry."

He looked at her through his blurry eyes. "So, I admire you for choosing *not* to drink."

"Danny, I know it must be difficult to talk about, even after all these years. Thank you for trusting me with your feelings."

"I never even told Matt that I don't drink," he said, rubbing the back of his neck. "And I'm supposed to plan his bachelor party." He stood up and leaned against the gazebo railing. He set his eyes on the gushing fountain perched in the lake. "Last Wednesday would've been my parents' thirtieth wedding anniversary."

Cﾃﾟﾃﾟﾂﾞ

Gianna remained seated on the bench. She wanted to give him his space. She knew about the accident from her parents, but she never heard him talk about it before. She couldn't imagine his heartache.

After a few minutes, she lifted herself from the bench and stood beside him, gazing into the evening sky. The summer moon revealed its orangey-red lover's face over the horizon.

"Sure, can't see this in the city," she gasped. Her body flinched as the cool breeze off the lake blew right through her chiffon dress.

"Nope, too many lights." He looked at her and touched her arms. "Brrr! You're freezing. Take my coat."

Before Danny could remove his coat, she drew herself into him. She wound her arms inside his coat and around his back. She rested her head on his chest and looked into his eyes. "I'm warm now."

Danny ran his fingers along her face and lifted her chin to his. His mouth barely brushed her lips when—

"Gianna! There you are," Mark hollered as he climbed the steps of the gazebo.

Gianna quickly stepped away from Danny and folded her arms across her chest. "Perfect timing, Mark," she mumbled.

"We've been looking for you two. The servers are taking dinner orders, and Father Anthony is about to make his opening speech. C'mon," he said, motioning them along.

Gianna held Danny's hand and strolled back inside the banquet hall. *My stars! What a turnout.* She had no idea that so many of her extended church family would be there. Although she preferred to stay outside with Danny, she was thrilled to sit next to him at the dinner table.

"Here are the love birds now," Luke announced, jabbing John in the side.

John let out a ridiculous laugh.

Mom glared at them. "Shush, boys. They'll hear you."

Gianna heated up with embarrassment. Leave it to Luke and John to be so immature. She was certain Danny heard them too, but she tried to play it cool by ignoring her brothers' childish behavior.

Danny pulled out a chair for her, and when she sat down, he pushed it in for her. She caught a glimpse of her parents watching. They smiled, and when she returned the grin, she felt her face blush. She quickly looked away trying to hide her own excitement.

The attention focused on Father Anthony as he approached the podium. Father Anthony, a compact man with mahogany brown hair and a benign appearance, spoke into the microphone.

"Good evening, everyone. I would like to welcome all of you to our annual church social. It's so nice to see so many of our extended family continuing fellowship outside of our parish celebration."

Gianna chuckled inside after hearing his welcoming speech. His introduction had been the same since he joined the parish twelve years ago. He was a respected priest, and his homilies were easy to understand and apply to everyday life. She always enjoyed attending Sunday Mass and really missed his sermons when she was away at college. She was sad that she had not been able to find a church in the city with the same small-town feel.

Father Anthony continued his speech. "Tonight, I'd also like to welcome back two of our parishioners: Miss Gianna Stefano and Doctor Daniel Christiansen."

Father Anthony paused briefly while the guests applauded.

"Gianna has just finished graduate school and will be moving to New York to teach, and Doctor Christiansen has just finished his residency and has joined a practice in Manhattan. We know their families are proud of them. So tonight, I'd like to wish them both the best in their endeavors. Let's keep these two young adults in our prayers."

Gianna thought it was an honor that Father Anthony mentioned her in his speech. *I'm really going to miss it here.*

Gianna and Danny gathered around the dinner table with their families and enjoyed the fascinating conversations. They discussed everything from medical procedures to weddings to country life and city life. Danny talked about the challenges of working in a large multicultural community and having to learn how to deal with language barriers amongst some of his patients. Gianna acknowledged similar concerns that she would face with some of her students.

When the servers finally brought the entrées, Gianna barely ate. She had butterflies in her stomach from the thrill and anticipation of her new-found friendship.

Her mother glanced over at her plate and whispered, "You didn't eat much tonight. Don't you like it?"

"I'm fine, Mom," she replied in a sour tone. She bit her lip nervously and looked away from her mother. She didn't want to listen to her nag about wasting food.

After dinner was over, the DJ kicked up the music, and the dance floor livened up. Gianna and Danny became the focal point at their table. Friends from church and high school mingled around them to wish them well.

"Talk about Grand Central," Gianna whispered to Jessica. With all these people swarming her, she felt like she was at her high school class reunion.

"Don't look now. Andrew's coming this way," Jessica muttered in her ear. "Do you remember him?"

"Oh, yeah. How can I forget?"

Andrew was a popular, outspoken preppy. He looked like a typical surfer dude with his bleached blond, curly hair, and sunbaked body, and he hadn't changed a bit since high school.

"If I recall, he had a crush on you," Jessica said.

Gianna cringed. "Oh, puhleez. He's not my type."

"Gianna!" Andrew said, showing off his row of perfect white teeth. "How're you doing, honey?" he asked, hugging her tightly.

She reluctantly returned the hug. "I'm fine, Andrew, thank you," she replied, firmly pulling away.

"Wow, you look incredible tonight!" he said, flashing his eyes like summer lightning.

Gianna recalled he was never shy. She wanted to be polite but really didn't want to converse with him. In high school, he never stopped talking, and it was usually about himself.

"Yeah, I'm a CPA now," Andrew said. "Hard to believe, huh?"

He rambled on for the next fifteen minutes, running his words together like rain.

Gianna yawned. Bored, she glanced around the table and realized everyone had left her again. But this time, she was stuck listening to a dweeb. She was desperate to be rescued. Andrew certainly didn't get the hint, and he continued babbling without mentioning what he was talking about.

While she tried to tune him out, her head was starting to ache. *Ugh! Someone, save me!* Then the DJ put on her favorite country song, and her mood instantly lifted. A gentle hand touched her shoulder. It was Danny, her knight in shining armor.

"Dance with me," he said.

"I'd love to," she said, quickly standing up.

She excused herself from long-winded Andrew and accompanied Danny to the dance floor.

"This is my favorite song."

"I know. That's why I requested it," he said.

She looked at him mysteriously. "How'd you know?"

"Jess told me."

Gianna smiled. How clever Jessica was trying to play cupid.

On the dance floor, she rested her head on Danny's chest. She could feel his heartbeat. It seemed so calm compared to how nervous she was. As they swayed, she felt her blood coursing through her veins like a raging river. It was at that moment she knew that he was the one for her. She tilted her head up and gazed into his eyes, hoping to pick up where they had left off hours ago in the gazebo.

Danny pulled her closer to him. He lifted her chin and kissed her slowly and tenderly. When the song ended, she didn't want to leave his embrace. Her feelings for him were intensifying.

As Gianna and Danny left the dance floor, Jessica rushed toward them and grabbed her arm.

"Come with me to the powder room," she said.

Gianna touched Danny's arm. "I'll be right back."

Jessica rushed Gianna into the powder room. She checked all the stalls to make sure they were empty. When she was certain they were all alone, she said, "You two looked sensational! People were even asking me if you two were a couple."

Gianna's mouth dropped open. "What people?"

"Uh, just about everybody," Jessica answered nonchalantly. "I told them you two were just friends, but I don't think they believed me after seeing that kiss." She clamped her lips together trying not to smile.

Gianna felt her cheeks heat up. "You saw us kiss?"

"Yeah, along with everyone else, even Father Anthony was blushing."

Gianna grabbed Jessica's arm. "He's the one! I know it." She closed her eyes, cherishing that moment on the dance floor. When reality hit her, she opened her eyes. "Oh, no! I hope my parents didn't see us."

"I *know* they saw you, but chill. Matt told me your father adores Dan," Jessica said.

"Jess, you KNOW my parents. They're conservative and wouldn't approve."

"Approve what?"

"Us. You know I was never allowed to date."

"That was high school. You're an adult now."

Gianna shook her head. "Not in my dad's eyes." She sighed. "I wonder what Danny thinks. I hope he doesn't think I'm easy."

"Get real, Gianna. He's not like that. He knows how your father is."

Gianna returned to the dining table where her mother and Mrs. Kendall were chatting. She tapped her mother on the shoulder. "I'm sorry to interrupt, but do you know where Danny is?"

Mrs. Kendall answered, "Daniel went outside with your father and Joe."

A chill ran up her spine. *Oh, this can't be good, can it?* She looked at Mrs. Kendall. "Ok, thank you."

Gianna turned to Jessica, but she was gone, too.

Ugh! Now where'd she run off to?

Gianna headed toward the exit, focusing on the floor to avoid any unwanted stares. She couldn't stop thinking about what Jessica told her in the restroom.

When she stepped outside, the pleasant fragrances of the cool breeze greeted her. It was refreshing compared to the stuffy air inside. As she walked down the pebbled path toward the gazebo, Danny was sitting on the bench with her father, Dr. Kendall, and Father Anthony. Her brothers and Jessica sat across from them. Their distant conversation was unclear, but they were obviously laughing and enjoying each other's company.

"Gianna!" Danny called, waving to her to join them.

Gianna was careful not to trip in her long, layered dress as she climbed up the steps of the gazebo. Like a gentleman, Danny held out his hand and helped her inside.

Her brothers hogged the entire bench, leaving her no place to sit, so she leaned up against the gazebo railing with her arms across her chest, awkwardly staring at the floor. Just then, Danny touched her arm and smiled. He placed his hands around her waist and drew her close to him, sitting her on his lap.

His outward show of affection stunned her. Nervously, she glanced at her father and expected an expression of disapproval, but shockingly he didn't appear uneasy. He just continued his conversation with Dr. Kendall and Father Anthony.

She shook her head in disbelief. *What's with Daddy?* He had always been overprotective and had frowned upon her dating. In the past, she would have had to sneak out to go on a date. And here tonight, she was wrapped up in Danny's arms.

Lost in her private thoughts, she was startled when Father Anthony called on her. "So, Gianna, your father tells me you're looking forward to moving to the city."

Gianna nodded. "This is a fantastic opportunity for me to begin my teaching career."

"It's a much different life than here," he said with a varied degree of warmth and concern. "But then again you know this having already been to college there."

"Yes, sir," she said.

"God be with you, Gianna."

Father Anthony glanced at this watch. Needing to wrap up the event inside, he excused himself from the conversation.

Dad rubbed his hands together. "Well, Stefano family. What do you say we call it a night?" he asked, rising to his feet. "I'll go get your mother."

Matt and Jessica nodded and followed him out of the gazebo, along with Gianna's brothers.

"Dan, I'm going to get Evelyn," Dr. Kendall said. "I'll meet you by the truck." He gave Gianna a wink and waved goodnight.

Danny rubbed her shoulders. "It's just you and me."

Gianna took a deep breath. "I guess so." She stood up and walked across the gazebo. She stared at the lake. *What happened tonight!* Her mind raced searching for answers. She spun around and asked, "So, what'd you and my father talk about?"

Danny stood up and walked toward her. He answered her casually. "Nothing much. Just that he's worried about you living in the city. He told me that if I didn't live there, he'd fight you tooth and nail to keep you home."

Gianna rolled her eyes. "Sounds like Daddy."

She always knew her father thought the world of him, so now it was clear why he didn't object to their blossoming relationship.

She looked intently into his eyes. "Tell me something. That kiss on the dance floor...that kiss meant *more* than just friends, didn't it?"

Danny reached for her hands and laced his fingers through hers. He captured her eyes and replied, "I'd like to think so. I want to spend more time with you."

He drew her body to his and kissed her again.

Chapter 7

Saturday rolled in. Gianna woke up at noon. She was exhausted from last night's amazing dance. She had just finished showering and getting dressed when her mother called her from the bottom of the stairs.

"Honey, Daniel's here!"

Gianna gave herself a quick onceover and rushed to the top of the staircase. She looked down and saw Danny in the foyer, dressed in a blue checked shirt, blue jeans, and cowboy boots. As she hurried down the steps, she noticed he was checking her out.

"This is a pleasant surprise," she said.

"It's a beautiful sunny day. What do you say we take a ride up to Gray Wolf State Park?" he asked, standing eagerly with both hands stuffed in his front pockets.

"Well, it'd be nice to see the view once more before we leave it all behind on Monday," she said, glancing at her mother for approval.

Mom stepped backward putting her hand to her chest. "You're asking me for permission? Go, get out of here, but be careful. Those roads have a lot of sharp bends."

"Thanks, Mom. We will."

Gianna kissed her mother goodbye. As soon as she stepped out onto the porch, she stopped short and stared at the driveway.

"What's wrong?" Danny asked.

She asked apprehensively, "You're taking me out on your motorcycle?"

"There's a first time for everything. Trust me." He stepped off the porch, straddled the bike, and put on his helmet. "Here you are," he said, handing her a helmet.

She shrugged her shoulders. "Ok, I trust you." She put on the helmet, hopped on the bike, and nervously leaned into him.

Two miles into town, they stopped at the deli to pick up sandwiches and drinks. After cruising on a long, desolate county road, they pulled off onto a narrow, gravel path that zigzagged through the tall evergreens. When they arrived at Gray Wolf State Park, Danny parked his bike. They walked through the pine trees until they reached the lake.

"Well, look at that, reserved seating provided by God," Danny said, pointing to a cluster of rocks at the bank of the lake.

Gianna nodded in approval. "It works for me."

After lunch, Gianna made herself comfortable on a slab of rock. She sat with her knees bent and her arms clenched around them. She inhaled the fresh mountain air while taking in her beautiful surroundings. The sky was a pretty blue, without a cloud in sight. A warm breeze blew, skipping off the lake, where momma duck and her babies were wading in the water.

"This is heaven," she said, thrilled to spend the afternoon with him.

Danny leaned back on the rock, holding himself up with his elbows. "Just listen."

"I don't hear anything except the ducks quacking and splashing in the water."

"Exactly, it's so peaceful here," he said. "I want to hold this moment in my mind, so when I'm in the noisy, sterile doctor's office, I can remember the sounds and smells of this day."

Gianna smiled as she recalled a memory. "Remember that time when you and Matt were playing cops and robbers, and you two chased me around the yard?"

"Oh, yeah, I remember," he said, laughing.

"You lassoed me, and Matt tied me to a tree, leaving me there. I screamed until my father came to my rescue." She closed her eyes briefly then carried on. "Boy, my dad gave Matt a licking he'd never forget."

"If you think Matt got a licking, Doc Kendall laid into me that night, too."

Gianna giggled. "My stars! That was a *long* time ago." The scene in her head was so clear like it was just yesterday.

"That was funny...uh, that is, at the time." He reached out and brushed her cheek with his finger. "Now if it were today, I would've tied myself up *with* you," he said with a spark of desire in his eyes.

Gianna gazed at the ground and continued reminiscing, "I was around ten, I think, when I realized I had a crush on you." She peered up at him, heat seeping into her cheeks.

"I knew it, and Matt knew it, too. He always teased me about it."

She flushed briefly with anger, "Oh, he—"

"Don't worry, I didn't mind. I always thought you were cute."

"You thought I was cute? I was such a tomboy back then," she said, staring at the ground again.

"Well, you're clearly not one now," Danny said, shifting his gaze over her figure. "There were so many good times. I hope there are more."

Gianna quickly changed the subject. "Oh, I forgot to tell you. My dad said he can drive us to the airport if that's ok with you."

"Cool! I'll help you get settled in at your hotel."

"Thanks. I really appreciate it."

She was grateful to have an instant friend in New York, but still determined to take care of herself.

"Hey, c'mon," Danny said, pulling her up onto her feet. "Let's take a walk one last time before we leave the *big sky country*."

"Ok," she said, eagerly.

CʒᴇꙄ

Dan held Gianna's hand as they strolled along the edge of the lake. As they walked, he silently reflected on

60

the past few weeks. Initially, he came back to Montana to visit his folks, pay respect to his parents, and to follow-up with Matt's wedding plans. That was it. But then, he attended a church dance. *Who would've thought I'd fall in love at a dance?* He couldn't discard his feelings. As crazy as it sounded, he was certain he had a future together with Gianna.

Together, they walked, talked, and laughed, as if they were never apart. It was just so comfortable and natural. Hours had passed, and before they realized, it was dusk.

"We best be getting back before your parents worry," he insisted.

Chapter 8

Sunday morning, Gianna awoke to the crackling rain slapping against the windowsill. Thunder rumbled in the distance.

Groggy, she trudged downstairs for breakfast. Her father was sitting at the dining room table drinking his coffee and reading the newspaper.

"Morning, Daddy," she muttered. She leaned forward and gave him a hug, then dropped herself into the chair across from him.

"Ah, see what I'm going to miss when you're gone tomorrow, bella?"

"Oh, what's that, Daddy?" she yawned.

"Your sunshine smile."

"Sorry, Daddy, but I feel like the weather." She sat upright and rested her elbow on the table with her chin in the palm of her hand. "I have a long flight tomorrow," she mumbled.

"You can always forget New York and stay here with us. The choice is yours," he said.

"Nice try, Daddy, but I have a job commitment. If it doesn't work out, I promise, I'll move back home."

Gianna's father took a sip of his coffee. "I give you credit, bella. I couldn't do it. New York City never sleeps. The noise, the traffic, the chaos would drive me crazy."

Gianna's mother walked in from the kitchen with a tray of assorted bagels, jellies, and cream cheese. She set it on the table and took a seat next to her husband. She glanced at him and took his hand. She then looked at Gianna and gazed into her eyes with love and sincerity.

"Gianna, honey, I know these last two days have been exciting for you as well as emotional—"

"Is this about Danny?" *I'm twenty-four and don't need a lecture.*

"Let me finish," Mom said with determination. "Watching you smile and laugh this summer gave us hope that you would stay here. Now that you met Daniel, we want to be sure that he's not the only reason you're moving to New York, and that it's still for the job opportunity."

"Mom. Dad." Gianna looked at both her parents. She reached across the table and took their hands. "Please don't worry. I believe this is where God wants me to be right now, and I believe that Danny and I have been reunited for a reason."

Gianna's father cleared his throat and glanced at his wife. "Dan is a dependable, young man whom I trust with my daughter. Someday he *may* even be my son-in-law." He looked at Gianna. His expression was unnerving. His tone was stern. "But, until then, I hope you remember your faith. Do I make myself clear?"

"Yes, Daddy. You don't have to remind me. This isn't the first time you preached to me. And I quote, 'If a man orders spaghetti in a restaurant, he doesn't want someone else's leftovers.' I get it, so please trust me. You raised me with good morals, and I don't intend to throw them away just because I am moving to the city. I won't disappoint you," she said with tears in her eyes.

Her father's eyes softened. "You were never one to lose an argument. Thank you for being honest, bella. I know Joe and Evelyn did an outstanding job raising Dan." A gentle smile crossed his face. "We best get ready for church now."

Later that afternoon, Gianna and her mother prepared the Sunday supper that they were sharing with the Kendalls and Danny. While Gianna set the table, a loud clap of thunder crashed over the house. Her heart leaped in her throat.

"Mom? Are you sure they're still coming? This storm is wicked!"

"They'll be here, honey. Not everyone panics like you when it storms," Mom said and gave her a hug. "Look, I've got this. Go finish packing."

"You sure?"

"Yes, now go!" she said, shoeing her out of the kitchen.

Gianna taped another cardboard box closed and wrote *fragile* on the side of the box with a black marker. *I can't believe how many knick-knacks I've collected over the years.* As she grabbed another roll of bubble wrap, there was a knock on her bedroom door.

"Come in," she yelled.

Oblivious that the door opened, Gianna inhaled sharply when two strong hands encircled her waist. Her body tingled from the contact. She turned around and gave Danny a look of panic. "What're you doing up here?"

"Your father sent me up," he said. He raised his eyebrows questioningly. "Why is there a problem?"

Gianna tried not to laugh and shook her head in disbelief. "My dad let you come up here? I was never allowed to have a boyfriend, never mind let a guy in my room."

Danny walked over to the window and watched the downpour. "Could it have something to do with buying a cow or getting the milk for free?" He scratched his chin and said, "Oh, yeah, and something about eating someone's leftover spaghetti."

Gianna stumbled as the room began to spin. "How'd you know about that?"

"The other night at the dance, in the gazebo, your father and I had a private talk." He stepped away from the window and stared at her. "You ok? You look like you just saw a ghost."

"Yeah, yeah, I'm fine," she uttered, sitting down on her bed. *Unbelievable! Daddy lectured him, too.*

Danny sat down next to her and held her hands in his. He gazed into her eyes with sincere honesty. "I respect you and your father's wishes. Besides, I don't blame him for wanting to protect his baby." He lifted her hand and kissed it. "Gianna, I'll wait for you."

She nodded. "Thank you."

"But for right now, I think we should go downstairs before your father thinks I'm milking the cow."

"Or sampling spaghetti?" she said, laughing.

Chapter 9

Dad called, "Bella, get up!" He knocked on her bedroom door. "We got to leave soon."

"O-k-a-y," she groaned then squinted at the clock. It was six thirty. "O-o-o-h, I hate mornings," she grumbled.

"It's foggy out, so it's going to take us longer to get to the airport," Dad said.

"Ok, Daddy. I'm moving."

Gianna dragged herself out of bed and looked out the window. Yesterday's storm left a heavy lingering fog. *I hope the flights aren't delayed.*

She showered, dressed, and carried her suitcases downstairs.

"I'll take your luggage out to the truck," Dad mumbled, wiping a tear from his eye.

"Gianna, honey," Mom called from the kitchen. "Come eat something before you leave."

Gianna wandered into the kitchen and hopped on the counter stool, joining her brothers for breakfast. "I'm really not hungry."

Dad came back inside and sat down next to her. He handed her an envelope. "Your mother and I want to give you this graduation gift before you leave."

Gianna stared at it blankly, then opened it. Tears clouded her eyes, and her voice choked as she read the card aloud:

> *"Our Dearest Gianna,*
> *Here's a gift card to help you begin your new life in the Big Apple. We are so proud of you and your accomplishments. May God continue to bless you in all that you do.*
> *Love, Dad, Mom, Matthew, Mark, Luke, and John."*

Gianna caught her breath, but could barely squeak out, "Thank you." A hodge-podge of emotions flooded her, and she broke into tears.

"I love you, and I'm going to miss all of you."

She pushed her plate away and rushed out of the kitchen.

When it was time to leave, everyone assembled in the foyer to say goodbye.

Matthew hugged Gianna. "Best of luck at your new job. Tell Dan to call me if he wants advice on buying a ring."

"Funny, Matt," she said, her voice choking.

His witticism was lacking humor and wasn't making her goodbyes any easier.

"Take care, sis," Mark said, hugging her. "Don't let city life change you too much. I'll send you a bunch of my framed photos of Sheridan, so you'll remember your roots."

Gianna faked a smile. "Thanks."

"Good luck staying out of trouble," Luke said.

Gianna rolled her eyes. "You and John should talk."

"Yeah, watch your back and your purse," John said. His amused look suddenly left his face. "We'll miss you."

"I'll be fine!" she said as the tears fell. She swallowed hard. "I'll miss you all, too. Love you, guys."

Gianna turned toward the front door. She tried hard not to look back. Inside the truck, she took one last look at the house. She saw her brothers looking out the window as they pulled away. She watched the house disappear into the fog as the truck carried her down the dark, wet road to the Kendall's house.

☌

Dan sat with Joe and Evelyn inside the screened porch while they waited for the Stefano's SUV to pull into the driveway.

"Here they come now," Dan said. He hugged Joe and Evelyn goodbye then choked on his words. "Take care. I love you both."

He grabbed his luggage and stepped off the porch. He greeted Mr. and Mrs. Stefano and tossed his bags into the truck. He glanced at Gianna and saw the emptiness in her face.

"It's ok to cry," he whispered.

She nodded, then cried softly into his shoulder. He put his arm around her and kissed her cheek.

"Hey, we'll be back at Thanksgiving for Matt and Jessica's wedding," he said.

Gianna sniffled, "I know, but right now, November seems like forever."

By the time Gianna and Danny arrived at the airport, the fog had lifted, and the planes were on schedule. After jockeying their way through crowds of hustling people, it was time to say their last goodbyes.

"Daniel, it was nice seeing you again," Mom said, hugging him. "Stay in touch."

Gianna's father shook Danny's hand and patted his shoulder. "A lot can happen in New York. Please take care of my bella ragazza for me, son," he pleaded with his brittle voice.

"I will. I'm honored that you asked."

Gianna noticed her father's painful gaze. She could tell he was trying to be strong.

"You don't have to hide the tears from me, Daddy," she cried, clinging to him.

"Don't be a stranger to your old man. You call me."

"I will. You know, the plane flies both ways." She felt his body quiver as she let go. "See you at Thanksgiving."

Gianna turned toward her mother and took her hand. She swallowed hard. "I love you, Mom. Thanks for everything."

"I love you, too, honey," Mom said.

As Gianna hugged her mother one last time, she cried uncontrollably, and Danny had to peel her away, so they could get through security.

Gianna stared pointlessly out the plane window. She never imagined saying goodbye to her parents would be so painful. Why were goodbyes so much easier during college? Perhaps coming home during semester breaks made the separation less permanent.

"Hey, are you ok?" Danny asked, rubbing her shoulder.

She nodded. "I'll be fine." She reached inside her purse for a tissue then blotted her eyes.

Danny smiled and took her hand. "Try and get some sleep. We have a five-hour flight ahead of us."

He leaned in and kissed her forehead. She smiled softly then rested her head on his shoulder. Not long into the flight, she dozed off into a sound sleep.

"Hey, sleepyhead, we're home," Danny said as he massaged her arm.

Gianna opened her eyes. When her vision cleared, reality set in. *More like far from home.*

The airport was crowded with faceless, voiceless people, each one busy on a mission. Gianna held onto Danny's arm in fear that she'd get lost in the shuffle. Once they found their luggage, they flagged down a taxi.

As the taxi cruised through rush hour traffic, Gianna stared out the car window at the endless moving crowds. It was all too familiar to her, as if she had never left.

At last, the yellow taxi pulled down a private, one-way, tree-lined street. There were clusters of four-story, cookie-cutter brownstone buildings enclosed by tall, black iron fences.

"Welcome to my abode. It's not a cattle ranch, but it has just enough space to hang my cowboy hat," he said, sounding certain it was his rightful place to be.

Gianna stepped out of the cab and looked around. She nodded approvingly. "A place like this would be ideal for me."

"C'mon, I'll show you which building I live in," he said, grabbing some luggage.

She followed him down the sidewalk.

He pointed straight ahead. "That's a gated lot where I have an assigned parking space. And...here we are," he said, turning to an end unit.

They climbed up ten steps to a covered porch where Danny had a security pass that unlocked the main entrance. Inside the lobby, Gianna was awestruck. Cathedral ceilings, whitewashed brick walls, and Italian marble flooring encompassed the space. The lobby even had a twenty-four-hour security desk. It was quiet too, except for the trickling sound of water coming from a three-tier garden fountain.

My stars! This place is nice. "Wow! This is quite different than I imagined," she said.

"I was hoping I could impress you."

Gianna and Danny rode the elevator to the second floor. They stepped out of the elevator and turned right. His suite was at the end of the hall.

"I'll give you the grand tour. Afterward, we'll grab a bite to eat, and then I'll help you get settled into your hotel room," he said.

Danny unlocked the door, held it open, and gestured Gianna inside. She stepped into the foyer and was amazed all over again. His place smelled fresh, looked clean, and felt comfortable. It was the total opposite of a typical man cave.

The living room was to the right. A crucifix hung above the gas fireplace. Family memories decorated the buckskin painted walls and glossy hardwood floors flowed throughout the space.

Gianna stepped into the porcelain tiled kitchen, which was to the left of the living room. She glided her hand along the white, polished quartz countertop.

"Oh, Danny, this place is fantastic!"

"Thank you. Can I offer you a drink?"

"Yes, water please."

Danny reached into the cherry cabinet and removed two tumblers. He opened the stainless-steel fridge and grabbed a gallon of bottled spring water. "No well water here in the city," he said, filling each glass. He handed one to her.

"Thank you."

She took a seat at the center island and sipped her water. She glanced around the room admiring his style.

"Your décor is beautiful, Danny."

"Thank you. Unfortunately, I'm not home much to enjoy it." He laughed. "So, would you like to see the rest of my place?"

"Sure!"

Danny led her down the hallway and showed her the half bath and the laundry closet. "I can do my laundry right here. No hauling baskets to a laundry mat," he said contently.

Gianna gave him a smile and two thumbs up. She knew having a washer and dryer at home was a great convenience in the city.

"Check out the two bedrooms. Each one has its own private bath," he said, leading the way.

She poked her head into the primary bedroom. "Nice closets. It beats my dorm room. I never imagined a place this extravagant in the city. I guess I shouldn't judge a book by its cover."

"I have the second bedroom set up for Joe and Evelyn for when they visit, but I haven't been able to get them out here," he said, his voice trailing off in disappointment.

Gianna placed her hand on his shoulder. "Sorry, Danny, but if they're anything like my parents—"

"I know," he said. "So, what do you think?" he asked, his tone suddenly buoyant.

"It's perfect. I hope to find a place just like it."

Danny wrapped his arms around her. "Not to bust your bubble, but prices run steep here in the city. It's not Sheridan."

"I know. My father warned me," she said, lowering her eyes in frustration.

"Hey, now, I didn't mean to discourage you. I'll help you find something suitable."

Danny drew her face to his and kissed her softly. A feeling of both passion and fear infused her. The changes in her life were overwhelming, and he was moving a little too fast. She gently pulled away from his embrace.

"It's getting late. I, uh, should check into my hotel now," she said, nervously.

"Ok." He took her hand and walked her back to the front door. "I'll take you out to eat, and then I'll drive you to your hotel, if that's ok with you."

Gianna nodded in agreement and stepped outside his suite door. While she waited eagerly for Danny to lock up, a friendly voice echoed down the hallway.

"Hey, cowboy! Welcome home."

Startled by the stranger's voice, she quickly turned around. A tall, muscular, dark skinned man wearing blue jeans and a green t-shirt walked toward them.

"What's up neighbor?" Danny asked and shook the man's hand. "Arrest any thugs while I was gone?"

The man laughed. "There's never a dull moment."

"Hey, I'd like you to meet my girlfriend, Gianna. She's moving back here from Montana," Danny said.

Gianna got goose bumps when he referred to her as his girlfriend.

"Hello, Gianna. I'm Detective Troy Evans. Welcome to New York City," he said, shaking her hand.

His hand was firm, yet gentle. She felt comfortable with him. "It's nice to meet you, Troy."

Troy pointed down the hall toward his suite. "Hey, my wife asked me to invite you over for pizza."

"Oh, uh," Danny said, looking at Gianna for approval. "Is that ok with you?"

She nodded and then looked at Troy. "Thank you."

"No problem," Troy said. "Follow me."

Troy led them down the corridor to his suite. He opened the door and invited them inside.

"Tracy," Troy called. "Meet Gianna."

Tracy was in the kitchen taking plates out of the cabinet. She turned and smiled. She gracefully walked toward Gianna and extended her hand. "It's nice to meet you."

"Likewise," Gianna said, gently shaking her hand.

Tracy's skin was soft and her freshly manicured nails were decorated with a traditional French tip.

"Welcome home, Dan." Tracy's petite frame reached up and greeted him with a hug. "C'mon, we have plenty for you two."

The four gathered in the kitchen and ate pizza. As they made small talk, Gianna studied Tracy. She seemed familiar to her. She had a cheerful voice that matched her liveliness. Her bubbly disposition made her believe they may have met before.

"Gianna, you look so familiar to me," Tracy said, searching her face for clues.

"That's so funny. I was thinking the same thing."

Gianna sat back in her chair and tried to figure out where they may have met.

"Well, Tracy's a teacher, too," Danny said. "Maybe you two met in college?"

Gianna sprung forward in her seat. "Yes! I've seen you at PS241. I did my student teaching there."

Tracy nodded. "Yes, you did, girlfriend! I knew I recognized your face. I teach English and Social Studies there."

"I'm going to be the new health teacher."

Tracy's smile grew warm and generous. "Yes! I heard they hired a new teacher for that position. Congratulations! If you need *anything*, please don't hesitate to ask."

Gianna smiled in appreciation. "Thank you."

After dinner, Danny and Gianna stopped back at his place to retrieve her luggage. As they walked outside to the secured parking lot, Gianna noticed the shiny black Ford pick-up parked in his spot. She smiled and shook her head. *'You can take the boy out of the country, but you can't take the country out of the boy.'*

Minutes later, Danny pulled his truck into a parking space at the hotel. He gazed up at the tall, well-lit building that stretched into the night sky.

"Well, this looks like the right place," he said.

"Yes, thank you," Gianna said, releasing her seatbelt. "I really had a wonderful time tonight. I'm so glad I had a chance to meet Troy and Tracy. It's so coincidental that she and I will be teaching at the same school."

Danny nodded. "Yeah, it is. I've known them for three years now. They're good people."

Gianna nodded. She was thrilled to have made a new friend and one who would also be her colleague. She knew she'd have many changes ahead of her, but she was beginning to feel more comfortable about her relocation to New York.

"I don't know *what* I was thinking when I accepted this teaching position," she said.

Danny shook his head. He had a flash of wonder in his eyes. "You're certainly free-spirited, Gianna. I hope you don't regret any of this."

She reached for his hand. "No, I don't, but I'd be lost without you here in my life."

"I'll *always* be here for you," he said and feather-touched her cheek with a kiss. "C'mon, I'll walk you inside."

Gianna checked in at the lobby and got her room key. Together, they took the elevator ten floors up to her room.

"Here we are," she said, opening the door. It smelled fresh and appeared clean. As she entered the space, she examined the room carefully, and concluded it was adequate for now. "Hopefully, the bed will be comfortable. It ought to be for the price," she said sarcastically.

"Unfortunately, everything here in the city is expensive," Danny reminded her. He walked across the room and glanced out the window. "Well, you have a beautiful view of Times Square." He pulled the drapes closed then stepped away from the window. "If everything's ok, I'll leave you to settle in."

Gianna sensed reluctance in his voice, and his uneasiness was contagious. "Is something wrong?" she asked nervously. "You seem jittery."

He rubbed her shoulders. "I don't like leaving you here alone."

Gianna sighed in frustration. She rested her head on his chest and looked up at him. "Please, Danny, don't worry about me. Had I not met you, I would've been in this place all alone. It's a blessing to have you near me."

"You know, I have the extra bedroom that you're welcome to stay in," he said. "No matter what you say, I'll still worry."

She gazed into his concerned eyes and said, "Thank you, but I'll be fine. Besides, it's not like I haven't been here before. You better get home and get some sleep."

Danny kissed her, his lips gentle, tender, and careful. "I love you, Gianna."

A shiver rushed up her spine. He had never told her he loved her before. She caressed his beard and whispered, "I love you, too."

As Danny walked toward the door, he paused and looked back at her. "You have my number. Call me if you need anything."

Gianna gritted her teeth. "I'll be fine."

"Make sure you lock the door," he said.

"Good night, Danny."

When he left, she locked the door behind him and sighed. *My stars! Sometimes I think he's just like Daddy.*

Gianna unpacked a few items from her suitcase and then took a shower. After she put on her cotton nightshirt, she climbed into bed under the stiff, cold sheets.

Even though she was exhausted, her eyes wouldn't close. She just stared at the popcorn ceiling. She couldn't turn off the commotion that surrounded her. Bright lights flashed through the window drapes, sirens screamed up and down the street, and worst of all, someone in the room above her pounded the floor. She hated all the noise and felt trapped inside the strange hotel room.

She watched the digital clock slowly approach midnight. *Daddy's right. This city never sleeps. This is ridiculous. Will I ever get used to this kind of life?*

Chapter 10

After a long, sleepless night, Gianna was jolted out of bed by her ringing cell phone. She yanked it off the charger without checking the caller ID.

"Hello?" she yawned.

"Good morning, babe. How'd you sleep?"

"Horrible. I forgot how hard it is to block out the sounds of this city."

"It takes time to readjust. It took me awhile to fall asleep, too. I just wanted to make sure you're alright."

"I'm fine," she insisted. "I'm going to browse the newspapers today for apartments and start the hunt."

"Don't schedule any appointments until after six, so I can go with you."

"Ok," she sighed. Danny's insistence miffed her. She understood his concern, but she wasn't a child.

"Listen, I got to go. I love you."

"Love you, too."

Gianna set her phone back down on the charger. *First things first.* She grabbed the newspaper and sat down at the round table. She was determined to find the perfect apartment. However, after she called half a dozen ads, she learned the places were either too expensive or no longer available. She finally stumbled across an ad that sounded promising. It was a one bedroom, one bath, 500 sq. ft. studio for $1300 a month. She called and set up an appointment to view it that evening.

Next, she planned to go grocery shopping and surprise Danny with supper. He mentioned that Troy and Tracy had a key to his suite, so she could borrow the key and make a nice supper for him.

She called Tracy to confirm she had the key. When she told Tracy about her plan, Tracy offered to go with her to the market.

After they browsed through the small store, Gianna realized how challenging it was to live in the city. Not only was everything expensive, but it was also hard to imagine carting all her packages to an apartment. However, she smiled at her current mission.

"I've always gone shopping with my mother, and we've always dreaded the task, but I have to admit, today I'm having fun."

Tracy gave her the strangest look. "That's because you're in love girlfriend." She busted out laughing. "Let me tell you something, it gets old fast."

After Gianna and Tracy trudged the groceries to Danny's home, she familiarized herself with his kitchen. She referred to her mother's homemade recipe for penne pasta with vodka sauce. She recalled how much he enjoyed it as a kid when he ate supper over the house. She followed her mother's instructions exactly. Even though she made it hundreds of times before, she was nervous about how it would turn out.

She cleaned up the kitchen and set the table with cloth placemats and two candles that she bought at the store. She glanced at the clock. *Danny should be home soon.* She wanted to make sure everything looked perfect before he walked through the door.

It was nearing six thirty when she heard him fumbling with his keys outside the door. When he opened it, his eyes lit up as if it was the Fourth of July.

"Just what the doctor ordered," Danny said, smiling from ear to ear. He set down his laptop bag and tossed his hat on the couch. "Baby, come here," he said with open arms.

"Tracy loaned me the key. I hope you don't mind. I made your favorite, penne pasta with vodka sauce."

He smiled. "This is so nice, really nice."

"I also picked up a few things for you at the store. Your fridge looks less empty now. Besides, I know you keep a busy schedule, but right now, I don't." She took his hand and led him into the dining room. "Let's eat while it's still hot."

Danny appreciatively dished out supper for them. As he lifted his fork, he said, "Thank you. This is a pleasant surprise." After he tasted it, he looked at her and winked. "Hmm, delicious. Just like your mother makes it. I feel right at home."

She was pleased to make him happy. Now, she wanted to tell him her good news. "I have an appointment downtown tonight to look at an apartment. It's a one-bedroom studio. Most places are either rented or too expensive for me. I didn't think this was going to be so difficult."

Danny wiped his mouth with his cloth napkin and responded with uncertainty. "Ok. We'll go if you want to, but downtown is so far from your school, and you should be closer to me."

His lack of enthusiasm puzzled her. She thought he wanted to help her find a place. She put down her fork and glared at him. "Look, I need to find something because that hotel is going to break me. Even at a discounted rate, I'll be broke in a month."

"I understand, but I don't want you to rush into anything either. I'll help you out if you get into a bind."

Gianna clamped her jaw tightly and tried hard to keep her composure. She didn't want to seem ungrateful, but she didn't want him bailing her out of her problems. She wanted to do it on her own.

"Danny, thanks for offering, but I'll be ok," she insisted.

After supper, Gianna and Danny went on their way to look at the apartment. According to the given directions, the apartment complex was on the opposite side of town. After they hunted for a parking space, Danny finally found one, over a block away.

"Good thing you don't have a car, because there wouldn't be any place to park," he said.

"Please don't sound so negative."

Gianna didn't think the walk to and from the school would be that bad. In fact, it would be good exercise.

"Here we are," she said, pointing to her right.

She stared at the double, eight-story stucco buildings that stood side-by-side. Their uniform ugliness was undeniable. They looked like a state-run institution, with only a narrow alley separating the gray buildings.

Gianna and Danny exchanged mutual expressions. He was obviously uncomfortable.

"Ok, so it isn't a Swiss chalet, but looks can be deceiving," she said, continuing to scan the surrounding area.

Gianna and Danny walked together. When they approached the main entrance, a group of punks landscaped the front steps, smoking, and drinking. The punks' conversation stopped, their heads turned, and they gawked at Gianna. When she detected their stare, she looked the other way, determined not to reveal her uneasiness. As she and Danny climbed the steps, she gripped his hand tighter.

"Hey, buttercup, come to daddy," howled the one punk who appeared to be the leader. He entreated her and made perverted gestures at her body.

Surprisingly, Danny kept his equanimity, but Gianna noticed a distinct hardening of his eyes and his posture tightened.

They entered the smoke-filled lobby. A plump, well-to-do man in his fifties was sitting behind a desk, puffing thoughtfully on his cigar. After the man extinguished his cigar, he stood up and shook Gianna's hand.

"You must be Gianna," he said. His voice was deep and husky. "Ralph Owens, landlord of this building. Nice to meet you."

"Same here, Mr. Owens. This is my boyfriend, Danny."

Danny tipped his hat in polite acknowledgement.

Mr. Owens stepped out from behind his desk. "You're here for the rental. It's on the sixth floor, room 6G. Come this way." He took them up the rickety, dark elevator to the apartment, and unlocked the door. "Look around, see what you think. I'll be at the front desk with the lease papers should you be interested. Pull the door shut on your way out," he instructed, then left.

Gianna and Danny didn't need to go any further than the front door. It was a tiny, stench-ridden, one-room studio. There was a heap of trash piled up in one corner. The once beige carpet was stained brown with who knows what, and a hole was worn through the center. There was a bucket positioned to catch rainwater as it dripped from the moldy ceiling.

"O-k-a-y. This can work," Gianna said, trying to sound positive as she inspected the apartment.

"No way!" Danny's tone was adamant.

"Why not?" she asked. Her voice was high-pitched. "This could just be a diamond in the rough." She placed her hand on his forearm and stressed, "I can work at it."

Danny possessively placed his hands on her shoulders. "I'm not letting you live here in this scrapheap with those wolves prowling at your door."

"Now you sound like my father. I'm not afraid of them," she snapped.

"Babe, you're not going to be my leftover spaghetti. Besides, I vouched for your safety. If something happened to you, every Stefano male would come after me and seriously hurt me. Now, let's get out of here."

Without waiting for a response, Danny strode to the door. Gianna groaned in discontent and followed him out. When they exited the lobby, Mr. Owens was behind his desk with another cigar in hand.

He called after them. "Hey, lady, aren't you going to sign the lease?"

"No, thank you, sir," Danny said. "The place is a dump."

Although dismayed, Gianna was surprised at Danny's clear defensive stance and hardened manners.

Meanwhile, the punks were still outside the door chugging their beer, staring at passers-by, and spewing obscenities in every direction. Their talking got louder and more boisterous. When they saw Gianna and Danny again, one of them yelled out in an arrogant voice.

"Hey, Buffalo Bill! You got one sexy ride. Mind if I look under the hood?" His speech was slurred, his laugh was evil, and his breath could intoxicate a breathalyzer machine.

Danny's protective arm pressed Gianna closer to him as they quickly walked past the punks. Ignoring their remarks, he muttered to Giana, "Don't look back. I don't want any trouble. I left my lasso back in Montana."

Although Gianna felt safe and protected by him, she picked up her pace. She was grateful that he insisted on going with her.

When they returned to the hotel, Gianna plopped down on the bed, disappointed. "Back to square one," she exhaled, blowing her hair out of her face.

Danny sat down beside her. "Gianna, it's only been one day. Something will turn up."

"I know, but I wanted to get settled in before I started my new job."

"You still have a couple weeks yet."

"I know. I have another place I'm interested in looking at tomorrow."

"Can I suggest that you concentrate your search near your school? You should look in mid-town or uptown."

Gianna nodded.

Danny's blue eyes pleaded with her. "Listen to me. Please do not wander into neighborhoods after hours."

"Ok, I won't."

He swept a few strands of hair out of her eyes. "Boy, you look exhausted."

"I am," she said, rubbing her eyes. "I don't think I slept more than four hours last night."

"Lie on the bed, and I'll massage your back."

Gianna nodded. Danny's offer was too good to refuse. The gentle, but firm touch of his palms sent warm tremors through her body. She slowly sank into the bed as her muscles relaxed.

"Hmm, where was this when I was cramming for finals?" she moaned, closing her eyes.

Danny stopped and mumbled that he had to leave. He kissed her on the top of her head and let himself out.

Chapter 11

Morning arrived, and Gianna woke up in the same position she passed out in. She felt like a million bucks, thanks to last night's soothing massage. Her incredible slumber allowed her to view life in a new light.

She looked out her window and saw what a beautiful sunny day it was. Today, her goal was to visit the school and get herself acquainted with her teaching position.

When she stepped outside the hotel lobby, a gentle breeze blew through her hair. It was too gorgeous of a day to ride in a taxi. Instead, she joined the other mobs of people and hit the pavement. The school building was only a few blocks down from the hotel.

She arrived at the familiar brick school building. She gazed up at the flagpole and watched Old Glory flutter in the wind. *Where did the time go? It seems like just yesterday I spent sixteen weeks student teaching.* She continued along the concrete sidewalk, up the old stone steps, and pulled open the front door. She stood inside the lobby and took a deep breath. *Ah, that memorable scent of crayons and glue.* It prompted a flashback of her childhood years in school.

When Gianna approached the security desk, she recognized the guard who had his nose buried in a book. Thirty-five-year-old Nick Cruz, built like a football player, had a shaved head, olive skin, and deep brown eyes. He had a powerful resistant look about him that kept the students in line. However, she knew he was a kind man behind his uniform.

"Good morning, sir," she said, gesturing him in a mock salute.

Nick peered up from his book. "Hey! Good morning, Ms. Stefano. How've you been?" He stepped out from behind the counter and welcomed her with a hug.

"Just fine, Nick."

"So, what brings you back?"

"A full-time job. I'm here to see Mr. Sterling."

"Well, congratulations! In case you forgot, it's the second door on your left," he said, pointing her down the hall.

"Thanks! See you later."

Gianna set off toward the central office. The click-clack sound of her heels rattled her nerves as she walked down the quiet corridor. When she reached the principal's door, she gave it a soft knock.

"Come in," a low, deep voice answered.

Gianna slowly opened the door. Mr. Sterling, a stout man, dressed in a blue power suit, sat hunched over in his chair shuffling papers.

"Good morning, Mr. Sterling," she said, trying hard to sound confident.

Mr. Sterling looked up from his pile of papers and smiled easily. "Nice to see you again, Miss Stefano." He stood up and shook her hand. "Please have a seat while I locate your personnel file."

Gianna took a seat in the only empty chair available. Relieved that their greeting went well, she sat patiently with her hands folded in her lap. She watched him thumb through his credenza in search of her file. She had a lot of respect for the man. It was only four weeks until the new school year, and his desk looked like a total disaster. Yet, he had everything under control.

"Ah, here we are," Mr. Sterling said, pulling out a folder with her name on it. He sifted through her file and verified receipt of her credentials, her criminal background check, and her signed contract. "It looks like all you need to fill out is your emergency contact information form and have your physician sign off on the medical clearance form," he said, handing her a packet and an employee handbook. "It's my pleasure to have you as part of our team."

"Thank you," she said.

"Do you have any questions?"

"No sir."

"Very well, then let me take you to your classroom so you can become acquainted with it. I trust you remember where the faculty room is located?"

Gianna nodded and followed him down the hall.

"Your classroom is the last room on the right in corridor B, next to the fitness room. You'll be across the hall from the gymnasium and locker rooms."

Gianna bit her lip. *That sounds like a horrible location.* "Won't it be noisy?"

"On the contrary, I believe you'll find it peaceful," he said, stopping midway. "You see, the gymnasium divides corridor A and corridor B. The students tend to use corridor A because B is off the beaten path."

"Oh, I see," she said, pleased.

"Well, here you are, Miss Stefano," he said, handing her the key. "I'll leave you now to look around at your leisure. If you need anything, please don't hesitate to ask." He smiled, shook her hand, and left.

Gianna unlocked the door and stepped inside. The morning sunshine beamed through the large windows. She walked toward the back of the room and took a seat at her desk. She placed her room key on her own key chain. *Just a few personal touches and this room will be perfect.* She stood up and counted the student desks. *Twenty-five. I'll rearrange the desks into groups of five. But first, I want to tackle the paperwork.*

She stayed about an hour filling out documents, leaving only the medical clearance form to complete. She placed her pen to her lips and questioned who she could use as a physician since the only doctor she went to was at the university clinic. *Maybe Danny can recommend someone.*

Finished for the day, Gianna packed up her belongings. Preoccupied thinking about curriculum ideas, she nearly jumped out of her skin when she turned and found an athletic man with light brown hair and gorgeous hazel eyes standing in her doorway. His six-foot stature was strong and powerful, and his shoulders were thickly muscled.

She stared blankly with her mouth open. *Is he for real?*

"Hello, there. I'm sorry. I didn't mean to startle you."

Gianna caught her breath. "Hi, Mister—"

"I'm Chad Garrett—one of the gym teachers here."

She smiled and shook his firm hand. "Hi, I'm Gianna Stefano."

"So, you're the new health teacher?" he asked, leaning against the lockers purposely showing off his physique.

"Yes. I did my student teaching here awhile back."

"Ah, I knew I've seen your pretty face and beautiful brown eyes around here before," he said, gazing over her with approval.

Gianna's cheeks burned. "Umm, if you could excuse me, I have another appointment."

"No problem," he said, standing there boldly, arms crossed against his chest, flexing his huge biceps. "I'm sure we'll be bumping into each other over the next couple of weeks."

"I'm sure we will."

Quickly, she locked her classroom door and rushed up the corridor. She glanced over her shoulder and noticed he was still standing there watching her.

Chad intrigued her. He was friendly, attractive, and she liked the attention he gave her. But she also knew not all that glitters was gold. Besides, she was in love with Danny. He had all the qualities she was looking for in a man: mature, responsible, honest, faithful, compassionate...the list goes on. She and Danny shared the same interests and religious values, too. She had a promising relationship with him, and she wasn't about to jeopardize it.

Gianna stepped out of the cold, air-conditioned school into a sauna. The sticky, noon city air was unbearable to breathe, so instead of walking back to the hotel, she flagged down a cab. As she opened the car door, her cell phone rang a familiar tune.

"Hi, Danny," she answered cheerfully.

"Hey, where're you at?"

"I'm leaving the school now, about to head back to the hotel. Hey, I need a medical clearance for work. Can you recommend a doctor?"

"Uh, yeah. Listen, I'm going to lunch now. Meet me at Jacob's Deli on Columbus Ave. We'll talk then."

"Ok, I'm on my way."

Gianna met Danny at a local Jewish deli that was well- known for its delicious overstuffed hot pastrami on rye. She was finally going to find out what all the hype was. It didn't take long for her to figure it out though. As soon as the door opened, the smell of pungent kosher dill pickles wafted through the air. There was no enticing needed to draw her inside.

They found a tiny round table to dine at near the front window. She looked around the overcrowded café. It was small and quaint, but terribly busy, even busier than the hectic streets outside.

"Hmm, what should I order?" she asked, browsing the menu.

"You've got to try the pastrami on rye. It may not be heart healthy, but it's delicious," Danny boasted.

"Ok, I'm up for a treat."

She reached for her satchel, pulled out a piece of paper, and handed it to Danny. "Mr. Sterling, my boss, gave me this list of clinics."

Danny quickly glanced at the paper and replied, "You can come to my practice. For obvious reasons, I can't see you, but I have a reputable colleague who can take care of you."

"Ok. Set me up."

"I'll call you when I get back to my office. It may be a week or two until your appointment though."

"Ok, thanks."

The server brought their plates to the table. When Gianna saw the size of the sandwiches, she practically fell out of the chair. "Yikes, these portions are huge! I'll have leftovers for the next two days."

"Wait 'till you taste it."

She took a bite of her sandwich. "Mmm, this is delicious."

"Told you," he said. "Oh, my request for time off for Matt's wedding was approved."

Gianna saw the enthusiasm in his eyes. "You mean Matt *and* Jessica's wedding," she said. "Well, I should hope so. You *are* the best man," she teased. "I can't wait!" She smiled, thinking about her brother and Jessica's upcoming wedding, and going home.

Chapter 12

Over the next two weeks, Gianna and Danny's paths rarely crossed. Danny was extremely busy between office hours and on-call obligations at the hospital. Gianna spent most of her days preparing her classroom, writing lesson plans, and pouring over students' records.

Gianna sat in her classroom, attached to her desk by a ball and chain. She was trying to create lesson plans from scratch for the family living part of her curriculum, but the task challenged her teaching skills. Fortunately, the health section already existed but needed tweaking. She only had one more week to get it together. *Why didn't I move to New York sooner? How am I going to get this all finished?*

Before she could think, her cell phone rang. The local bridal boutique had let her know that her bridesmaid dress for Jessica's wedding was in. *No way has it been ten weeks since we picked out the dress in Montana.* She scheduled a fitting and blocked off a time slot in her appointment book. *Ugh! Now I have another task to do.*

Gianna leaned back in her chair and rubbed her forehead. *Oh, and then there's the quest for an apartment.* She twirled her hair. *There's no time. I'll just have to postpone the hunt.* After her last adventure, she wised up and realized she should wait for Danny to go with her, but in his busy world, that could be another month.

She escaped from her desk chair to take a breather. She rounded the building once and was on her way back to the classroom when her cell phone rang again.

Ugh! Who's calling me now? She pulled her phone out of her pocket. *It's Jessica.* "Hello?" she huffed in a strained voice.

"Hey, chickadee! What's wrong?" Jessica asked. "You sound stressed."

"I am," she sighed. She closed her classroom door so she could talk in private. "I'm not prepared to teach. Four weeks in New York just isn't enough time to get my act together. I can't find a decent affordable apartment. I haven't seen Danny in two weeks. My bridesmaid dress just came in, and I don't have time for fittings."

"Whoa, Gianna, slow down! You sound like a typical New Yorker."

"I can't. There's not enough time in the day."

"C'mon, chill. First off, the dress can wait. There's plenty of time left for alterations. Second, forget about the apartment search for now. I heard about your ordeal through Matt. Just wait for Dan. I don't want to hear about you on the news. And, as for Dan, he has a lot on his plate right now, but I do know he misses you."

Gianna sniffled, "You think so?" The lack of time spent with Danny was what bothered her the most.

Jessica half-laughed, "Girl, I know so. Trust me."

"I feel better now, thanks. Thanks for listening, Jess."

"I'm always here for you. Take care of yourself."

Gianna ended her call and grabbed a tissue. She couldn't believe she blubbered like that to Jessica. She decided she had enough fun for the day and packed up her stuff. She needed to go back to the hotel and rest.

In her room, she lounged in bed. She broke down in tears again. All she wanted was a few days to explore the city with Danny, but all she had seen so far was the cold block walls of her classroom. She was lonely and homesick. Her college classmates moved on, and she had only met a handful of friendly people since. She had less stress and more friends in graduate school than now. New York just didn't feel like home.

The week before school started, Gianna buckled down and finished organizing her classroom. She sat in her desk chair and studied the room. *This will have to do.*

"Hi, brown eyes," a deep voice called out.

Gianna glanced up and saw Chad standing in her doorway. He looked macho, dressed in his navy-blue workout pants and gray, fitted t-shirt.

"Hi," she said casually.

"Room's looking good," he said, eyeing her up and down. "Just stopped in to see if you need anything."

I need lots of things, but nothing from you. "Thanks, but I'm managing," she said.

"Ok, then. I'll see you tomorrow in orientation."

That evening, Gianna curled up in bed while she watched a romance-comedy on television. *Why can't real-life relationships be as simple as the movies?* She was immersed in the story when her cell phone rang. *Shoot! It's Mom. Oh, this ought to be good. I haven't called her in three weeks.*

"Hello, Mom...please don't yell! I admit, I'm guilty for not calling. I'm sorry."

"Honey, I was worried sick about you. I left you messages, and you never called back."

Gianna clicked off the television. "I know. I apologize. It's been nuts here getting ready for school."

She filled her mother in on the details of her life. Two hours later...

"Mom, I love you, but it's almost midnight, and I have orientation tomorrow," she said.

Morning came soon enough. Gianna, like all newbies, arrived at school early. She was glad to be there. It turned out to be a highly informative day. Mr. Sterling discussed classroom management, organization, and scheduling.

During the lunch break, she joined her colleagues in the crowded teachers' lounge for a special catered lunch. As she enjoyed a baguette stuffed with roast beef, she reflected on her accomplishments. Although it had been a long, grueling three weeks, she felt prepared to teach. *Thank you, God, for your guidance throughout this challenging undertaking.*

"Hi, brown eyes. Mind if I sit here?" Chad asked.

Without hesitation, he pompously parked himself down next to her. Gianna cringed at his persistence.

"Not at all," she said not wanting to be rude.

Chad tried to drum up a conversation. He asked her if she was nervous about teaching tomorrow. Then he pried into her personal life, like where she was from, and why she moved to New York. She was surprised he didn't ask her if she was seeing anyone. She was glad he didn't because she preferred keeping their relationship at a professional level.

Before lunch concluded, Gianna learned that Chad grew up in Long Island, attended college on a football scholarship, and taught in this school for six years.

After a long productive day, Gianna returned to her hotel room, exhausted. Just as she climbed into bed and clicked on the television, Danny called.

"Hey, babe, how are you?"

Hearing his gentle voice made her heart race.

"I'm excited and nervous about teaching tomorrow."

"Just our luck, I have tomorrow off," he said with a heavy sigh.

"Go figure. School ends at three. How about I stop by your place sometime after four?"

"Sounds like a plan. I'll see you tomorrow then," Danny said eagerly. "Listen, good luck. I love you."

After they ended their call, Gianna turned off the television and switched off the light. She tried to get a good night's sleep, but her eyes wouldn't close. She stared blankly at the ceiling, wide-awake again, just as she did on her first night in the city. However, this time it wasn't the city noise keeping her awake, it was anxiety. Afterall, it was her first day of school, too. *How are my students going to behave? Will they take advantage of me because I'm an inexperienced teacher, or will they be courteous?*

She couldn't turn off her thoughts about school, and when she finally did, she began stressing about her diminishing savings. *This hotel is draining me, and I need a paycheck.*

Chapter 13

When morning arrived, Gianna's eyes popped open to the blazing sun that glared through the openings in the drapes. She glanced at the clock and saw it was six thirty. She was exhausted. All night she flopped around in bed unable to sleep. *Why is it, I can fall asleep easily now, but couldn't last night?*

Gianna dragged herself out of bed and took a shower. Afterward, she applied her make-up. She was never much for wearing cosmetics, but she figured she'd look more mature and professional with it, especially since most middle school girls wore make-up already. It would also hide the dark circles under her tired eyes. She quickly pulled her damp, long hair back into a clip.

What should I wear? She had planned to pick out her clothes last night, but her phone call with Danny distracted her. So, in a tizzy, she tried on three different outfits before she selected a three-piece suit. She studied herself in the mirror and concluded that a gray pinstriped pantsuit, with a raspberry-red camisole, made her look sophisticated enough to take on her class.

She arrived early to work and reviewed her schedule and lesson plans. Not long after she sat at her desk, there was a knock on her door. Chad poked his head inside her room.

"Good morning, brown eyes." He walked in and placed a cup of coffee and a donut on her desk. "I thought you might like some breakfast."

"Thank you, but a donut for the health teacher?" she asked sarcastically. "Now I'll have to exercise twice as hard."

"Oh, please! You look fantastic. But, if you ever want to work-out, the fitness room is open after school for faculty use, and I could give you a special workout routine," he offered with a wink. "One of the perks of being a teacher here, I guess."

Flustered and not being able to respond wittingly, she said, "Thanks for breakfast. I'll keep it in mind." She smiled and straightened her posture.

"Good luck, brown eyes."

Chad smiled and then strutted out the door.

Gianna rolled her eyes. *Oh, brother!* She leaned forward, covered her face with her hands, and prayed.

Dear God, please help me to have a positive first day with my students. Also, I'm so confused. Chad seems like a nice guy—someone I wouldn't mind getting to know better if I wasn't dating Danny. I know I'm in love with Danny, but he's so busy lately, and I'm lonely. Will we ever have time to be together? Please show me the way. Thank you, Amen.

Just when Gianna finished her prayer, the sound of high heels tapping outside her classroom startled her. She glanced at her door and saw Tracy standing there.

"Hey, girlfriend! It's been a while. So, are you ready to begin your first day?"

"Yes, I think so," Gianna said, deeply inhaling.

"I don't mean to pry, but are you and Dan still dating? I haven't seen you around lately."

Gianna's attention perked up at the mention of him.

"We've both been so busy lately, but I am going to his place tonight. We don't really have any plans yet."

"Cool. Maybe I'll see you," Tracy said.

"Yeah, maybe," Gianna said, then pointed to her desk. "Would you like a cup of coffee and a donut?"

"No, thank you, but why'd you buy it if you don't want it?"

"I didn't. Chad Garrett did."

"Ooh, ooh girl, Dan's got competition!" Tracy teased with her hand raised and her finger up.

"What's that supposed to mean?"

"It means Chad is in pursuit of you, so Dan, look out!" A flash of humor crossed Tracy's face.

Gianna flipped her wrist. "Danny has nothing to worry about. My heart has his name on it."

She refused to let temptation get the best of her.

"I'm just teasing you. Chad is conceited. All the teeny boppers flirt with him constantly, only swelling his ego even more," Tracy said, shaking her head in disgust.

The morning bell rang and the familiar sounds of yakking, giggling, and hollering filled the corridor.

"Now the fun begins," Tracy said, patting Gianna on the shoulder. "Good luck. If you need anything, I'm in Room 135," she said, rushing out the door.

Gianna grabbed the schedule off her desk. *Good! I don't have homeroom duties, but I do have an eighth-grade class coming in first period.* She studied the class roster and saw that it was a large group of twenty-five students. She took a deep breath. *I can handle it.*

When the first period bell rang, she jumped from her chair. Her stomach quivered as she waited in the doorway to greet each student. After all the students took their seats, she walked to the front of the class and introduced herself.

"Good morning. Welcome to *Health and Family Living*. My name is Miss Stefano, and I will be your teacher," she announced assertively.

She discussed her classroom rules and then handed out a fun, get-to-know-you activity. Her goal was to motivate and energize her students.

"I'm handing each of you a lined piece of paper. Please take a few minutes to list ten positive attributes about yourself."

A few of the boys in the back of the room groaned at the task. One called out, "Hey, *Miz* Stefano. Does this count for a positive attribute?" As the youth asked this, he pointed to his groin and gestured provocatively. Many of the students snickered loudly.

Gianna realized that her authority was being challenged, and how she handled this was important to earn their respect. Although her cheeks burned from embarrassment, she turned to the whiteboard. She wrote the words *POSITIVE ATTRIBUTES* in big letters and announced, "It's only a positive attribute if there is a man standing behind it."

"Ooooo!" The entire class howled.

"Another remark like that and you'll be taking a hike to Mr. Sterling's office, and that goes for anyone else who's disrespectful in my classroom," she said.

Determined to keep control of her class, she spun on her heel and asked the girl in the first row what was on her list.

"Good friend and listener," she answered in a timid voice.

Gianna nodded her head in approval and kept the class focused on the topic. Although the rest of the period was uneventful, she questioned why this seemed so much harder than her student teacher assignment. Back then, she was under the guidance of a seasoned teacher. Now, she was inexperienced and on her own.

During her third period class, she was stunned when an obviously pregnant, fourteen-year-old girl sat in the front row. She knew these were significant issues in schools, but she didn't think she would be dealing with this with girls so young. She now realized that she would need to readjust some of her lessons. It was clear that many of these kids were more advanced than she was at twenty-four.

During her fifth period break, she ventured into the teachers' lounge. Harried from a tough start, she sat down and started to look at the lesson plans she had been working on for the past month. Glumly, she began to change some of her lessons.

An overweight Hispanic woman noticed her and sat down at her table. She introduced herself. "Hi, I'm Juana Gomez. You must be the new health teacher. I teach English as a second language to many of the kids here."

Gianna looked up and smiled weakly. "Yes, I am. My name is Gianna Stefano. It's nice to meet you."

Juana asked, "How's it going? Tough day?"

Is it that noticeable? Gianna nodded and told her how her day started.

Juana laughed and said, "That's classic. There are many wise guys here. Some are harsh, but mostly, they are just trying to find themselves in a hard city. Many of these kids come from single parent homes or have parents who are both working one or two jobs each. They have few role models and those who don't, have gang members to look up to. It's sad but a reality."

Silently, Gianna promised herself to light a candle on Sunday. She thanked God for her wonderful family and her good Christian upbringing.

Juana patted Gianna's hand and said, "Hang in there. It isn't all bad. There are terrific kids here, too.

The great part of teaching is finding the gems in the pile of rocks and being able to polish them into the true diamonds they are.

The afternoon carried on without any nonsense. Gianna lost track of time and was startled when the dismissal bell rang. Her last period students filed out of her classroom like a herd of cattle. Chaos filled the hallway. Backpacks hit the floor, locker doors slammed shut, and the thundering voices of boisterous preteens quickly faded into the distance.

She sat down at her desk, closed her eyes, and massaged her temples. Her head pounded from too much stimulation. *I did it, though. I somehow made it through my first day of teaching.* She rested her head on her desk when suddenly a familiar voice shouted outside her door.

"Whoa there, partner!"

Gianna's heart jumped, and her pulse pounded at Danny's voice. What was he doing there?

He stood in her doorway with his cowboy hat in hand. "A person can get trampled on out there," he said, pointing at the hallway.

In an instant, Gianna pushed to her feet. With one forward motion, she wrapped herself up in his embrace.

"How'd you get past security?"

"The guard dog at the door took one look at me and knew I was here for you."

"Ah, I see you met Nick." Lost in his eyes, she said, "I've missed you!"

"So, how'd your first day go?"

"Good, I think. Although I'm tired, I liked it. I have no regrets!"

"Now that's music to my ears."

Gianna walked over to her desk to gather up her papers and books. "But I thought I was meeting you at your place?"

"There was a change in plans," Danny said with a wonderous look on his face.

"Oh?" *What is he up to?*

Outside in the school parking lot, Danny opened the passenger door. The delicious aroma of fried chicken wafted through the air arousing Gianna's growling stomach.

"What's all this?" she asked.

"I made your favorite—fried chicken and corn bread."

Gianna put her hand to her heart. "Oh, Danny! You are such a romantic. Thank you," she said, giving him a kiss for his thoughtfulness.

Danny and Gianna strolled along a path in Central Park until they reached a quiet spot that overlooked a lake on Cherry Hill. They spread out a blanket underneath the tall cherry trees and enjoyed a picnic supper together.

"It's not Gray Wolf State Park, but it's the company you keep that matters," Danny said.

"So true," Gianna said, enjoying their scrumptious meal. "Thank you, Danny. This is the perfect ending of a hectic, first day of school."

Later, Danny drove Gianna to his home. As they entered his unit, she grabbed the picnic basket from him and said, "I've got this. Please go and relax."

"Yes, ma'am."

"The least I can do is clean up," she said, carrying the basket into the kitchen.

Danny lounged on the couch with his laptop when his cell phone danced a Texas two-step across the coffee table. He answered it. "Hey, can I call you back?"

When he abruptly, ended his call, Gianna walked in from the kitchen. "Who was that?"

"Your brother," he said, focusing on his laptop as if to dismiss the conversation.

"Oh," she said, confused as to why he didn't want to speak to Matt.

"Come here, baby," he said. He set is laptop down on the coffee table and pulled her onto his lap. He cuddled her in his arms and gazed at her starry-eyed.

"What's that look?" she asked.

"Suddenly, being a bachelor doesn't feel right anymore."

Although they hadn't dated very long, she craved to hear those words from his lips. She hoped he would mention the M word, but before she could question it, there was a knock at the door. She groaned and reluctantly rolled herself onto the floor.

Danny sighed heavily then ambled to the door and opened it. It was Troy and Tracy.

"Perfect timing," he mumbled.

Tracy poked her head inside the doorway and smiled at Gianna. "I was hoping you'd be here tonight. So, how'd your first day go?"

Gianna bounced to her feet, and in a spirited voice, responded, "Fantastic!"

Tracy stepped into the living room. "Girl, I need to talk to you." She grabbed her arm and pulled her into the kitchen.

Gianna scrunched up her nose. What was this, high school? What could Tracy have to tell her that was so important and secretive?

Tracy whispered, "I stopped by your classroom after you left. Guess who was looking for you?"

Gianna raised her eyebrows and thought for a moment. "Mr. Sterling?" she asked. She crossed her arms. "I have no clue. Tell me."

"Chad!" Tracy blurted out in a loud whisper.

"Chad? What did he want?"

Gianna's temperature spiked. *Well, at least I'm not fired.* Mixed emotions assailed her as she tried to process what she was hearing. She was glad she missed him. After tonight's amazing supper with Danny, she was certain God had answered her prayer.

Tracy pressed her lips together to keep from giggling. "Chad asked me if I knew who the *country boy* was that you left with."

Gianna widened her eyes. "No way!" A sudden reprieve came over her. Hopefully, he got the hint that she wasn't available.

"Whoa there!" Danny bellowed from across the room. "First day of school and you're already gossiping." He shook his head. "I can never figure out why women need to know everything."

Troy shrugged his shoulders dismissively. "You and me both, brother."

Gianna and Tracy looked at each other and laughed.

Tracy pranced back into the living room and put her arm around Troy. "We're not gossiping, honey. We're just talking about Gianna's new friend, Chad, the gym teacher."

Gianna gave Tracy a cold stare then skated across the room in her socks, trying to hush her before she spilled the rest of it.

"This guy, Chad, has been flirting with Gianna for weeks. He even bought her breakfast this morning."

Danny's attention shifted to Gianna. He swallowed hard. "Should I be jealous of this city slicker?"

A tingling sensation swept up Gianna's neck and across her face. She did not intend to make Danny feel insecure. She sat down beside him and gazed into his eyes. "No, Danny. I swear, nothing is going on with Chad."

Tracy spoke up. "I'm only kidding, Dan. I admit Chad's physically attractive, but it ends there. He's a cocky, dominating, shallow creep. I know this because two of my colleagues once dated him."

A sudden chill hit Gianna. That was news to her. Obviously, Tracy knew Chad better than she led on.

"It sounds like Chad is twenty pounds of manure packed in a ten-pound bag," Danny said with a contagious laugh.

After Troy and Tracy left, Gianna cuddled on the couch with Danny. "Now, where'd we leave off?" she asked in a honeyed voice.

"Right here," Danny whispered. He kissed her lips and then sprinkled kisses down her neck.

Her body tingled from his touch. She appreciated the attention but hoped he would mention the bachelor thing again.

"I really missed you," he whispered in her ear.

"And I missed you, but you're always so busy."

Danny sighed. "I know, baby, but a new doc has to pay his dues."

Gianna gazed into his sad, puppy dog eyes. She couldn't be angry with him. She took a deep breath and said, "I understand."

"I promise I won't always have to work sixty hours a week. It's just that I have a lot of catch-up work to do. Listen, I'll make it up to you. I'm off this weekend. We'll do whatever you want."

"Whatever I want?" Gianna asked. That was too good to pass up. She rested her finger on her lips. "Hmm, since we can't fly home, how about we drive upstate to a horse stable and go riding?"

"Sure, anything for *my* girl."

After a long exhausting week at school, Saturday finally arrived. Gianna was more than ready for her date with Danny. He kept his promise and took her to a horse stable to ride.

When she mounted the horse, she cracked a huge smile. "Back in the saddle again," she sang. "Well, he may not be my horse, Gemma, and this may not be Montana, but this is going to be fun." She leaned forward and patted the Tennessee Walker.

"You really miss home, don't you?" Danny asked. They set off on the trails. "I hope you don't have regrets about moving here."

"No, I don't. I just wish we had more time to spend together."

"We will, babe, soon—real soon."

Gianna didn't ask him what *soon* meant, but she was happy to hear it, nevertheless. The day turned out to be memorable. It was a nice outing away from the chaotic city.

The next day after church, Danny took Gianna out to look at an apartment. It was uptown. The two-bedroom rental was well kept, unlike the scary studio she had scoped out weeks ago. However, she hesitated to sign the lease due to the high monthly rent. It was just as expensive as the hotel she was rooming at.

"Something will turn up," Danny said with optimism. "This place just isn't meant to be."

"I suppose," she said.

"C'mon, I'll take you out to dinner."

Chapter 14

The next few weeks were a whirlwind. September rapidly turned into October. The city air turned ruthlessly sharp. There was no doubt that it was autumn; but that was Ok, it was Gianna's favorite season.

Everything was perfect in her life. Her career as a teacher was extremely rewarding, especially when her students grasped a concept that she'd been trying to pound into their heads for a month of Sundays. Even better, Chad Garrett was no longer a nuisance. He had become preoccupied with a newly hired math teacher, Mandy. His involvement with her distracted him from Gianna. Gianna was happy for him.

There was no question in her heart that Danny was the one; however, his career was less than perfect in her eyes. His schedule as a doctor continued to be rigorous and demanding, but he made up for it. The little time that they did have together was well spent. They often volunteered at a food pantry, explored the city, or just lounged around at his place.

Even with the busiest of schedules, Gianna and Danny always found time for church. After they attended several churches, they settled into a smaller, less affluent parish where the priest and parishioners knew each other. Gianna and Danny developed a strong friendship, strengthened with their faith in God, and their commitment to each other.

Time flew by faster than ever, and it was now the day before Thanksgiving. Danny and Gianna were eating breakfast together at the hotel where she was still living.

Slumped in her chair, Gianna stared at the bowl of oatmeal placed in front of her. She stirred it instead of eating it.

"For someone who's flying home today, you sure look unhappy. You Ok?" he asked.

"I..." She looked up at him and mumbled, "I dread facing my dad. I thought I'd be doing better financially by now, but I'm not. This hotel is draining me even with a discounted rate." She put down her spoon and sighed. "I can't afford a decent apartment here, and my dad's going to say, 'I told you so'." She turned away to hide her tears. "I'm a failure."

"Gianna." Danny reached for her hand.

She was comforted by his gentle touch. She looked at him through her blurry eyes. His serene expression was warm and understanding. A sense of strength came over her, and her despair seemed to lessen.

"I've been thinking. Move in with me," he said. His voice was serious, his gaze steady.

Gianna stared at him blankly, her jaw dropped. In a loud whisper, she asked, "What?" She wiped her tears. "Are you *crazy*, Danny?"

"Baby, I'm crazy about you."

"Sorry, but I can't. It's against our faith."

"Gianna, I'm not asking you to sleep with me. Well, I mean...you know." His face colored fiercely. He shook his head. "Listen to me. I've known you since you were born. You're not a stranger off the street."

"Danny, it's wrong!"

Danny gently squeezed her hand. "Look at me." He had honest eyes. "You'll have your very own bedroom and bath. I promise to respect your privacy." His tone was sincere. "Besides, I don't want you living alone in those apartments you looked at. I'd feel better knowing where you are."

"No, I can't. What would I tell my parents?"

"The truth. We're not living in sin."

Gianna ran her fingers through her hair. His suggestion intrigued her.

"Listen, babe," Danny said. "As long as we don't expose ourselves to temptation and avoid anything immoral, it's ok to share the same home."

"Yeah, but—"

Danny threw his hands up. "I promise, no fringe benefits."

"I don't know." She dropped her head and rubbed her eyes. She stewed at the idea. *Danny does work insane hours, and I would have my own space. Plus, I'd be able to replenish my savings.* She looked up at him and nodded. "How much rent do you want?"

"Nothing."

"Danny! I must pay something to live there."

"Ok, you can buy the groceries."

"No. I have to do more than that."

"Look, you're just starting out, and that's challenging enough. I know, I've been there. And believe me, the last thing you need is to be burdened with debt."

Gianna sighed. "Ok but remember what my father told you." She tried to remain serious. "Why buy the cow…"

Danny laughed. "I promise no monkey business."

After breakfast, Gianna gathered up her personal belongings and permanently checked out of the hotel. When they arrived at Danny's home, she quickly unpacked her stuff and hung her clothes in the huge wardrobe closet. She sat down on the bed and admired her new cozy room. Finally, she was home sweet home. She knelt beside her bed and prayed.

Dear God, I have so much to be thankful for. I have a loving family, a fulfilling job, and most of all; I've been blessed with Danny, the love of my life. Now that I've moved in with him, please help me to avoid temptation. Thank you. Amen.

Late afternoon, Danny and Gianna were on a flight home to Montana. Contented, Gianna gazed out the plane window. Through the breaks in the clouds, she could see the handcrafted landscape below. She then glanced at Danny and smiled.

"You're glowing, babe," he said.

She touched his arm. "My little world is a much happier place, thanks to you."

"You're welcome."

Hours later, the plane landed. Gianna and Danny scrambled through the crowded airport to baggage pick-up. A familiar voice caught Gianna's attention.

"Bella! Dan!"

Through a sea of bubbly faces, Gianna spotted Matthew and her father. "Daddy!" she cried, giving him a hug.

"Oh, I've missed you, Bella," he said. He turned to Danny with a huge smile on his face. He shook his hand and said, "Welcome home, son."

Matthew hugged Gianna and patted Danny's shoulder. "Everyone's at the house waiting for us," he said, grabbing a bunch of suitcases. "C'mon, let's get out of here!"

"Matt, slow down. You're like a bolt of lightning," Gianna yelled. She had never seen her brother so fired up before. She sighed. It must be pre-wedding jitters.

The next day was Thanksgiving. It was bitterly cold. The sun tried to peek through the clouds, but it was too cold to melt the snow that dusted the ground. Gianna loved this time of year: the change in weather, the anticipation of the upcoming holidays, and most of all, the company of her loved ones.

In the dining room, Gianna dressed the rustic oak table with a pumpkin-colored linen cloth then placed a cornucopia with fruits and vegetables in the center. Everything looked perfect.

The mouthwatering aroma of roasted turkey flowed through the house, announcing dinner was almost ready. Meanwhile, rowdy cheers from the boys in the family room were becoming unbearable. It must have been some wild football game on TV.

Gianna headed into the kitchen where her mother, both her grandmothers, and Mrs. Kendall were preparing the side dishes. "Need some help?" she asked.

Mom handed her the breadbasket. "Tell me about your apartment. You talked so much about your job. What's your place look like?" she asked.

Immediately, Gianna's face heated up. Not knowing how to respond to her mother's question, she quickly carried the breadbasket into the dining room.

When she returned to the kitchen, she said, "I, uh, haven't found a place yet." She went on to describe the apartments she considered but declined. "Anyway, Mom, once I get back to New York, I'm sure the right place will turn up."

"I suppose," Mom said with uncertainty.

"You must be paying an arm and a leg staying at a hotel," Mrs. Kendall said.

"I'm managing ok for now," Gianna assured them. Hastily, she changed the subject. "I wish Matt and Jessica could've joined us for dinner."

"Matt and Jessica shared Thanksgiving with us last year, so this year they're spending it with her family," Mom said, putting the last of the side dishes on the table. "Gianna, please tell the boys that it's time to eat."

"Sure, Mom."

Hours later, the Kendalls and Danny were preparing to leave. While Dr. and Mrs. Kendall warmed up the truck, Danny and Gianna said their goodbyes.

She stood on the front porch, her arms crossed. In a blah voice, she said, "I wish you didn't have to go."

"Yeah, I know," he said. He lowered his head and let out a heavy sigh. "You didn't tell your parents that you moved in with me."

Gianna's stomach tightened. "I don't think they'd approve of our living arrangements. Besides, I *just* moved in yesterday."

"If I recall, your folks were always fair as long as you were honest."

"I know," she said, dropping her chin to her chest. "I need more time." She glanced at the truck. "They're waiting for you."

"Yeah," Danny said, putting on his cowboy hat. "Goodnight."

It was Friday. In celebration of Matthew's last day of bachelorhood, the men had an adventurous day planned. They were going hiking. The bridesmaids, on the other hand, were going for massages, manicures, and hairstyling. Gianna and her mother were meeting Jessica and the girls at the health club.

Entering the spa was like stepping into a candle shop. The inviting aroma of lavender scented candles filled the air. The dimmed lights and soft music added to the ambiance, promptly muting her vibrant mood. It was what Gianna needed.

During her private massage session, Gianna reflected on all the changes that occurred in her life over the past four months. Although she missed her family and Montana, she was pleased with her teaching career in the city, and her promising relationship with Danny. She was happy with the way her life was unfolding, except for moving in with Danny. It was wrong, and not telling her parents the truth was wrong, too. Her body tensed up at the thought of their disapproval.

But as the therapist rubbed her shoulder blades, her body sank into the warm, padded table, sending her into a deeper state of relaxation. During this tranquil phase, she prayed. She asked God for guidance in her life. She knew that if it were His will, she and Danny would someday become one.

After a morning of pampering, the ladies gathered around a corner booth at a local coffeehouse for brunch and a little socializing before wrapping up their day.

Jessica's younger sister, Heather sipped her coffee, then looked at Gianna with her cutesy grin. "So, Gianna, is it true your relationship with Dan has moved to the next level?"

Gianna nearly gagged on her hot chocolate. How did she find out she moved in with him? She glanced down at her new French manicure and said, "Our friendship is blossoming nicely."

Sarah, Jessica's fifteen-year-old sister, said, "Maybe there'll be wedding bells in your future."

"I'd like to hope so...someday."

Sarah exchanged meaningful glances with their youngest sister, Amanda, and giggled.

Do they know something that I don't? Gianna looked across the table at her mother and Mrs. Duncan. They were busy in their own conversation, oblivious to the bridesmaids' idle chitchat.

Gianna swallowed hard. She needed to change the subject before her new living arrangement leaked out. She touched Jessica's forearm and asked, "Are you anxious about tomorrow?"

"No," Jessica said, adjusting her posture. "When you're with Mr. Right, there's no need to feel nervous because you know you're doing the right thing."

Gianna nodded. Jessica had a point, but that didn't explain why she still felt nervous about telling her parents about moving in with Danny.

When Gianna and her mother arrived home, the SUV was backed in near the garage.

"Oh, the guys are home," Mom said.

"It's early. I wonder how their day went."

Mom looked at the house and shook her head. "The house looks too quiet. They're probably sleeping."

Gianna laughed and nodded in agreement.

They walked along the snow-covered sidewalk. The only noise was the snow crunching under their boots. When they reached the covered porch, Mom unlocked the front door. Pure silence surrounded them.

"You're right, Mom," Gianna whispered. "They must be sleeping."

Mom took off her coat and boots and glanced at the staircase. "I think I hear your father snoring."

Gianna suppressed a giggle. "That's him."

She hung her coat in the closet and noticed Danny's heavy winter coat on the hanger. *I guess he's here, too.*

She closed the closet door and wandered down the hall toward the guest suite. She gave the door a knock, but there was no answer. Quietly, she opened the door a peeked inside. Danny was sound asleep on the bed with his cowboy hat tipped over his eyes.

She stood in the doorway and listened to him breathe. *Poor guy. The freezing cold must have knocked him out.* She left the door ajar, then tiptoed to the bed and sat down on the edge. She leaned into him and kissed his cheek.

Danny put his arm around her. "You're finally home."

"Yeah, what time did you guys get in?"

He lifted his hat and rubbed the sleep out of his weary eyes. "Noon. It was so cold. We hiked four miles then gave up. We stopped for lunch, then came home." He adjusted his pillow. "I took a hot shower. Been sleeping since."

"We were so spoiled today," she said, feeling a bit guilty. She gazed at him and noticed a spark of passion in his eyes.

"Babe, you look beautiful! Your hair is down—just the way I like it."

His smile made her heart race.

"Thank you." She stepped away from the bed. "I better go get ready for rehearsal."

Danny sat up in bed and reached for her arm. "No, come here." He eased her onto his lap and held her in his arms. "I really missed you today."

"Aw, I missed you, too."

He kissed her.

Gianna's mouth burned with hunger. Aching for another kiss, she cradled his face in her hands. She kissed him back, this time more fervently, savoring the sweetness of his lips. Shocked at her own eagerness, she pulled away from his embrace.

"I'm so sorry. I shouldn't be doing this."

"It's ok, I understand," he said. "Can't blame a guy for trying," he mumbled.

"Gianna?" Her mother's abrupt voice echoed down the hallway.

Gianna leaped off the bed and headed for the door. She looked back at Danny and cried half-heartedly, "I'm sorry." She poked her head out the door and answered, "I'm right here, Mom."

"I thought I might find you here," Mom said, warily. "We need to leave soon, so you best get ready." She put her hand on Gianna's shoulder and scooted her along.

Chapter 15

Wedding bells at the church chimed. Jessica and her bridal party arrived in a white, stretch limousine. Since they were early, they waited in a little room just left of the vestibule while the rest of the guests could be ushered to their pews.

The sound of hymns resonated through the inner church doors. Gianna stepped into the vestibule and caught a glimpse of the inside of the church. *My stars! It's beautiful.* White satin ribbons adorned the pews. Dozens of red and white poinsettias festively decorated the altar.

"Jess, there are a lot of guests here."

"It's ok. I'm not nervous."

"I am."

Gianna paced back and forth inside the little room waiting for their cue, when suddenly she heard the clicking of heels inside the vestibule. She peeked out the door and saw a young woman wearing a white, low-cut, clingy blouse and a black suede mini skirt that bared her long legs. Her spiked heels hiked her up so much, that she was taller than the young man who accompanied her. *Really? Who dresses like that to a wedding?*

Gianna looked over her shoulder. "Jess, who is that?"

Jessica glanced out the door. "Oh, that's Angel. My cousin, Tommy's girlfriend." She shook her head. "I don't know what he sees in her."

"Isn't it obvious?" Heather asked, standing with her hands on her hips. "Don't let her innocent name fool you."

Gianna bowed her head. *Please forgive me, God. I know I shouldn't judge.* She peered out the doorway again. She caught Angel eyeing Danny from head to toe. *Well, at least she has good taste in men.* He looked stunning in his black tuxedo.

John walked over to Angel to escort her to a pew, but she declined. Instead, she approached Danny. She linked her arm through his and then wiggled her hips into the church, leaving her boyfriend behind. Danny, always the gentleman, guided Angel to a seat, then took his position at the altar.

Gianna's blood boiled. Her cheerful mood veered sharply to anger. Weakened by jealousy, she stood there, arms crossed, fuming. When she seized John's attention, she gave him a look of fury, but all he did was shrug his shoulders.

Jessica touched Gianna's arm and whispered, "Don't worry. Angel is no contest. Dan loves you."

The wedding coordinator signaled the bridesmaids to line up. When the organ sounded the wedding march, Sarah began the procession. When it was Gianna's turn, she focused her gaze on Danny. Immediately, her fiery eyes softened, and her mood lightened.

All heads turned and focused on the bride as she strolled down the aisle with her father. Gianna shed happy tears over her brother marrying her best friend. She gained a sister.

After the lovely church ceremony concluded, the wedding party formed a receiving line in the vestibule. Matthew and Jessica stood together with both sets of parents next to them. The bridal party lined up on the opposite side and greeted the guests as they left the church.

Gianna felt honored to be there, especially since she met extended family that she hadn't seen in years. She was all smiles until Angel and Tommy appeared. While Tommy congratulated Jessica and Matthew, Angel paraded toward Danny to introduce herself.

"Hi, I'm Angel," she said in a vivacious voice. "I'm a friend of uh, uh, Jessica's family."

Danny stepped backward, obviously shocked by her abruptness. Swiftly, he put on his charm and cheerfully introduced himself. "I'm Dan and this is my girlfriend, Gianna." He wrapped his arm around her and possessively pulled her close to him.

Gianna smirked. "It's so nice to meet you, Angel."

Angel's smile deflated. She flipped her long blond hair, grabbed Tommy's arm and left.

Gianna couldn't help but display a contented smile. When she looked up at Danny, he winked at her. Her heart sang with satisfaction, knowing that he wasn't interested in Angel.

The reception was held at the Swan Lake Inn. During cocktail hour, Gianna munched on hors d'oeuvres and punch, mingling with the wedding party in a private room until it was time to make their grand entrance into the ballroom. There were no shadows across her heart, until her twin brothers stirred up doubt.

John sat at a small corner table sipping his soda and making snide comments about who knows what. In response, Luke cackled and blew bubbles through his straw.

"Ok you two, what's so funny?" Matthew asked.

Luke had been laughing so hard that tears ran down his face. "You missed it, Matt. When we were ushering people into church, this chick with a short skirt and skimpy top showed up."

Mark joined in laughing, too. "Yeah, she took one look at John and ditched him for Dan."

John retorted, "Hey, that's almost true. Anyway, that's not the funny part. You should've seen Gianna. Her brown eyes turned an *ugly* green when that chick approached Dan."

"Yeah, she was madder than an old wet hen," Luke squawked. He clucked at her a couple times, then cackled on some more.

Gianna patted her forehead with her cloth napkin. Suddenly, the room felt ten degrees warmer. "So what? The green-eyed monster attacked me."

"Angel was out of line," Danny said. "But I think she got the hint when I introduced Gianna as my girlfriend."

"Well, *who* is she?" Matthew asked.

Jessica explained to Matthew who Angel was. Meanwhile, Heather invited Gianna to go with her to the powder room to freshen up. As the two left, Jessica called out, "We'll be along shortly."

☙❧

Dan stood by the doorway and watched Gianna as she greeted friends and family along the way to the powder room. Once she was out of sight, he gave Jessica the signal to discuss her plan.

"Now, listen up girls," Jessica said to Amanda and Sarah. "I need you two, and Heather, to surround Gianna when I throw the bouquet. Hopefully, I can toss it directly to her."

"What if someone else catches it?" Amanda asked.

Jessica shrugged her shoulders and looked at Matthew baffled.

"Then, the plan is off," Matthew said. "But, if she catches the bouquet, I'll fling the garter to Dan." Matthew pointed to his brothers. "You three play blocker. Got it?"

Luke shook his finger at Dan. "You'd better catch it. I'm not going there with my sister." He put his finger to his mouth to show himself hurling.

John smacked Luke. "Dude, you're gross."

In a low, timid voice, Sarah asked, "But, Dan, what if she catches it and you miss it?"

"Don't worry. I've got this," he said, then swallowed hard. *I'd better catch the garter.* He reviewed Jessica's plan in his head and imagined it running smoothly. He also played out what could go wrong. His stomach dropped at the thought of some other man putting the garter up her leg.

The wedding coordinator poked his head into the room, ripping Dan from his thoughts. "It's show time in five minutes, folks!"

☙

Gianna lined up with the wedding party outside the ballroom. While they waited for their cue, she glimpsed through the double glass doors and saw how exquisite it looked inside. There were white icicle lights that dangled from the ceiling along the perimeter of the room. The banquet tables were decorated with gold linen cloths and silver bell centerpieces. The four-tiered wedding cake was decorated like Christmas gift packages; each layer wrapped with edible ribbons and bow accents.

When the DJ announced the wedding party, they entered the ballroom in pairs, then stood alongside the dance floor while the bride and groom danced for the first time as husband and wife. Warmth radiated through Gianna as she watched her brother and Jessica. They were so in love.

The evening moved quickly. Gianna mingled with friends and family, enjoying exciting conversations with her loved ones. No doubt, this joyous day would stay in her heart forever.

Gianna returned to the bridal table and kicked off her shoes. Just as she sat down and rubbed her sore feet, the DJ invited all single women to the dance floor for the bouquet toss. Gianna cringed. *I'm not going out there. There is no way I'm going to make a fool out of myself. Those shenanigans are for drunken, party girls.*

Danny approached the table and prodded her. "Babe, go up there."

"No thank you," she said, shaking her head.

Heather hurried to the table. "Come on, Gianna." She grabbed her hand and pulled her away from Danny onto the dance floor.

"Heather, I'll never forgive you for this!" *Ugh! Why me?* Having a strong urge to flee, she scanned the ballroom for the nearest exit, but Heather had a tight grip on her wrist.

CB&EO

Dan stood on the sidelines and watched Gianna and Heather join the already crowded dance floor of frolicsome, single women. While Angel stood front and center, Heather steered Gianna toward the left side of the crowd next to Sarah and Amanda.

Dan rubbed his chin. *I hope this plan works.* There were quite a few spirited women waiting impatiently for Jessica to toss the bouquet. *Ok, good. Jess pinpointed Gianna's location.* He waited with anticipation. When she tossed the bouquet into the air, it landed right into Gianna's arms. *Perfect!*

"Y-e-a-h!" he hollered from the sideline.

He noticed Gianna's bulging eyes. She shook her head in denial. "Not me, nuh-uh, no way," she said, holding the bouquet like a hot potato. She even tried to pass it off to Heather before Jessica raced over to her.

Dan heard Gianna tell Jessica that she didn't want it. He noticed her hands shaking and she looked a little pale.

"Oh, yes, you do. Just wait here with me," Jessica said. She wrapped her arm around Gianna and pulled her aside from the dance floor.

Dan's stomach tightened. *Am I a monster for putting her out there?* His intention was not to embarrass her. To make it right, he had to be certain that he would catch the garter.

Just then, the DJ announced all eligible men to come onto the dance floor. With no hesitation, he stepped up. He made eye contact with Matthew and got into position. He was cool in his boots until six wasted men staggered to the dance floor. They whistled at Gianna, then gestured that they were going to catch the garter. The pressure was on, but Dan was determined to follow through with the plan. He glanced at Gianna's brothers. "We've got an over-excited bunch here. Get between me and the drunks and play blocker."

Matthew whipped the garter through the air. Mark leaped forward to block a drunk but was clobbered in the head. Following suit, Luke and John tripped over Mark and fell to the floor.

Dan focused on the garter as it soared through the air. He stretched his arm out as far as he could reach and caught it with his finger, then tumbled to the floor.

He stood up and shouted, "Victory!" twirling the garter on his finger. He heard a few groans of defeat as the drunks dispersed off the dance floor.

Dan grinned while walking over to Gianna. She was frozen in place. Her trembling hand covered her mouth in obvious shock. He swept her up into his arms and carried her to a chair in the middle of the dance floor.

While the DJ played a tune, the crowd chanted his name, urging him to put the garter on her leg.

Dan's heart pounded at the task. He knelt in front of Gianna, smiling with eagerness. He playfully inched the garter up her leg. When he reached her mid-thigh, he noticed her face was beet red. Out of respect, he stopped.

"Higher, higher," the drunks hollered from across the dance floor.

◕◖

Gianna burned with embarrassment and motioned Danny to remove the garter. She hated being in the spotlight, especially with her parents and grandparents watching. After he removed the garter, he placed it on his wrist like a bracelet, then leaned forward and kissed her. The tension in her body released. *Thank goodness, the show is over.* She wanted to bolt off the dance floor, but before she could stand up, she saw Matthew handing Danny a small box. Her eyes filled with tears. *No way!*

Danny knelt on one knee and took her hand in his. "Gianna, I love you, and I know that this love is from God. Because I know this, I want to be your husband. I promise to always be faithful and true to you. Will you marry me?"

Butterflies fluttered in her stomach. He was everything to her, her best friend, her life. She gazed into his eyes and said, "Yes! I will marry you!" Tears of joy streamed down her face.

Danny's eyes welled up as he placed the heart-shaped diamond ring on her finger.

"It's so beautiful! Thank you, Danny," she cried. She sprung from her chair and threw her arms around him. "I love you," she said, kissing him recklessly, forgetting that she was still the focus on the dance floor.

"Ahem." Jessica cleared her throat.

Gianna turned and saw Jessica and Matthew standing there. She pointed her finger at them. "You two set me up!"

Matthew smirked. "Well, mama didn't raise any dummies!"

"It was my idea," Jess said.

"Yeah, I hung up on Matt a few times because you walked in on our call," Danny said.

Gianna smiled. "I had no clue."

"Congrats, bella," Dad said, giving her a hug.

Mom hugged her. "Congratulations, honey."

"You mean you two knew about this?"

"Of course," Dad replied. "Dan *asked* my permission to marry you."

"Thank you, Daddy, for your blessing. I love you."

Her father placed her hand in Danny's hand. "I want to see my best girl dance before she leaves tomorrow."

Gianna and Danny set out on the dance floor one last time. As they swayed back and forth, she gazed into his eyes. "We need to pick a date."

"How about July? We can have it here in Montana," he said, his eyes gentle and dreamy.

"Ok," she said with no hesitation. She rested her head on his chest. *I will cherish this evening forever.*

Chapter 16

Gianna and Danny's plane landed at Newark Liberty International Airport late Sunday afternoon. They managed to muddle through the baggage pick-up area, and shortly after, they were riding in a taxi. Gianna stared out the cab window in a daze. The all-too-familiar sensations of reality came back to her.

"We're home, babe," Danny said.

"Home." The word sang in Gianna's heart. This was a moment in time that all the pieces of her life seemed to have fallen into place. She was so happy.

When Gianna and Danny arrived at their front door, Troy and Tracy rushed over to greet them.

"Welcome home," Troy said.

Tracy gave Gianna a hug. "Ok, girlfriend, show me the ring."

Gianna held out her hand. "Why am I not surprised that you knew about this?"

"Oh, it's beautiful!" Tracy said, admiring the diamond. "To answer your question, girlfriend, the day of your in-service, Dan asked me to meet him at the jewelers."

"So, that's why you kept picking my brain about engagement rings. And here I thought you were giving me input for my lesson plans on relationships."

Troy put his hand on Danny's shoulder. "Not to break up this little chat, but we have a little spread over at our place for you both."

"Thanks, bud," Danny said. "You've got to see the video of my proposal."

"Now this I've got to see," Tracy said.

Hours later, Gianna and Danny returned home. Finally, able to relax after a long, exhausting day, Danny flipped on the gas fireplace, clutched Gianna's wrist, and led her to the couch to cuddle. Wrapped in each other's arms, they watched the shadows of the flames dance across the wall.

"What do you think about asking Troy and Tracy to be in our bridal party?" Gianna asked.

"Yeah, I think we should."

"Do you think they'd accept? Montana's a little far."

"I'll offer to pay their airfare," Danny replied easily.

"Ok, I'll ask Tracy tomorrow at school."

"And I'll talk to Troy."

"I'm going to ask Jessica to be my matron of honor."

"Ok, and Matt will be my best man."

Gianna gave Danny a quick kiss on his cheek then leaped off the couch. She grabbed a pocket calendar out of her purse and plopped down next to him.

"Here's July. What day should we pick?"

Danny glanced at the dates and pointed to Saturday. "Let's do the 26th."

She stared at the date. Why did it sound familiar? She smiled. "Oh, that was the date of the church social."

"Exactly," he replied with a wink.

"Ooh, you're so romantic."

She caressed his face with her fingertips. The stubble of his designer shadow made her stomach flutter.

Danny held her face in his hands. He brushed his lips against hers and whispered, "I can't wait 'till July."

He sprinkled a mini kiss on the tip of her nose, her cheek, and then down her neck and shoulders. The soft touch of his lips on her skin sent chills through her body.

She buried her face in his neck. The scent of his cologne made her desire him more. She breathed, "I love you."

As her passion grew stronger, so did his. He held her tighter, and she could feel the warmth of his body and his pounding heartbeat. He pressed his lips against hers and covered her mouth with a kiss. The refreshing taste of his minty breath left her hungry for more. But a voice in her head told her to stop. She was supposed to avoid temptation.

"Danny, we can't do this," she uttered through heavy breaths. She wiggled out of his embrace. "We have to wait."

Danny reached for her hand. "It's ok."

He seemed pensive, not disturbed, or angry.

"I think I should go to bed now," she said, pushing to her feet.

Gianna entered her bedroom and closed the door behind her. She sat on her bed and took a deep breath. Her heart ached with emptiness. *I knew it was going to be difficult to resist him once I moved in.*

She knelt by her bedside and prayed that the Holy Spirit would help her grow in virtue.

Afterward, she showered, climbed into bed, and listened to the silence. There weren't any doors slamming, luggage rolling, or muffled voices outside her room. It was weird, but it was a good weird. She felt safe in Danny's home.

It was Monday morning, and Gianna woke up earlier than usual. She slept well in her new room. For once, she didn't have to force herself out of bed.

She rummaged through her closet in search of something festive to wear. She chose a red sweater and a black pair of jeans.

She found her way to the kitchen, hoping to join Danny for breakfast, but instead spotted a note on the counter.

Good morning, Gianna. Have a wonderful day back at school. I'll be home by 8:30. Love, Dan

She smiled and twirled the ring on her finger. Her heart raced thinking about him. *I love him so much.*

When Gianna stepped outside, she quivered at the brutal temperature. It seemed colder in New York than in Montana. She shrugged her shoulders and carried on. The weather set the tone for the holiday season.

She assumed that returning to work after a week off would be difficult, but her enthusiasm for planning her wedding kept her motivated.

She arrived at school early and had time to chat with Nick and review her lesson plans. As each class period got underway, her students at once spotted the dazzling rock on her ring finger. Her exciting news prompted a discussion on relationships and marriage which turned out to be an appropriate topic for her class.

The morning flew by, and it was noon. Gianna was in the cafeteria buying her lunch. Rumors about her engagement spread to the faculty, so when she entered the teachers' lounge, she was the highlight of the discussion. When the dust settled, she sat down at a round table in the back corner to eat her sandwich. Just as she took a bite, Tracy strolled in.

"Oh, there you are," Tracy said as she tossed her lunch bag down on the table. She took a seat beside Gianna and placed her hand on her forearm. "Thought you might like to know there is a gorgeous hunk in the main lobby looking for you," she said in a low playful voice.

Dumbfounded, Gianna asked, "Who, Chad?"

Tracy's eyes protruded. "Where's your mind, girlfriend?" She shook her head. "No, Dan's here."

A tingling feeling raced up Gianna's back and into her face. "But...how? He had a full schedule today."

"Well, he's here," Tracy said.

A rush of adrenaline stormed Gianna's body. She leaped out of her chair and sprinted to the door, nearly colliding with Chad who had just entered the teacher's lounge with a tray full of food.

"Where's the fire?" Chad asked.

Gianna stopped dead in her tracks. "Oh, sorry, Chad. Please excuse me."

"It's all good," Chad said, lifting his lunch tray out of her way.

Gianna snaked her way through the noisy crowds of students. When she reached the front lobby, she caught sight of Danny speaking to Nick. She stood back and admired him from a distance. She agreed with Tracy. He was a hunk. What was it? The way he held his cowboy hat in his hands, or how he presents himself in his black leather duster, jeans, and boots? Whatever it was, left her pulse in her throat.

She snuck up behind him and wrapped her arms around his waist. "Hey there, cowboy. This is a pleasant surprise."

Danny turned and greeted her with a peck on the cheek. "A few patients canceled, and the office closed for lunch. Thought I'd stop by to visit."

"Aw, so sweet," Nick teased.

Gianna gave Nick a playful smirk then turned to Danny. "Well, I'm happy you're here."

She reached for his hand and led him through the lively cafeteria to buy him lunch. As they weaved through the mingling cliques, she noticed the admiring stares from her students and heard a few snide comments.

She invited him into the teachers' lounge and joined Tracy and Chad at the corner table where she had left her lunch minutes ago.

"You made it back," Tracy said.

She kicked Gianna under the table and motioned her to introduce Danny to Chad.

Gianna, deliciously alive, glanced at Chad who looked all buff in his red, snug-fitting t-shirt and black workout pants. "Chad, I'd like you to meet my fiancé, Doctor Daniel Christiansen." She placed her hand on Danny's forearm and said, "Danny, this is Chad Garrett, one of our gym teachers here."

"Nice to meet you, Chad," Danny said in a friendly, civil voice. He reached across the table to shake his hand.

With hesitancy, Chad placed his water bottle down on the table. He firmly grasped Danny's hand, and in a glittering, false smile, responded, "Likewise." He stood up from his chair and in a brusque tone muttered, "Excuse me, I have a class." As he started to walk away, he looked back at Danny with a tinge of jealousy in his eyes and said, "You're one lucky *country boy*. Congrats on your engagement."

"Thank you," Danny said, looking a bit stunned by Chad's persona. He scratched his chin and asked, "Not the friendly sort, is he?"

"That's because *you* have what *he* can't have," Tracy said, wriggling her shoulders. "I'm afraid you're a bit outside the box for him."

Gianna, feeling her cheeks flush, sat back in her chair. *Whoa! Tracy certainly has a way of saying things without beating around the bush.*

"So, that's Chad?" Danny asked.

"That would be him," Tracy said. She looked at Gianna and said, "Before, when you ran out to find Dan, Chad asked me where you were going in such a rush. When I told him your fiancé was here, he suddenly became irritated and asked, 'you mean that country boy proposed? What the heck does she see in him?'"

"Excuse me?" Gianna asked, stunned. "What happened to that math teacher he was dating?"

Tracy folded her hands and rested them on the table. She leaned forward and whispered, "Oh, he's seeing her, but in his world, it's an open relationship. His eyes are free to wander, along with his hands." Tracy turned to Dan. "I'd say Gianna's rejection tarnished his pompous ego just a bit."

Gianna swallowed hard. *If Tracy's right, then Chad's an animal.*

Danny narrowed his eyes as if he was red flagged. He folded his hands and rested them on the table. "Maybe I should talk to him."

Gianna turned to Danny and swept a few strands of hair out of his face. "Don't bother. Chad's a big boy. Besides, I think he finally got the hint."

The period bell rang.

"Crab apples!" Gianna said, springing from her chair. "I have to get to my next class."

Chapter 17

December was a hectic month for both Gianna and Danny. Gianna was busy with school projects, Christmas preparations, and planning their wedding. Danny's schedule was ludicrous with an outrageous number of couples having babies. He spent many nights on-call at the hospital. However, regardless of his unpredictable schedule, he and Gianna always made time to fit in Sunday Mass.

Gianna and Danny managed to have one free weekend together, so they arranged a road trip upstate to cut down a Christmas tree. Despite the wind and cold, the weather cooperated, and there was no snow. Together, they relived childhood memories and picked out the perfect tree.

When they returned home that evening, they brought the beautiful Douglas fir inside. Because of its size, the tree barely fit through the doorway and nearly touched the nine-foot ceiling. The scent of the freshly cut pine tree lingered in the living room.

Danny hauled out the box of decorations from storage. Together, he and Gianna strung the colored lights and hung the ornaments. Afterward, they crashed on the couch and admired their festively decorated home.

Gianna leaned into Danny. "It's so beautiful. I love all the colorful twinkly lights. As a kid, we always had white lights."

"Uh-huh, my folks did, too," he said. "I think I like color lights better, maybe because all I see here in the city are bright white lights."

"Makes sense," Gianna said.

She excused herself for a moment and came back with a small box wrapped in gold paper and a velvet bow. She sat down and gave it to Danny. She kissed him on the cheek and told him to open it. Quietly, he opened the gift. His eyes sparkled, and his smile broadened as he lifted the customized cowboy and cowgirl ornament from its cushion.

"Babe, it's perfect!" Gently, he grabbed her hand and lifted her from the couch. Together, they hung the ornament inscribed *Our First Christmas – Danny and Gianna.*

She tapped his shoulder. "Notice the lasso?"

He nodded and said, "Yup, and don't think I won't use it if you think about running away from me."

After a long embrace at the tree, they settled back on the couch, lost in their own thoughts about the future. They gazed at the tree long enough to fall asleep.

The next morning, after church, Gianna and Danny stopped for brunch then came home. While Danny settled into his recliner with his laptop and paperwork, Gianna went into her room to change out of her Sunday dress into a pair of leggings and an ugly Christmas sweater. She was all about comfort, especially when working in the kitchen. And today, she decided to bake a variety of holiday cookies.

She ventured into the kitchen and turned on the Christmas music. As she kneaded the cookie dough, she heard snoring from the living room. She shook her head. *My poor guy is whipped.*

By early evening, Gianna had baked sugar cookies, chocolate chip cookies, and gingerbread cookies. All she had left to do was decorate them. Engrossed in her creations, she sensed Danny's presence over her shoulder. "I know, I know. The kitchen is a disaster," she said, standing there under his scrutiny.

He stepped backwards and threw his hands up as if to surrender. "What? I didn't say anything!"

Gianna scanned the kitchen at the mess she had made. Mixing bowls, utensils, and cookie sheets filled the sink. A layer of flour covered the countertop as well as the floor. "Mom would've had a fit if I did this in her kitchen."

"I'm not excited. I know you'll clean up when you're done," Danny said. He took a long glance at her then shook his head and smiled. "You're a sight. Your ponytail's askew, your forehead's dusted with flour, and you're still the prettiest girl I've ever seen."

Lost for words, Gianna wiped the flour off her forehead and tidied her hair aimlessly. She looked at him and smiled. "Oh, you." She dipped her finger in a small amount of frosting and playfully dabbed it on his beard, starting a flirtatious feud.

Danny looked at her, and his double gaze was obvious. She dashed around the center island. As he chased her, she slipped on a blanket of flour and tumbled to the floor.

"Are you ok?" he asked.

She looked down at her ankle, still half-laughing. Her smile grew serious, and her voice became shaky. "I don't think I can stand up. Ooh, it hurts."

Danny carefully pulled her sock off and examined her ankle. "Most likely you sprained it." He picked her up and carried her over to the dining room chair.

"It's my fault. I started it," she said, regretting her careless behavior.

"You're only half right. You should've kept the kitchen clean like your mother does," he teased. He took an icepack out of the freezer and wrapped it in a towel. "Here, hold this on your ankle."

Danny disappeared briefly and returned with Ibuprofen and a cup of water. "This will help relieve the pain and keep the inflammation down."

He walked back into the kitchen to sweep up the mess, fill the dishwasher, and grab a cookie. "Yum, these are delicious!" he said, walking over to her. "So, how's that ankle feel?"

"Cold and sore," she said.

"You'll need to continue applying a cold pack for the next twenty-four hours, and you're to stay off of it."

Gianna pressed her lips tight at his recommendation. She had so much to do between school and volunteer work. "But I have the toy drive to run, and on Friday, I'm supposed to sing Christmas carols at the nursing home."

"Take it easy, baby. Give it a couple of days."

"Fine," she sighed.

A week and a half later, it was Christmas Eve. Gianna and Danny attended Midnight Mass together. It was crowded but lovely. The dominant sound of the pipe organ, and the harmonious church choir, announced the glorious birth of the Christ child. The aroma of the burning candles and incense, and the festive red and white poinsettias, gave the cathedral a beautiful, enchanting spirit. Gianna and Danny were very blessed to share in the ceremony but missed the joy of celebrating with their families.

That night, Gianna was in a deep sleep, when she felt someone tugging at her shoulder. She groaned, then rolled over. She rubbed her weary eyes and saw Danny sitting on the edge of her bed. *What's he doing here?* All sorts of catastrophic events flashed through her head.

She sat up. "What's wrong?"

"One of my patients is in labor."

Gianna sighed. *It's Christmas, and we should be together.* But she realized she was being selfish. *Having a baby is a miracle, especially on the day we celebrate the Savior's birth.*

She nodded. "I understand."

"I'll be home as soon as I can."

When daybreak welcomed her, Gianna kept her original plans and volunteered at the local soup kitchen. Afterward, she returned home and prepared a small turkey. While it roasted, she lounged on the couch and called her parents. After their call ended, she imagined her future with Danny. She sighed. *I'll just have to get used to his unpredictable schedule.*

Suddenly, her phone played a Christmas tune. She grabbed it off the coffee table and answered it. "Danny, hi, how's it going?"

"Hey, I'll be home soon. My patient just delivered a healthy baby boy!"

"Oh, wonderful news! I'll see you soon."

Gianna smiled, imagining what it was like to hold a precious newborn in her arms. She prayed for all Danny's patients, and then thanked the Lord for him being a part of their lives and hers.

Chapter 18

Luckily, for Gianna, winter was mild in New York. She didn't have the hassle of schlepping through the snow, store-to-store, browsing for wedding trinkets.

She was a frugal shopper. When she saw something she liked, she noted the ordering information and compared the price to stores in Montana. When she found her dream-wedding gown, she arranged for the bridal shop in Montana to order it. She expected a trip home once the dress came in.

Although it had been an easy winter, Gianna happily welcomed spring. Danny continued to work ridiculous hours while she took on tutoring after school to help her parents pay for the wedding.

It was soon Easter break, and Gianna had a week off from school. One afternoon, she was spring-cleaning her bedroom. As she organized her closet and sorted her clothes, she found an old pair of blue jeans crumpled in the corner that had fallen off the hanger. *My jeans! These are my favorite.*

Thrilled to have discovered her missing jeans, Gianna held them up against herself in front of a full-length mirror. *I can't wait to try these on.* She recalled the last time she wore them. It was autumn, when she and Danny had gone horseback riding.

She stepped into her skinny jeans and wiggled them up over her hips. She inhaled deeply, sucking in her stomach, but she couldn't button them. She shook her head and sighed.

She trudged into the bathroom and stepped on the dreaded scale. A sudden chill hit her core. She gained thirteen pounds. *But how did I?* She scratched her head. *I know. It's all those pit stops after school at the street vendors for kettle corn.* She frequently craved the sweet and salty taste.

She marched back to the full-length mirror and analyzed every curve of her body. She pushed her shoulders back and straightened her posture. *Ugh! Today, I'm starting a diet, and I will shed these pounds before my wedding.*

She changed into a black pair of yoga pants and a purple t-shirt. She turned on the television and clicked on an exercise program. After just three minutes of jumping around, she stopped. *This is so boring.* She switched off the television and cranked up the stereo.

She dropped to the floor and started doing stomach crunches. She managed to complete ten before the music abruptly shut off. She glanced over her shoulder and saw Danny standing there with a half-smile on his lips.

Gianna jumped to her feet and shrieked, "Jumpin' Jehoshaphat! Don't sneak up on me like that!"

"I didn't. How could you hear me anyway with that metal music vibrating the walls? I thought you were partying without me," he teased. His eyes roamed up and down her figure. "Since when did my country girl turn bad girl anyway?"

"It's the only music that keeps me motivated to exercise. Look at me. I've got a big butt, big thighs, and a gut." She twirled around so he could check her out. "I need to lose weight before our wedding."

Danny stood there with his head cocked, an eyebrow raised, and his mouth wide open. "Why? You're at a healthy weight, and you look fantastic," he insisted. "It wouldn't be healthy for you to lose any weight."

"Fine, I'll weight train then. Tracy and I will workout in the fitness room after school."

"I can see your mind is made up, but promise me that you won't overdo it," he pleaded.

"Ok, I promise."

Danny pulled her close and kissed her. "I love you just the way you are."

Later that evening, Gianna and Danny sat down for supper. She had prepared her mother's recipe for pot roast.

"What's new with the wedding plans?" Danny asked. "It seems like I haven't been around much to help lately."

Gianna put down her fork and patted her face with her napkin. "Don't worry about it. Everything's great. Mom called me today. My gown's in already."

"So, did your gown trigger your sudden desire to lose weight?" he asked with a smirk.

"Funny," she said. "It was the jeans that I found on the closet floor."

Danny shook his head. "We'd better get those plane tickets for Memorial Day weekend. I already have the time off."

Gianna nodded. She knew the importance of being in Montana to finalize their wedding plans. "Ok, so we're leaving on that Friday and coming home on Tuesday, right?" she asked.

"Yes. That Saturday is our Pre-Cana encounter with Father Anthony."

"Ok. I'm on it tonight," she said.

Over the next few weeks, Gianna and Tracy met three days after school for forty-five-minute workouts. Gianna felt great and enjoyed exercising. Most of the time, she ran on the treadmill, but there were days where she'd weight train, too.

Two days a week, Chad Garrett offered to coach Gianna and Tracy. They appreciated his guidance. He was very encouraging and supported their efforts. In just a few weeks, Gianna and Tracy started a trend. They inspired other teachers to exercise as well.

"In just four weeks, I'll be going home," Gianna said. She breathed heavily as she ran on the treadmill. "I can't wait to try on my wedding gown!"

Tracy was on the elliptical trainer. Winded, she said, "That's so exciting, Gianna. I wish I could be there to see you." She hopped off the machine and dropped onto the floor to stretch. "My bridesmaid gown came in." She paused to catch her breath. "And yesterday I went for a fitting. I'm so excited that they must take it in at the waist another quarter inch. These workouts are paying off."

Gianna finished her program on the treadmill and stepped off. She sat on the floor and rested a moment letting her mind stray. She was so grateful for her family, especially her mother. She had done so much planning the wedding. She reserved the banquet hall, ordered the flowers, booked the photographer, amongst a million other things. Gianna also realized how lucky she was to have the perfect fiancé and how much she loved him. Her eyes welled up in appreciation for the life she had.

Chapter 19

Another two and a half weeks passed, and it was now mid-May. Gianna woke up to a beautiful clear Wednesday morning. Temperatures were supposed to reach eighty degrees. She couldn't wait for the end of the school day, so she could work out again with Tracy.

Gianna sat at the kitchen counter eating a bowl of cereal. "Only nine more days until we go home," she said, enthusiastically.

"Baby, I'm so ready to go that I'd leave today if I could," Danny said without any hesitation. He poured himself another cup of coffee. "I'm dreading this conference I have this afternoon."

"That bad?" she asked, placing her bowl in the sink.

Danny sighed and ran his fingers through the back of his hair. "There's this one difficult doctor that has ideas for making more money, but I don't agree."

"I'm sorry," Gianna said. She stood behind him and massaged his shoulders. "Ooh, *you are* tense. Meet me after school. We can work out together and relieve some stress." She leaned forward and kissed his cheek.

Danny turned and wrapped his arms around her. "I can't. The meeting is at three thirty. But I wish I could. I'd like to observe Chad coaching you."

Gianna sensed he was a little envious but did not intend to make him feel that way. "Danny, I love *you*, not Chad," she said, sealing her vow with a kiss.

"I *know*, and I *trust* you," he said confidently. He stood up and mumbled, "It's Chad I could live without." he mumbled. He walked her to the door. "I love you, too. Have a good day."

Gianna held his face in her hands and kissed him. "Good luck at your meeting." She tucked her satchel under her arm and trekked out the door.

Gianna had a rough day at school. Her students were rambunctious and inattentive, making it difficult for her to cover her lesson plans. *Good grief! Is it the summer-like weather making them nuts?*

"Oh, c'mon, Miz Stefano! Why do we have to do this stupid assessment anyway?"

"Zack, it shows me how much you've learned."

"This is so boring," Wyatt said, tipping his chair back.

"Wyatt, all four chair legs on the floor, please."

"Sorry," Wyatt said, putting down his chair.

"Boys and girls, only a few more minutes left."

The three o'clock dismissal bell rang. Her students charged out of the building like cattle from a chute.

Gianna met Tracy in the locker room. "Phew! It's been one heck of a day!" she said, wiping her forehead.

"You ain't kidding, girlfriend," Tracy said. "I think I already had my work-out."

After the two changed into their workout clothes, Tracy pulled the door open to the fitness room and eyed the bike. "Looks like we've got this place to ourselves."

"Fine by me."

Gianna stepped on the treadmill and began her warm-up program. Within forty-five minutes, and a lot of oomph, her petite frame jogged three miles. She stepped off the treadmill. *I'm so proud of myself.*

She took a break and sat down on the gym mat. She closed her eyes and imagined herself at the bridal shop trying on her dress. She hoped it would be too big.

"I lost almost twenty pounds since we started this."

"You worked hard, girlfriend. You earned it," Tracy said. "But you'd better start eating more. What does Dan say about your weight loss?"

"I don't think he noticed. He's been on-call at the hospital a lot lately. He's covering hours now, so we can take a two-week honeymoon at a resort in Montana. If he knew *how* much weight I lost, he'd be angry as a bull, so don't say anything, ok?"

"Gianna, being *too* thin is not healthy."

"Save the lecture, Tracy. I already got it from Danny way before I started this."

Gianna began her sit-ups. In the middle of one, she caught a glimpse of Troy's reflection in the wall mirror. *Oh, crab apples! I hope he didn't hear me.*

Gianna tried to act casually. "Oh, hi, Troy."

"Hey, how y'all doing?" Troy asked. He glanced at Tracy and said, "I'm on my dinner break and thought I'd take my *beautiful* wife out for a bite to eat."

Tracy hopped off the bike. After she straightened her stiff legs, she wobbled over to him. "Well, thank you, but I need to shower first," she said, wiping her face with a towel.

"Well, I don't have *that* much time, honey," Troy said, glancing at his watch. "You smell...*lovely*," he added, trying to mask his grin.

"Nice save, sweetie," Tracy said, patting him on the shoulder. "Would you like to join us, Gianna?"

"No, thank you. I'm going to take a shower and head home. Danny should be home from his meeting by then."

"Ok," Tracy said, waving goodbye.

A few minutes later, Gianna pulled the fitness room door closed then cut through the gymnasium to the girls' locker room. The place was deserted. *Oh well. It's a beautiful day outside. I'll be out of here, too, after a cool, refreshing shower.*

As she moseyed through the locker room to her locker, her hot, sweaty body suddenly turned stone cold. It was too quiet. Shaking off her uneasiness, she dialed the combination to her lock. She opened her locker and pulled out her clean clothes, a towel, and beauty supplies.

On her way to the shower, a cold chill ran down her spine. She stopped at the shower stall and listened. Nothing. *Why do I feel so creeped out? Maybe I should just pack up. I can take a warm, relaxing bath when I get home.*

Gianna returned to her locker, grabbed her duffle bag, then proceeded to leave the locker room. As she opened the door, she crashed into Chad, who was on the other side pushing a cart full of tennis rackets through the gymnasium.

"Oh, sorry, Chad."

"No harm done. That's what I get for walking too close to the door." He laughed gently. "Hey, sorry I missed you this afternoon. I had a meeting with Mr. Sterling."

"No worries," she said.

Gianna was relieved he wasn't there. After Danny's comment this morning, she felt guilty.

"Well, I should be going. I have to stop at the market on my way home," she said.

"Have a nice evening, brown eyes," Chad said, moving forward with his cart.

Before Gianna left the school, she stopped back in her classroom to grab a stack of tests that needed grading. While she stuffed the papers in her satchel, her cell phone beeped, indicating a voicemail message. She scrambled through her purse for her phone. She dialed her voicemail and listened.

"Babe, sorry I missed you. It's, uh, three thirty, and I'm heading to that conference. Listen, don't worry about supper. I'll bring home a pizza, uh, hopefully around six. I love you."

Gianna smiled at Danny's thoughtfulness. She glanced at the clock. It was four thirty. *Gee, he's probably still in his meeting. I don't want to disturb him.* Instead of calling him, she texted him. *Ok, thxs. Luv & miss you.*

When Gianna arrived home, she couldn't wait to get out of her stinky gym clothes. She drew herself a warm bubble bath and soaked in the tub for a good half hour. *Well, time to tackle my homework.* She dried off and changed into a cozy pair of flannel pajama shorts and a t-shirt. She pulled her damp hair into a ponytail and went out to the dining room to gruel over test papers.

"Oh, come on, Zack," Gianna mumbled. "You knew these answers." She put a big red X on his paper. She rubbed her forehead. *How do I get through to this kid?*

It was five thirty. She was halfway through grading papers when she heard the lobby intercom system buzzing in. *Who in the world?*

She sprung from her chair to answer the call. "Yes?"

"Front desk security. I have...Chad here to see you. May I send him up?"

Gianna's mind swirled with emotions. *Chad? What's he doing here? How does he know where I live?* Her pulse ramped up. "Umm, uh, yes, please," she said.

In a matter of minutes, there was a knock at the door. She opened it and greeted Chad. "Hi!" She raised her eyebrows. "What...brings you here?"

Chad held up her wallet and said, "You left this in your classroom."

Gianna merely stared, speechless. *How did I manage that?* She reached for her wallet and thumbed through it.

"I assure you it's all there," Chad said. His caustic tone made her face burn.

"Ok, I trust you," she said. Dumbfounded, she shook her head. "Where are my manners? Come in."

Chad nodded and stepped inside. She closed the door behind him and offered him a seat at the dining room table where she was grading papers.

"May I get you something to drink? A glass of iced tea, lemonade, uh water?"

"Iced tea sounds good," Chad said, sitting down.

As she poured a glass of iced tea, she stewed on the wallet incident. "I know. I was digging through my purse for my cell phone. I pulled out my wallet. I got sidetracked with a message and never put my wallet back in my purse. Wow! It's a good thing I never went to the market."

"Hey, forget it. We all make mistakes," Chad said, walking toward her.

When Gianna turned to hand him his iced tea, he was right in her face. He reached up and touched her hair. "Your hair looks pretty up," he said in a sensuous voice. He leaned into her and whispered, "You smell nice, too."

A familiar cold knot formed in her stomach. She put her hand up and politely pushed him away. "Uh, Chad, please, stop!"

She stepped backwards, right into the kitchen counter.

"What?" Chad asked, giving her a black, layered look. "You can't take a compliment?"

"Chad, you need to leave," she demanded.

"But you didn't thank me yet for bringing you your wallet. Isn't that why you invited me in?" he asked, wedging her up against the counter.

"No!" she gasped.

Panic seeped into her body. Her eyes scanned the kitchen. *Where's my cell phone?* She noticed the microwave clock read five forty. *Danny, where are you?* She eyed the knife set on the far counter but couldn't reach it. Chad had her cornered. She needed to try a different approach.

She took a deep breath and said, "Chad, thank you for bringing me my wallet, but you need to leave now."

"That's my thank you?" He chuckled and shook his head slowly. "How about a little," he asked, reaching under her shirt to cop a feel. His cold, rough hands startled her, and she screamed.

Chad slapped his hand over her mouth. His chilling, emotionless voice reprimanded her. "You scream like that again, and I'll kill you. Understand?"

She nodded. Her body quaked as horrible images of what he might do flashed through her mind.

He cautiously removed his hand from her mouth, and whispered, "Good girl, brown eyes."

Like a bull in a China closet, she charged at him with all her might. But, before she could escape, his powerful hands gripped her arms.

"Like it frisky, do you?" A satanic grin spread across his lips.

"Please, let me go," she cried.

Anger flared in his eyes. He raised his hand to her face and struck her. Her vision went blurry, and she lost her balance. She fell to the cold tile floor.

Gianna moaned. Her head throbbed as if a stampede of cattle trampled her. *What happened? Where am I?* She opened her eyes. Everything around her was hazy.

"Don't move!" Chad's harsh, familiar voice shouted.

When her vision cleared, she recognized him. He was standing over her, removing his shirt and loosening his pants. A more terrifying realization washed over her. *He's going to rape me.* She needed to move, and fast, but all too quickly, he straddled her and pinned her down.

His strong, corded body molded into her soft curves. She was in pain, sandwiched between his hard body and the unforgiving floor.

Gianna looked into Chad's eyes. They were as dark as a stormy sea. Perspiration streamed down his face. He reeked of sweat and musk, a putrid combination that will burn in her memory forever. She tried to stay calm, hoping he wouldn't kill her if she did what he ordered.

"Good girl," he muttered.

Short of breath, she choked on her words, "Please...let...me go!"

He whacked her in the mouth. "Shut up! You're going to like this."

"Please...don't...hurt me," she pleaded between breaths. "I'm still a..." her words broke as she sobbed.

With an evil laugh, Chad mocked her. "I'm supposed to believe a hot—" his profanity hurt her ears. "—like you and that rodeo guy never—" He laughed. "Well, sweetheart, I'm going to brand you with *my* mark."

Chad's mouth covered hers hungrily. He forced her lips open. His tongue lunged and explored her aggressively. She nearly choked from his vinegary taste.

His cruel hands fondled her. He squeezed her so hard that she couldn't help but cry in pain. He deliberately mistook her muffled cry as a moan of satisfaction and continued to pinch her even harder. When he finally let go, he slithered his hands to her waist and yanked off her shorts. Her body, crushed beneath him, squirmed to escape. At the same time, her limbs shuddered as she fought diligently to prevent his hands from opening her legs. His attempt was firm and persistent.

With pain coursing through her body, she screamed in hopelessness, "Somebody please help me!"

She remembered the front door was unlocked. *Where is Danny?* She was exhausted, and her body was going numb. About to give up, she asked the Lord for help. Then, with a sudden burst of energy, she screamed again, "Help me, please!"

Cʒꝏ

Meanwhile, Dan arrived home and parked his truck in the gated lot. As he entered the main lobby carrying his pizza, he saw Troy and Tracy retrieving their mail.

Troy shouted, "Hey, cowboy! Pizza night?"

"Yep. I'm giving Gianna a night off from kitchen duty."

"I'll have to tell her that the offer doesn't last long after the honeymoon," Tracy said, elbowing Troy in the side.

Dan grabbed his mail and tossed it on top of the pizza box. The three of them took the elevator upstairs to their floor. As the elevator door opened, Dan heard Gianna's blood-curdling screams.

"Help me!"

"What the—?" Dan's heart thundered frantically. He dropped the pizza box, along with his mail, and barreled through his front door.

When he realized what was happening, he sprang into action. With quick reflexes, he grabbed Chad like a tornado uprooting a tree. He laid his fist into him and pounded his head into the floor.

"Cowboy, that's enough!" Troy shouted, prying him off Chad. "You'll thank me later."

Dan backed off, his chest heaving as he struggled to hold his anger.

Tracy panicked. "She needs a doctor!"

"Dan, go to her. I got this," Troy insisted as he restrained Chad. "Tracy, call 9-1-1."

Dan sprinted to Gianna, who was sitting with her knees bent, pulled to her chest, and her face buried in her hands. She was sobbing, rocking back and forth.

Quickly, he unbuttoned his outer shirt and removed it. "Babe," he said, draping his shirt over her back. He gently pulled her hands away from her face and noticed her beautiful brown eyes had darkened with pain, and her bottom lip was split and swollen. "I'm here, baby. You're safe now." Blood trickled from her forehead. He grabbed a kitchen towel and held it to her head. "You're going to need stitches." He felt the bump on the back of her head and said to Tracy, "She may have a concussion."

"Just hold me," Gianna cried.

Gently, Dan cradled her in his arms. When he looked into her eyes, his own blurred with tears. "What did he do to you?"

She shook her head in dismay.

Dan's eyes burned with anger. "Tell me! I need to know," he demanded.

"Dan," Troy said, shaking his head.

Gianna wouldn't speak. She clung to him desperately and sobbed.

"It'll be ok," he whispered, gently massaging her back.

Dan's heart pounded. He imagined the worst and became sick to his stomach. When Chad moaned in obvious pain, Dan shot him a look of death. *Oh, do you think you're in pain? Your pain is nowhere as severe as the pain you caused Gianna.*

Chad glared at Gianna with his dark, toxic eyes and shouted, "That tramp seduced me! She asked for it!"

Irritated and hostile, Dan thundered, "You lying snake!" Rumbling like a volcano, he stood up and lunged at Chad, but, before he could erupt, Troy intervened.

"Dude, he's not worth it!" Troy said, trying to control him.

Finally, the two dispatched officers arrived. As they handcuffed Chad, his face darkened with defiance. He scowled at Dan and sneered at Gianna with hatred in his eyes.

"Get him out of here!" Dan demanded.

After the two officers whisked Chad away, a female officer and a detective arrived along with the medics.

Troy crouched on the floor next to Gianna. In a sympathetic voice, he introduced the female officer to her. "Gianna, this is Officer Christie. She needs to question you."

Gianna looked away and remained somber.

Troy motioned Tracy and Dan to step back into the living room. "Let them do their job."

Dan dimmed his eyes and shook his head in disgust. "She won't speak to me. Maybe she'll talk to them."

"It's ok, cowboy. She's in shock. Besides, Officer Christie's good," Troy said.

Dan watched as the medics tried to check Gianna's vitals, but she refused treatment. "No, I want to shower first. I feel dirty," she said.

"Gianna, sweetie," Officer Christie said. "We need you to get checked out at the hospital first, and then you can shower."

"Why? Chad didn't..." She buried her face in her hands and cried.

When Dan heard her speak, he stepped back into the kitchen. He could feel the pain that he heard in her voice. For peace of mind, he just wanted to know *what* happened and *why* Chad was in his home.

Gianna uttered, "Danny got here before Chad..." She began sobbing again. "I tried to fight him off as long as I could."

Dazed, Dan watched as the medics carefully helped her onto the stretcher. As they moved her out, Tracy said to Gianna, "I'm riding with you."

Gianna nodded with approval.

"We'll meet you there," Troy said. He patted Dan's shoulder. "It's ok, cowboy. Detective Scott and I will finish up here. Go pack her a bag."

"What? Oh, yeah. I'll do that..." Dan's voice trembled as his words trailed off. He wandered a short distance down the hallway before he turned around. He entered his bedroom and sat down on his bed. He pulled his cell phone out of his jean pocket and scanned his text messages. He read Gianna's last reply.

Ok, thxs. Luv & miss you.

Dan dropped his head and wiped his tears.

"Yeah, I love you, too," he mumbled.

He grabbed a duffle bag out of his closet then made his way into Gianna's room. He glanced around her room and rubbed his chin. *What clothes do I...?* He opened her closet door and took out a pair of pants and a t-shirt. When he opened her dresser drawer, his chest tightened. As he pulled out her intimates, he felt his temperature rise. *If only I went to the gym with her, this wouldn't have happened.*

Chapter 20

When the ambulance arrived at the hospital, the E.R. staff immediately triaged Gianna to a bed. The intake nurse instructed her to change into a gown.

"I'll be back in a moment with some paperwork to fill out," the nurse said.

Officer Christie followed the nurse out, while Tracy stayed with Gianna.

Gianna, consumed by a sensation of intense sickness, moaned in misery. Her head pounded with excruciating pain. As she slowly sat up, her vision began to swim. "I can't do this," she cried.

"Let me help you," Tracy said.

Gianna nodded, then removed Danny's shirt. As she pulled off her tattered t-shirt, she moaned. Perpetual waves of pain plunged deeply through her body.

Tracy unfolded the hospital gown and opened it up. When Gianna slipped her arms into the sleeves, she caught a glimpse of the bruises on her arms. The black and blue blotches journeyed up to her shoulders. *Boy, he really did a job on me.* It wasn't until she reached up to gather her hair, that she felt the goose egg on the back of her head. *Ooh! That explains the pain.*

"I just want to go home," she cried.

"Soon," Tracy said as she buttoned up the gown. "Here, lie back down on the gurney."

As Gianna repositioned herself, she groaned from the pain in her inner thighs. They ached horribly from squeezing them so tight during her ordeal.

There was a knock at the door and Officer Christie returned with an evidence bag to bundle up her clothes.

"While we wait for the doctor, can you tell me what happened?" she asked.

Gianna sighed. "No, I have a headache and I'm tired." She turned away and closed her eyes. *Can't everyone just leave me alone?*

Shortly thereafter, the nurse returned with the intake paperwork. She handed Gianna the clipboard. "We need you to fill out these consent forms."

Gianna groaned. All these requests were overwhelming, and her head pounded too much to think. Tracy must've read her mind because she took the clipboard and offered to fill out the information for her.

In a matter of minutes, Tracy handed back the pen and clipboard to Gianna and said, "Sign here."

The nurse gave Gianna a new gauze pad for her forehead and began taking her vitals. "This is quite a laceration you have. Can you tell me your pain level?"

"A ten," she said, licking her lips. She tasted the dried blood. "What does this exam consist of?"

The nurse answered her forthright. "The doctor will perform an external and internal exam and then take pictures of your bruises for evidence. We use special lighting to search for hair, clothing fibers and any traces of semen."

Gianna sighed. *This isn't necessary. Chad never got that far.* The realization of another stranger touching her again, made her nauseas.

"The doctor will be in shortly," the nurse said, before leaving the room.

Gianna closed her eyes and tried to rest. *I just want to forget all of this.* As she floated into that twilight state of sleep, she heard Tracy's soft-spoken voice.

"She just dozed off."

There was a muffled response, and then Tracy raised her voice. "Are you kidding me, cowboy? This place is a zoo, so unless you have some pull around here, we'll be here 'till morning."

That was the last voice Gianna heard before she slipped into the darkness of sleep.

Gianna fussed in her sleep trying to get comfortable. When she rolled to her side, she groaned in pain. The agony she felt reminded her that she wasn't in her own bed. A fractured reality appeared when she heard the shuffling of feet and muted voices.

"I found the attending physician. She's on her way."

Gianna recognized Danny's calm voice. She opened her eyes and tried to focus on his face. She painfully raised her arm and motioned him to her bedside.

Danny sat beside her and held her hand. He leaned into her and whispered, "I'm right here, baby."

"I'm sorry. I—" emotionally unstable, she sobbed.

"Shh, just rest now," he said in a gentle voice.

"Dan, stay with her. I need to make a phone call," Tracy said. She stood up and pulled Troy out of the exam room.

A moment later, there was a tap at the door. A tall, blond woman dressed in green scrubs walked into the room. "My name is Doctor Pamela Rice. I am the attending physician this evening."

Danny kissed Gianna's hand. As he stood up to leave the room, she grabbed his arm. "Don't leave me," she pleaded.

"Doctor Christiansen, you can stay. I'm going to stitch her laceration first," Dr. Rice said.

Danny nodded and sat back down. He rubbed Gianna's hand and reminded her that everything was going to be okay.

Dr. Rice examined the laceration on her forehead. "Can you tell me how this happened?"

Gianna swallowed hard. She closed her eyes and recalled her fall. "Chad hit me. I lost my balance. My head hit the edge of the counter—I think." She winced in pain as Dr. Rice prepped her forehead.

"Hmm, that would explain the lump on the *back* of your head but not this gash. Was he wearing a ring? Did he have a weapon?"

"I don't know," she mumbled. She flinched as the needle poked her.

"Does your head hurt?"

"Yes. Everything's blurry, and I'm tired."

"Sounds like you have suffered a slight concussion," Dr. Rice said, documenting the chart. She noticed her swollen lip. "Do you remember what happened?"

"He hit me," Gianna said. She glanced down at the colorful bruises that embellished her arms, provoking her mind to recall the attack. "He grabbed me and cornered me." Through her tear-filled eyes, she caught a glimpse of Danny's fiery eyes. *Do you blame me?*

"Gianna, I'm going to examine your body for injuries, and Officer Christie will be taking pictures for evidence. Then I'll perform an internal exam and take some samples. It will feel just like a normal gynecological exam," Dr. Rice said. "Do you have any questions?"

"No, but Chad didn't..." Gianna took a deep breath and squeezed her eyes closed. "I...never had one before."

"I'll wait outside," Danny said. He nervously stood up and left the room.

Dr. Rice said, "Gianna, this is standard procedure for sexual assault. I'll explain everything as I examine you."

She reclined the bed, pulled out the stirrups, and replaced the blanket with a privacy drape.

When Dr. Rice performed the internal exam, Gianna tensed up. The procedure was cold, awkward, and uncomfortable.

"You can relax now, Gianna. The exam is complete."

"Please, can I go home now?"

"Not just yet. I believe you have a concussion. I'd like to keep you overnight for observation. Unless—" she raised her pen to her lips. "If someone can check on you every two hours during the night, I can discharge you."

"Danny can," Gianna said.

"Very well. I'll consult with Doctor Christiansen. Meanwhile, you may get dressed."

Officer Christie handed Gianna the duffle bag that Danny had brought her. "Here you are, sweetie. Do you need any help?"

"No thanks."

"Ok, then. I'll leave you to your privacy."

After Officer Christie left the room, Gianna unzipped the duffle bag and pulled out a complete change of clothes. She clutched her stomach. It was unsettling knowing that Danny had dug through her dresser drawer for her undergarments. As she pulled on her t-shirt, she burst into tears. The shirt was one she had bought in Montana. It had a beautiful lake scene with pine trees and mountains in the background.

Why did I leave home? Did I invite this to happen? Was Daddy right about the city? As she carefully pulled her pants over her battered body, she cried miserably.

Not more than a few minutes later, there was a knock at the door. "May I come in?" Danny asked.

"Yes," she said, lying back down on the bed.

"How're you feeling?" he asked, sitting beside her bed. "Do you think you can give Officer Christie your statement before I take you home?"

"If it gets me out of here."

"I have a wheelchair outside the door for you. There's a private room where we can meet."

Tears blinded Gianna's eyes. Her voice choked, "Fine." She stood up with Danny's aid, but weakened by emotions, she collapsed in his arms. "Danny, I'm so sorry. Please forgive me. I didn't know he—"

"Let it go. It's not your fault."

Danny's sympathetic response, his soothing heartbeat, and gentle arms comforted her.

Danny wheeled Gianna into the conference room where Officer Christie, Troy, and Tracy were sitting around a small oval table. Once Gianna settled in, Officer Christie started the interview.

"Did Chad ever threaten you before?"

Gianna looked directly into Officer Christie's eyes and responded softly, but clearly, "No! On the contrary, he's been pleasant to work with." She glanced at Tracy and added, "Chad has been a tremendous help coaching us in the weight room."

Tracy nodded. "Yes, he has been training us in the fitness room for weeks, and his behavior was nothing less than professional."

Officer Christie scribbled her notes and moved on to the next question.

"Did he display any odd behavior prior to the attack?"

"No! He was his normal, friendly self," Gianna said.

"Ok. I understand you and Tracy worked out in the fitness room today. Troy stopped by and left with Tracy. With your permission, I'd like to record the events that took place *after* you left the fitness room this afternoon. Would you describe what happened," Officer Christie said.

Danny placed his hand over Gianna's. "You got this, babe."

Gianna took a deep breath and acquiesced. She closed her eyes and recalled her nightmare. "I went into the locker room to shower. There was no one around. When I set out my clean clothes, I had a bad vibe. Something scared me, so I decided to go home and take a bath instead. When I left the locker room, I bumped into Chad in the gym. He apologized for not coaching us."

She paused. "Afterward, I stopped by my classroom to gather up some papers. That's when I heard my voicemail. It was Danny. After I texted him, I went home. I took a bath, got dressed, then graded papers. That's when security called me to say Chad was downstairs. I had no idea how he even knew where I lived. When he came to the door, he handed me my wallet that I unknowingly left at school. Not thinking, I invited him in."

Gianna shook her head. "I offered him a glass of iced tea, but as I poured it, he approached me. He touched my hair then told me I smelled good." Her body began to shake, and her voice trembled. "I tried to push him away, but he pinned me against the counter. I told him to leave, but he got angry. He said I didn't thank him for returning my wallet."

Gianna hesitated. Her stomach felt sick thinking about the details. "Chad put his hands up my shirt, and when I screamed, he threatened to kill me." She wept hopelessly. "I didn't know what to do. I was scared for my life."

Danny handed her a tissue, and whispered, "It's going to be ok." He gently put his arm around her to comfort her.

"No, it's not!" she shouted.

Calmly, Officer Christie asked, "What happened next, Gianna?"

After Gianna caught her breath, she continued. "I tried to fight back, but he was so strong. He knocked me to the floor, and that's when I hit my head."

She dropped her face into the palms of her hands. "I must've blacked out. I...I remember him yelling. He was on top of me. Oh, he was too strong for me to push off. I begged him not to hurt me, but he hit me. He told me to shut up and...and he told me that I'd like it. He started kissing me. Then he grabbed me. He tore off my shorts. I fought him..."

She sobbed as she recalled the details. "I screamed, and the next thing I knew, Chad was ripped off me. That's when I realized Danny was there."

She wiped her tears. Humiliated, she looked away.

In a rigid voice, Officer Christie asked, "Did he penetrate you?"

Gianna looked directly at Officer Christie and answered sharply, "No, Danny came home just in time."

Officer Christie moved right on to the next question. "At what time did you leave the school?"

"I don't know. Right after I texted Danny."

Danny pulled out his cell phone and checked his messages. "Uh, four thirty."

"What time did Chad arrive at your home?" Officer Christie asked.

Gianna was irritated having to recall specifics and with all the repetition. Her head pounded, and she really didn't care. She ran her fingers through her matted, sweaty hair and said, "Last time I glanced at the clock it was five forty, and that was *after* Chad cornered me in the kitchen."

"The security desk would have the time that Chad signed in," Troy said.

Officer Christie jotted a few more notes in her report. "Thank you, Gianna. I have no further questions," she said, turning off the recorder.

"Can we go now?" Gianna asked, giving Danny a look of disgust. She was tired of being drilled and just wanted to forget everything that had happened to her.

Danny cupped his hand under her chin. "You're a strong, brave woman," he said, nodding. "Yes, we can go home now."

It was after Midnight when Troy and Tracy drove Danny and Gianna home. As they arrived at Danny's front door, Troy asked, "Is there anything we can get for you?"

"No. Thanks, bud, for everything."

"Gianna, I spoke to Mr. Sterling. I requested tomorrow off in case you need me," Tracy said.

"Thanks," Gianna mumbled.

Danny unlocked the door and opened it slowly.

Feared gnawed at Gianna again. "I…I can't go back in there."

"I'm here, and I'm not going to let anything happen to you. Let's take one step at a time."

Unsteady and fragile, she held on to Danny. She buried her face in his side while he guided her to her bedroom.

"I want to shower. I feel dirty."

"Ok, but you need to keep your stitches dry, so I recommend a bath. I'll help you in and out of the tub if you need me to. Baby, I don't want you to fall," he said in a concerned voice.

Gianna could hear the *doctor* in him talking, but still, he was the last person she wanted to see her naked.

"I'm not dizzy. I'll be fine," she insisted.

"Please don't be stubborn. If you need me, please call me. It would be so much worse if you fell. And don't make the water too hot."

"I won't," she said.

Gianna closed her bedroom door and ambled her way into the bathroom. She filled the tub with warm water and carefully lowered herself into the tub. In the water, she felt better but kept adding hot water. She scrubbed her body until her skin wrinkled. The smell of Chad was all over her, no matter how hard she scrubbed. *Why me? Did I lead him on?* Confused, she just cried. She was so overshadowed with grief that she didn't hear the bathroom door open.

"Gianna, are you alright?"

"Not really," she quivered. She poked her head out from the shower curtain and cried, "I still feel dirty."

Danny sighed with exasperation. "You've been through a lot, and it's going to take a while for you to heal." He waited a moment before he proudly announced, "I heated up the pizza. Would you like a slice?"

She cracked a tiny smile of appreciation. "No, I'm not hungry. I think I'll just go to bed."

"Ok," he said, closing the door.

Gingerly, Gianna climbed out of the tub, dried off, and headed to her bedroom. While she pulled on her pajamas, she glowered at herself in the mirror and then broke into tears. *How could I have let this happen? I trusted Chad. He was supposed to be my friend.* She knew he once liked her but believed he moved on. *Is this what men are like when they don't get what they want?* She shoved that thought out of her head at once. She didn't want to think like that. She climbed into bed and pulled on the covers. Once she calmed herself down, she fell asleep.

The next morning, Gianna woke up to the gentle touch of Danny's fingers stroking her hair. With fear ripping through her, she grabbed the comforter to cover herself. "What are you doing in here?" she asked.

"I'm sorry if I startled you. I was checking to make sure you're ok. How's your head?"

She swallowed hard. "A little shaky and I'm still tired, but my vision seems ok." She carefully sat up. "What time is it?"

"It's noon. Relax, you need your rest," he said, laying her back down.

"But I never called out of work. I—"

"It's ok. Tracy took care of it last night. You just need to take care of yourself."

"But I—"

"Have to rest," he said, finishing her sentence. "I'm home today and tomorrow." He leaned over and kissed her cheek. "I'll check in on you in a little bit."

On Friday, Gianna stayed in bed until late afternoon. When she got up, she wobbled into the bathroom. She was extremely light-headed from not eating, and her body still ached from the attack. After she washed up, she dressed into sweatpants and a sweatshirt. She studied herself in the mirror. The laceration on her forehead still looked raw around the stitches. Her swollen lip looked a little better but was still tender. She touched the back of her head. The bump was huge and still very painful.

She realized that she had to face the crime scene, the kitchen. It was the one place she used to enjoy. *How can I ever go back there?*

She meandered to the dining room where Danny was reading the newspaper. "I look like a train wreck," she muttered as she carefully lowered herself into a chair.

Danny looked up from his newspaper and smiled. "Hey, you're up." He rose from his chair. "Can I fix you anything to eat?"

"No, I'm not hungry."

"Gianna, you must eat something. How 'bout I make you some eggs and toast?"

"No thanks."

"Would you like a bowl of cereal?"

"Fine," she answered reluctantly.

Danny went into the kitchen and got her a bowl of cereal. He poured her a glass of milk and a glass of orange juice. After he put them on the table, he crouched down beside her and stroked her arm. His gaze was as soft as his touch. "I love you so much, Gianna." A tear rolled down his cheek.

"You don't blame me for this, do you?"

Danny stared, completely surprised. His eyes filled with tears. "Oh, Gianna." He shook his head repeatedly. "No, no, never...in fact, this was not your fault. You understand that, right?"

She tried to nod her head, but the pain was excruciating. She sniffled, "Uh-huh." Tears welled in her eyes. "I love you, too."

He took her hand and asked her to pray with him for strength. "Heavenly Father, have mercy on us and see us through this grim time. Amen."

Gianna lounged on the couch and watched television late into the evening. Danny sat at the dining room table with his laptop and paperwork when her phone rang.

"Your phone has been ringing continuously for the past two days," Danny said.

"I know it's my parents calling," she said half-heartedly.

"Aren't you going to answer it?"

"No. Why?" she asked, pretending that she didn't know what he was getting at.

"If you don't return their calls, they're going to worry. I'm surprised they haven't called me yet," he said with fear in his voice.

"If they do, just tell them I'm sick."

"Baby, I'm not going to lie. They need to know."

"No! I'm not telling them." She looked away not wanting to see his reaction.

Danny sprung from the dining room chair and walked into the living room. "Oh, Gianna! It's one thing not telling them about our living arrangements, but you can't hide this."

She heard the disappointment in his voice, but her feelings were like a raw, open wound, and she wasn't about to expose them anymore. She sat up straight, grabbed his hands, and begged him. "Please, Danny. I can't tell them. Remember, doctor-patient confidentiality."

"Gianna!" he exhaled heavily. He painfully closed his eyes. "You've always been able to talk to your folks...about everything." His voice was strained. "Besides, because of our relationship, I can't be your doctor."

"My parents mustn't know, ok?" Tears streamed down her face. "I just want to forget this happened, and I don't want to talk about it anymore." She stood up, stumbled her way down the hallway to her room, and slammed the door.

CʒʒᏰᎴ

Dan felt like a dagger had just gone through his heart. Never did they have an argument like that. He refused to let her go to bed angry, so he raced after her. He tapped on her door then opened it slowly. She was lying on the bed with her back facing him. He entered the room and sat beside her. He rubbed her back and whispered, "I'm sorry."

She sat up. She closed her eyes to fight back the tears. "Me, too." She pulled him close and motioned him to lie down next to her. With a tired voice, she said, "Stay with me tonight. I don't want to be alone."

He touched her lips with his finger. "Shh, I'm here for you." He wrapped his arms around her like a warm blanket until she fell asleep. He softly kissed her cheek then slipped out of her room.

It was Saturday morning. Dan woke Gianna up early for a counseling appointment that he had scheduled, but she was unenthusiastic about going.

She sat on the living room couch with her arms crossed. "I don't see why I need to go. I'm fine now."

"Gianna, please!" Frustration crept up his neck like a hot hand. "They can help you."

She sighed. "Fine, I'll go if it makes *you* happy."

She picked up her purse and ambled to the door. Dan could see she was still in a lot of pain. When he helped her into the truck, her cell phone rang.

"If it's your folks, you should answer it," he said.

Gianna inhaled sharply, put on a happy face, and then answered the phone. In one breath, she said, "Mom, I can't talk. I'm late for a doctor's appointment."

She held the phone away from her ear as her mother lectured her.

"Mom, I'm not feeling well. You know, headaches, body aches, and fatigue. Got to go. Love you, Mom," she said before ending the call.

Dan stared at her, shocked at her attitude. It irked him that she treated her mother so rudely. Without saying a word, he started the truck. Neither one of them spoke the entire drive to the behavioral health clinic.

At the clinic, Dan sat in the waiting room while Gianna went inside. Silently, he prayed to God that someone, *anyone*, could get through to her, to help her deal with the assault.

૦ૐ૦

During the hour-long session, Gianna told the counselor that she was coping fine and that she didn't feel it was necessary to return.

"Gianna, here is a note excusing you from work next week. Please take it, just in case. Call me if you feel you need to talk. I will squeeze you in," the counselor said.

"Thank you, but I'm sure it won't be necessary," she replied, taking the script.

On Sunday, Gianna stayed in her room for much of the day. She only came out to grab an apple from the fruit bowl, and she would only go as far as the dining room. *How am I ever going to go back inside that kitchen?* She sat on her bed and replayed every detail leading up to the attack. *If only I met Chad downstairs in the lobby, this would never have happened. I should never have invited him in. But I trusted him. He was my friend.* Thinking about *what if* made her stomach churn. Urgently, she rushed to her bathroom.

૦ૐ૦

That evening, Dan was in the living room researching *sexual assault* when he heard a knock on the front door. He got up to answer it. "Hey, Troy. Come in. What's up?"

200

Troy stepped inside the foyer. "I just wanted you to know Chad admitted his guilt."

"Well, that's a no-brainer. He was caught in the act."

Troy put his hand on Dan's shoulder. "In order to get the guilty plea, the prosecution dropped the attempted murder charge and terrorist threats charge."

Dan scratched his head. "So, what does this all mean? He gets away with this?"

"No. Chad is guilty of attempted rape. He will stay in jail until his sentencing. In my professional opinion, he'll get some time in an upstate facility for sexual offenders, nine to twelve months. He'll then be remanded to a halfway house. He's now branded as a sex offender, so he'll never step foot in a school again. He really ruined his life. The best part of that guilty admission is it spares Gianna a nasty trial."

"Oh, yeah. Great," Dan said with sarcasm. His blood boiled thinking about what happened in his house.

"How's Gianna?" Troy asked.

Dan shook his head. "Scarred—Chad messed up her head bad. She's playing the denial game right now. If she got nothing else from the counselor, at least she got excused from work until Friday, which is when we fly home."

Troy sighed. "Give her time. It's only been a few days. Did she tell her parents yet?"

"No, she won't talk about it at all, not even to me."

"Are you sure you still want to go home?"

"Bud, I have to get her out of here. Besides, we have Pre-Cana, her gown fitting, and her surprise bridal shower."

"All my prayers to you, cowboy," Troy said.

Chapter 21

Dan returned to his rigorous work schedule trying to make up for the time he had missed. In addition, he needed to prepare his colleagues for his impending weekend absence. Meanwhile, Gianna stayed home from work, using the written excuse that her therapist wrote.

It was Friday morning. Dan woke up early and took a much-needed walk. The air was brisk, but the sun was shining. It was going to be a cloudless, warm day for their flight home to Montana.

He strolled through Central Park, hoping to lift his spirits, but instead, his melancholy only seemed to deepen. In only a few hours, they would be on their flight. *What are Gianna's parents going to think when they see her? What will she tell them? What am I supposed to say?* This burden weighed heavily on his heart. If only he knew what tomorrow would bring. But, for now, he needed to be strong for Gianna.

On his walk home, he stopped at a coffee shop to buy fresh bagels for breakfast. When he returned home, he set the bag of bagels down on the kitchen counter. He looked up at the ticking clock in the living room. *Gianna can't still be sleeping. If I don't wake her up, we're going to miss our flight.*

Dan knocked on her bedroom door.

Gianna's tired voice answered, "Come in."

He opened the door. "Good morning. I bought us breakfast...French toast bagels...your favorite."

"Thanks, but I'm not hungry."

He nodded glumly. *What a surprise.*

Gianna sat up in bed. "I had another bad night."

"I know," he said, sitting down beside her. He gazed into her tired, swollen eyes. "I checked on you twice last night. You were tossing a lot and fussing in your sleep."

"Thank you for that." She linked her arm through his and rested her head on his shoulder. "I'm ok now."

"But you're not." He knew she was still hurting physically and emotionally. "You don't eat, you lock yourself away in your room, and you sleep all the time. I miss you."

"I..." Her voice broke.

"Gianna, talk to me. Don't shut me out," he begged.

"I can't. I'm afraid," she shouted. She grabbed her pillow and clutched it in her lap.

"Come here." He invited her into his arms. "I would never hurt you. I love you more than life itself."

He held her as if he was holding a precious newborn so fragile and helpless. When he thought about the pain Chad caused her, he suddenly felt weak and vulnerable to temptation. He wanted desperately to hunt him down and kill him.

Gianna backed out of his embrace. "Maybe things will be different in Montana."

"Maybe." He reached for her hand and patted it gently. "If you need anything, I'll be in the kitchen."

೦ಣ೮

Gianna remained in bed. She was exhausted. *How am I going to face my family in a few hours?* She crawled out of bed and dragged herself into the bathroom to wash up.

Afterward, she dug through her closet for something to wear. She found her favorite pair of worn blue jeans. They were the ones she worked so hard to fit into. Then she pulled out a long sleeve western blouse and put it on. She wanted to wear something that would conceal her bruised arms.

She styled her hair down and combed wispy bangs over her forehead to try to camouflage her healing wound. She put on make-up that she normally didn't wear. She was adamant about hiding the dark circles under her weary eyes and masking her swollen lip. When she finished, she studied herself in the mirror. *What is everyone going to say when they see me?*

Gianna sat down at the dining room table where Danny was finishing his bagel and cup of coffee. "I guess I should try to eat something before we leave," she said softly.

Danny's face lit up. "Breakfast coming right up!" He jumped out of his chair and went into the kitchen.

A moment later, he returned with a bagel and a cup of milk and placed it down in front of her. "Anything for my girl." He leaned forward and kissed her cheek.

He's too good to me. She cracked a tiny smile of appreciation and said, "Thanks."

Danny poured himself a second cup of coffee. As he sat down, he gave Gianna a once-over. "Don'tcha think it's a bit warm outside for long sleeves?"

"Well, the plane is air conditioned. Besides, I look like I was in a barroom brawl," she said, trying to defend her choice of clothing.

Gianna and Danny arrived at the airport by cab. While the two of them scurried through the terminal, Gianna latched onto Danny's arm as if he were her bodyguard. She walked with her head down, avoiding eye contact with strangers. She felt as though the world knew what had happened to her.

She slept most of the flight and only stirred when she felt Danny's gentle fingers caressing her cheek.

"Hey, we're just about home," he said.

"Are we on time?" she asked, rubbing her tired eyes.

Danny glanced at his watch. "Yep, it's eleven thirty, Montana time."

"Does Dr. and Mrs. Kendall know where to meet us?"

"Yeah, I spoke to Joe last night."

"Ok," she said.

"Babe, I..." Danny said, floundering his words. "I told him...what happened."

He squinted hard and leaned into the seat aisle.

"Oh, Danny! I didn't want anyone to know about this." She looked away to hide the pain in her eyes. *He betrayed me.*

Danny took a deep breath. His voice was blunt and exact. "Gianna, you may fool your parents with your tale but not Doc Kendall."

She stared out the window. *I'm done arguing with you.*

When it was time to exit the plane, Danny stood up and offered her his hand. She refused but followed him closely out the terminal gate.

Danny searched for Joe and Evelyn. When he spotted them, he broke into a wide, open smile. "Hey there, it's so good to see you both," he said, giving them a hug.

Gianna managed a faint smile and a meek, "Hello." She stiffened with pain as she hugged them.

Dr. and Mrs. Kendall led them to the parking garage. After cutting through rows of vehicles, they finally found their dark blue Ford Explorer.

While Dr. Kendall and Danny tossed the luggage in the back, Mrs. Kendall placed her hand on Gianna's shoulder. "Daniel told us what happened. We're so sorry. If there is anything that we can do to help you through this, please let us know."

Gianna gulped hard. Hot tears slipped down her cheeks. She took Mrs. Kendall's hand and said, "Thank you." For a brief second, she was lost for words then pleaded, "Please don't say anything to my parents. I need to figure this out first."

"Take your time, dear. When you're ready to talk about it, the words will come," Mrs. Kendall said.

On the drive home, Mrs. Kendall discussed the weekend plans. "Gianna, are you sure your parents don't mind Daniel staying with you? He's can stay with us."

"No, ma'am, it's not a problem. Mom says he can stay in the guest suite."

"Now, Daniel, let me get this straight," Mrs. Kendall said. "You're dropping off your stuff then riding back with us?"

"Yes, ma'am. I want to pick up my motorcycle."

When they arrived at the ranch, Gianna's mother was sitting on the front porch swing. As soon as she saw the truck, she dashed across the porch and flagged her arms at her husband, who was in the pasture.

Mrs. Kendall rolled down the window and apologized to Gianna's mother for not being able to stay and visit. "Joe needs to do his rounds at the hospital. We'll be back tonight for the tuxedo and dress fittings."

Danny prodded Gianna to hop out of the truck and greet her mother. "I'm going," she said in a loud whisper. She quickly checked her make-up and hair before opening the door.

"Hi, Mom," she said, slowly lowering herself out of the truck. "I missed you so much," she said, gently hugging her.

"I missed you too, honey."

Out of the corner of her eye, Gianna saw her father running toward them. He was filthy from head to toe.

He clapped the loose dirt off his hands. He was about to offer Danny a handshake but figured a friendly smile would have to do. "Welcome home, son," he said. He glanced at Gianna with a warm smile and said, "Oh, my bella ragazza, I'd love to hug you, but I'm—"

"A sight, Daddy," she said, finishing his sentence. "I'll take a rain check on that hug."

Gianna's father studied her closely. "My bella ragazza, you not eat?" He looked at her suspiciously. "What, uh, happened to you?" He reached up to touch her forehead.

Gianna quickly backed away. A chill raced up her spine. She looked at Danny and chose her words carefully. "I, um, it was stupid of me." Her words sped up. "I fell off the treadmill and cut my forehead on the weight bench." She looked down at the ground hastily not wanting to see her father's reaction.

"Treadmill? That looks bad," he said, looking at Danny for insight.

Danny swallowed hard. He scratched his scruffy chin and responded, "She'll be fine in time. The stitches were removed yesterday." He shot daggers at Gianna and then lowered his eyes.

Gianna knew Danny was disappointed that she didn't tell her parents the truth, and that she placed him in an awkward position where he had to help cover up her lies.

"Stitches? She needed stitches?" Dad asked anxiously.

"The stitches were used to promote healing and reduce infection," Danny reassured him.

"Honey, you need to be more careful," Mom said calmly. "Come inside. I'll fix you lunch."

"Sounds good," Dad bellowed.

"Not for you buster," Mom said with her hands placed firmly on her hips. "Not until you wash-up."

Gianna and Danny followed Mom inside the house.

"Daniel, you can stay in the guest suite."

"Thanks, ma'am," he said.

Gianna led Danny down the hallway to the guest suite with his luggage in tow.

"I don't want to keep Joe and Evelyn waiting. I'll be back as soon as I get my bike."

"Ok, but I might not be here when you get back. I'm going to ride Gemma to the creek."

"I'd rather you not ride alone in your current condition," he said in a critical tone.

Gianna put her hand on her hip and snapped, "Since when have *you* become my doctor?"

"Gianna, baby, please don't," he begged.

"Danny, just go," she demanded.

Danny's expression was tight with strain. He took an unsteady deep breath and strode out the door.

Gianna dropped her arms to her sides and sighed. *Oh, great. Now I screwed things up with him.* She slammed the guest suite door and stormed down the hallway to the foyer where she had left her luggage.

Mom walked in from the kitchen. "C'mon, honey. Let's get you fed."

"I'm not hungry," Gianna said.

Without waiting for her mother's response, she lugged her suitcase up the stairs to her bedroom. When she opened the door, her eyes brightened with exuberance. Her mother had organized all her wedding favors and supplies. On her dresser laid her garter and her satin handbag. On the floor near her closet were her bridal shoes and slippers, and on the desk was her tiara and a box of leftover invitations.

She sat down on her bed and imagined her wedding day, which was only nine weeks away. She pictured herself walking down the aisle and seeing her prince dressed in his white tuxedo. She felt warm and peaceful inside, and for the briefest second, she forgot about her calamity with Chad. Then suddenly a dark cloud blackened her happy thoughts. She visualized Chad's evil eyes staring at her. Feeling scared and alone, she buried her face in her pillow and wept until she fell asleep.

⊂੩੪⊃

Dr. Kendall pulled into his driveway. As Evelyn and Dan climbed out of the truck, Joe said, "If you need anything, I'll be at the hospital."

"Thanks," Dan said, waving goodbye.

"Daniel, dear, how are *you* doing?" Evelyn asked.

He rubbed his tired eyes. "I don't know...frustrated. I feel like I lost her." He shrugged his shoulders. "I can't

211

get through to her. I don't know *how* to get through to her."

"Daniel, give her time. She's hurting in many ways."

He nodded than gave Evelyn a hug. "Let me get going. I'll see you tonight."

"Oh, and please be careful. You always worry me on that bike," Evelyn said.

"I will," he said, pushing his motorcycle out of the garage. He put on his helmet, straddled his bike, and took off.

Twenty minutes later, he arrived at church. He went inside and knelt in the first pew and prayed. *God, my life is falling apart. Gianna's slipping away from me, and I don't know how to reach her.*

Suddenly, a firm hand touched his shoulder. He peered up and saw Father Anthony standing there.

"Welcome home, Daniel."

"Thank you, Father. Listen, do you have a minute?"

"Certainly." Father Anthony sat down beside him. "What's on your mind, son?"

Dan explained what had happened to Gianna and how she wouldn't confide in him or tell her parents. He explained the frustration he was feeling, and the anger he had toward Chad.

"Father, it was a good thing we came home today, because I was tempted to find Chad and kill him. I've never had such raw emotions before. I'm a doctor. I became a doctor because I want to help people, not cause

212

them bodily harm. Forgive me, but I can't shake what I'm feeling."

Father Anthony patted his shoulder. "Recall the words of Jesus in Matthew, 5:44. 'But I say to you: Love your enemies and pray for those who persecute you.'

Daniel, keep reminding Gianna that you are there for her. When the Spirit moves her, she'll talk. Have faith. Let us pray together."

Chapter 22

Gianna woke up from a restless slumber. Even in Montana, she couldn't sleep soundly. She glanced at the clock on the nightstand. It was already three o'clock. She fixed her hair and make-up and went downstairs to the kitchen where her mother was preparing supper.

"Hi, honey. Did you sleep well?"

"Yeah sure, Mom," she grumbled. She opened the refrigerator door. "Did Danny come back yet?"

"Yes, about an hour ago. He's out baling hay with Dad and the boys."

Gianna sat down at the counter with a glass of milk.

"Did you see I arranged all your wedding stuff?"

Gianna's mind was preoccupied. In a colorless tone, she answered, "Yeah, thank you. Looks perfect."

Her mother sat beside her. "Are you ok, honey? You don't seem yourself. Is this wedding stress, or are there problems with you and Daniel?"

"No, I'm fine. I guess the wedding, my job, everything has me worked up, that's all."

"You don't look well. How much weight have you lost?" Mom asked.

Annoyed, Gianna let out a heavy sigh, then answered her mother in a lie. "I don't know, like fifteen pounds."

Mom's eyes grew wide. "Fifteen pounds! Since when? What does Daniel say about that?"

"Since Easter. I've been working out every day, until I got sick. And...*what's* Danny going to say? Ok, so he didn't want me to lose *any* weight." She gulped down the rest of her milk and slid off the stool. "If I'm going to ride Gemma, I'd better get going."

As Gianna hurried out of the kitchen, her mother shouted, "Be home by six thirty for supper."

Gianna had been riding horses ever since she was a little girl. When she was just ten years old, her father had given her a beautiful bay horse. She had named him *Gemma,* which meant *gem or jewel* in Italian. The first time she met him, they were instant companions. Whenever she was lonely or needed to get away from her obnoxious brothers, she rode Gemma along the trails that bordered her father's property, trotting away from her loud, noisy reality to a place of serene tranquility.

Today was one of those days that she needed a retreat, so she traipsed up to the barn to saddle Gemma. After she went into the tack room to get her riding gear, she realized there was no way she could pick it up, let alone, mount him. *Whom am I kidding?* She flipped her wrist. *Oh, forget it.* Just as she turned to leave, Brody, her dad's farm help, walked in.

"Hey there, let me help you with that," he said. He grabbed her saddle and tack, carried it out, and saddled up her horse. "He's already been out today, so you're all set to ride."

"Thanks, Brody," she said.

Gianna watched him leave the barn. Her determination to ride was like a rock inside her. She stepped up on the horse-mounting block, put her foot in the stirrup, and stubbornly pulled herself onto the saddle. She groaned from excruciating pain. Although winded, she took hold of the reins and muttered, "Easy boy," and gently tapped Gemma in his side. Gemma, a calm horse, began walking.

"Good boy," she said. She really wanted to trot him, but her sore thighs ached too much to hold on. Also, she knew the bouncing would only make her head throb more. Instead, she walked him across a meadow and headed to Buffalo Creek to her favorite quiet spot.

Now, how am I going to get off him? When she swung her leg over the saddle, she cried out from pain. But willfully, she slid off the horse. Gemma sensed something was wrong and gently nuzzled her face. She patted her faithful companion and then ground-tied the reins, allowing him to graze on the lush pasture grass. She perched herself on a rock at the bank of the creek and listened to the trickling water. She closed her eyes. It was so peaceful there.

Although she sat in the shade, she was warm. In fact, she was hot wearing long sleeves. She rolled them up, exposing her seriously bruised arms that were still sensitive to the touch.

Last week's horrible incident played in her head. Since she couldn't focus on the future, she dwelled in the past. It had been a year ago when she contemplated her move to New York. She remembered how she prayed for the right decision. When she met Danny, everything had seemed to have fallen into place. Today, however, she was second-guessing her choice. What would have happened if she hadn't moved to New York? She wouldn't have met Chad. But would she be engaged to Danny today?

She cupped her hands over her face and prayed. *Dear God, why did this happen to me? Why do I feel so dirty and ashamed? Please give me the strength to get over this, so I don't have to carry the burden of this secret any longer. Amen.*

Gemma stirred. Gianna turned around to see what he was fussing about. "What's the matter boy?" She saw nothing but the tall blades of grass rippling in the warm, whispering breeze.

A firm, yet playful hand patted Gianna's shoulder. "I thought I'd find you here. Welcome home, city girl," a familiar, energetic voice lilted.

Gianna jumped a mile high in her boots. "Jumpin' Jehoshaphat, Jess! You scared the living daylights out of me. I could've fallen in the creek!"

"I'm sorry. I didn't mean to startle you. But it would've been funny to see you swim." Jessica giggled.

Gianna frowned, and her eyes welled up. Through her tears, she noticed Jessica's weakening smile and her darting eyes as they traveled from her forehead to her arms.

"What happened to you?"

Gianna quickly pulled her sleeves down and looked away. "I'm alright. I had a little accident with the treadmill last week."

"What?" Jessica asked.

"Yeah, I, uh, fell off and hit my head on the weight bench. I'm just a little banged up, that's all." Gianna spoke as convincingly as she could manage.

"Gianna," Jessica said, shaking her head. "You can talk to me. We're best friends, remember?"

"I'm fine, really. It was a stupid accident on my part. I should've worn the safety clip." She stood up and dusted the dirt off her jeans. "Look, I'll see you back at the house. I, I, came out here to ride." She stumbled toward Gemma. Unable to mount him, she grabbed his reins and walked off leaving Jessica to speculate.

⚮

Alone, inside the barn, Dan worked earnestly, carefully tossing each hay bale, layering them tightly in rows. After stacking several rows to the ceiling, he slung another bale, starting a new row.

Dang, it's hot as the devil. He removed his sweat-drenched denim shirt, leaving on his black tank top, hoping to get some relief from the sweltering heat. He pulled his bandana off his head and wiped the sweat off his face and neck.

He looked up at his progress then back at the hay bales that had been dumped off the wagon. *Only half a dozen more to go.* Just then, he caught a glimpse of Matthew and Jessica marching in together.

"Hey, newlyweds! You two are a welcome sight," he said, tossing his work gloves aside.

When neither one responded, he glanced back at them and noticed Matthew wearing his tough-boy face.

"I know that look, Matt. You got the tractor stuck in the mud again, didn't you?"

"We need to talk," Matt said.

"Ok. I need a break anyway," Dan said, grabbing an ice-cold water bottle out of the cooler. "Do either of you want one?"

"No," Matthew said.

Dan took a long chug of his water then parked himself down on a hay bale. "Have a seat," he said, pointing to a hay bale.

Matthew and Jessica, both looking as mad as a hornet, sat down across from him.

"So, what's going on?" Dan asked.

"I saw Gianna at Buffalo Creek," Jessica said.

Dan grimaced. *What the heck was she doing there?* He had assumed she was in the house with her mother.

He shrugged his shoulders. "And?"

220

"Dan, I know something's wrong, but she won't talk to me," Jessica said. Her voice quivered with uneasiness. "Perhaps *you* can tell us what's going on."

Dan stared at the ground and nervously ran his fingers through his hair. "You really need to hear it from her. She swore me to doctor-patient confidentiality."

"She told me that she injured herself on a treadmill. I saw the bruises on her arms. Who's she fooling?" Jessica asked, challenging him.

Dan rubbed his eyes and shook his head in anguish. He really hated being in this position of covering up the truth. The situation was getting uglier by the minute.

"Dan, we're talking about my sister here," Matthew shouted. "Jessica says it looks like someone abused her. Did you hit her?" he asked, flat out, accusingly.

Matthew's allegation left Dan disconcerted. He knew for the sake of their friendship; he would have to reveal the truth. His broad shoulders heaved as he breathed. "No one, especially Gianna, must know I told you this."

"Well, out with it then," Matthew demanded.

Dan clasped his hands together tightly and sighed. "A week ago, Wednesday, she was sexually assaulted by a colleague...and I walked in on it." His own eyes blinded with tears. The emotional pain was still all too real, even for him.

Matthew and Jessica sat there stunned as they listened to him explain in detail what had happened to Gianna. Matthew's face turned red with anger and Jessica just cried. They both gave him their profound apology for accusing him of causing Gianna's pain.

"I'm so sorry, bud. It's just...it looks bad for you," Matthew said.

"I know. I know. I saw the way people stared at me when they saw me with her. Matt, I would never, never hurt her or any other woman for that matter. Joe and Evelyn raised me better than that. Besides, I love her."

Dan just welled up with tears again.

Jessica put her arm around him and said, "Oh, Dan, I feel bad for you, too. If we can do anything, let us know. I just wish she'd talk to me. I could get her help."

"Thanks. I tried that. She won't talk to me either, Jess. She'll come to us on her own terms when she's ready. Tomorrow, we have Pre-Cana. Maybe she'll open her heart then," he said, checking his watch. "You said she was at the creek?"

"Yes, but she became ticked with me and walked off. I don't know where she went," Jessica said nervously.

"Don't worry. I'll find her."

"Want us to go with you?" she asked.

"No, it's ok."

"Well, call me if you need help," Matthew said before leaving the barn with Jesssica.

Feverishly, Dan stacked the last few bales of hay, then headed to the tack room to saddle up a horse.

☙❧

Gianna entered the barn with Gemma clopping behind. She tied him in the aisle, so she could brush him out.

222

"I was just about to go look for you," Danny said, stepping out of the tack room. A hint of annoyance hovered in his voice.

"I told my mother I was going riding."

"But you didn't tell her the truth. Babe, we both know you shouldn't have been riding."

"I know, but I needed to get away," she argued.

She reached up to take the saddle off, but a shot of pain zapped her upper body. She groaned in agony. When Danny noticed her struggling, he rushed over and grabbed the saddle from her.

"Thank you," she said, short of breath.

He shook his head in disgust and carried the saddle into the tack room. When he returned, a sudden gust of wind whipped through the barn aisle, nearly lifting his cowboy hat off his head. "Whoa there, feels like a storm brewing," he said, catching his hat.

Gianna stood alongside her horse, brush in hand, in a daze. She studied Danny as he put on his denim shirt. As he rolled up his sleeves, his shirttail flapped in the breeze. She gazed completely in awe. *I don't deserve him.* A part of her craved his touch, but part of her was afraid of what she might feel.

"Danny, come here." She held out her arms, needing to feel his gentle embrace.

Danny looked at her mystified, "You may want to wait for that hug until after I shower," he said.

She shook her head. "No, I need you now."

Danny walked toward her. She wrapped her arms around him like a ribbon on a gift package. It didn't matter that his sweaty, sticky body didn't smell like fresh pine shavings. What mattered was that she felt protected in his strong arms.

"You ok?" he asked.

Gianna moaned. "Not really. You were right. I shouldn't have ridden today. Now I'm even more sore."

Danny sighed and nodded in agreement. He swept her hair away from her face and examined her healing laceration. He pulled back her sleeves and examined the bruises on her arms. "Take some ibuprofen, but make sure you *eat* something with it." He glanced at his watch. "Go on. It's getting late."

Gianna was glad he never uttered the words 'I told you so.' "But I still have to brush Gemma," she said.

"I'll take care of him," Danny said, gently stroking her hair. "Babe, go inside now."

As Gianna walked back to the house, it suddenly dawned on her that she had to go to the bridal shop after supper. *I can't let anyone see me like this.*

She went straight upstairs to her bedroom and grabbed her bathrobe. She hurried down the hall to the bathroom and drew a bath. The warm, sudsy water soothed her sore, broken body.

She closed her eyes. *Just a few weeks ago, I couldn't wait to try on my gown. Now, I have no desire to do so. It's amazing how one careless mistake can ruin everything.* She rubbed her eyes in despair.

After her bath, she took ibuprofen, then returned to her bedroom. She applied make-up to her face and styled her hair. Next, she took her full-length fingerless gloves off her dresser. She could wear them during her fitting. When she finished doctoring herself up, she felt a little more confident.

୧୫

After Dan's rejuvenating shower, he sat on the edge of his bed and bowed his head. *Lord, please help me help Gianna.*

He joined Gianna's brothers in the dining room for supper. "Hey, guys," he said, sitting across from Mark and the twins.

Mr. Stefano walked into the room and patted him on the shoulder. "Thanks for your help this afternoon, son," he said, taking a seat at the head of the table.

"It was a good work-out, sir." *I needed to blow off some steam anyway.*

Mrs. Stefano and Jessica walked in from the kitchen with the main dish, followed by Matthew with a bottle of wine. "Gianna's not here yet?" Mrs. Stefano asked.

"I'll check on her," Jessica said.

"No need," Luke said, pointing at the doorway. "The beauty queen has arrived."

"It's about time, sis," John said. "No amount of make-up can fix your stupidity."

Dan shuddered inwardly at the twins' cruel remarks. He peered up at Gianna and noticed a glazed look of devastation had spread across her face.

"Boys, that's rude," Mrs. Stefano said. "Accidents happen."

"Knock it off, you two," Mr. Stefano said.

"Sorry," Luke quickly said, dropping his gaze.

"Yeah, me too, sis," John said.

Mr. Stefano sprang from his chair to greet Gianna. "My bella ragazza." He stretched out his arms. "I didn't get to hug you today."

A faint smile tipped the corners of her mouth. She gave him a much-needed hug. Dan noticed that she stiffened when her father's strong arms crushed her tender body.

"Daddy, I missed you," she said with a tear-smothered voice. It was as if the little girl inside her had escaped.

"I missed you, too, bella, but what's with all the crying?" he asked suspiciously.

Gianna carefully dabbed her eyes. "I guess I'm just homesick," she said with an artificial chuckle.

"Well, supper's getting cold," Dad said, offering her a seat next to Dan. "Your mother made your favorite, homemade meatballs with gravy on Italian bread."

When Gianna sat down, Dan noticed her nervous eyes gazing at him. He sensed her discomfort and placed his hand over hers. He winked at her with confidence, then exchanged concerned glances with Matthew and Jessica. It pained him that she denied her parents the truth. When he looked at Mrs. Stefano, she was clueless. As for Gianna's little brothers, they were too insensitive to notice and too young to understand.

CB80

After supper, Gianna and Jessica offered to clean up the dishes, so her mother could freshen up before leaving for the bridal shop. Gianna's brothers corralled to the living room to watch a baseball game, and Danny and her father went outside to wait for Dr. and Mrs. Kendall.

As Gianna cleared the table, Jessica loaded the dishwasher. She detected Jessica's silence and sensed her concern. Ashamed by her curtness earlier, she apologized. "Jess, I'm sorry for snapping at you before."

Jessica's eyes softened. "We all have our moments." She touched her shoulder. "I want you to know that you can talk to me about anything."

Gianna stared at the floor and replied, "Thanks for offering, but I'm fine, really." Her stomach churned, and she became light-headed. "Excuse me. I, I, need some fresh air," she said, stammering her words.

She scurried out of the kitchen. It seemed everyone knew something was wrong. Was she that transparent?

Chapter 23

Gianna grabbed her purse and a shoebox of bridal items and stepped out onto the porch. It was dusk and the rapidly approaching storm clouds blackened the sky hovering over the mountains. The sharp air howled through the trees. Instantly, a chill ripped through her body. *Oh, I hate this weather.* She sat on the porch step next to Danny and set her stuff down beside her.

She crossed her arms. "I hope we get back before it rains," she said, resting her head on his shoulder.

"I love the smell of the air just before it storms," he said, watching the distant lightning dance across the sky. He wrapped his arm around her waist and pulled her close to him. "You ok?"

From across the porch, Gianna's dad said, "Bella is terrified of lightning and thunder. She used to hide in her closet with her teddy bear. She wouldn't come out until the storm was over." He chuckled with the happy memory.

Gianna's face warmed up. "I still do," she said in a low, passive voice. She buried her face in Danny's sleeve.

Dr. and Mrs. Kendall's truck pulled into the driveway followed by a minivan. As the dark sky lit up, Dad read aloud the shiny lettering on the van's side. "Austin's Tuxedo Formalwear. That would be for us." He rose to his feet and opened the front door. "Arianna and Jessica—Evelyn is here."

Dan walked Gianna to the truck. He took her left hand in his and manipulated her engagement ring with his finger. He gazed into her eyes and whispered, "Promise me something?"

Gianna nodded.

"When you try on your gown, you'll think of me and smile." He lifted her left hand and kissed it.

Gianna's eyes pooled tears. "I love you," she whispered. She pressed her lips to his renewing a connection she had missed.

"I love you too, babe. Now, have a fun evening out."

On the way to the bridal shop, it began to drizzle.

"Hopefully, it doesn't downpour," Jessica said.

"We're almost there," Mrs. Kendall said, exiting the dark county road.

It was another two miles before they reached the one-horse town. Old historic Main Street consisted of the town hall, the post office, and the bank to name a few. There was a local café, a gas station, and a more modern grocery store on the newer end of the street. The next block over, was a small enchanting little village composed of a dozen mom and pop shops.

Since most stores closed early, there was ample parking. As they hopped out of the truck, Gianna looked up at the gold leaf inlaid sign: Melissa's Bridal Boutique. The last time she was there was for Jessica's gown fitting.

The ladies made it to the store entrance right before the sky let loose. When Gianna opened the door, the aroma of potpourri lured her inside. It was a cute store, very neat and organized. The left side of the store displayed a rainbow of bridesmaid dresses. The right side of the store had an array of mother-of-the-bride dresses. The back wall of the store featured a variety of white or ivory wedding gowns. Throughout the store were assortments of shoes, veils, and accessories. She couldn't believe all this could fit in one tiny shop.

"Hello, Gianna," an ebullient voice called her name.

Gianna looked up to find a tall, very pregnant woman waddling toward her. She didn't recognize the young woman at first, but the woman obviously knew her. It took Gianna a minute, but then she remembered. She was the shop owner who helped Jessica with her gown purchase.

"Missy, hello," Gianna said. "You look well. When's your baby due?"

"Thank you. Eight weeks, but I wish it were sooner," Missy said with a laugh. "Congratulations on your engagement. Your mother and I have everything set for your special day." She pointed toward the back of the store and led them to the fitting area. "Gianna, if you need help getting into your gown just give a holler," Missy said.

"Thank you, but I can manage," Gianna said, firmly closing the door behind her. When she saw her gown, her mood lifted, her heart warmed, and all her pain seemed to fade. *Oh, it's beautiful!* It was as elegant as she remembered in New York.

She gently pulled off her clothes and tossed them on the bench. She reached into her purse, grabbed her satin, fingerless gloves, and put them on. Next, she carefully removed the gown from the hanger. She stepped into it, pulled it up, and slipped her arms into the sleeve holes. She tried to zipper it up, but her aching body only allowed her to manipulate the zipper halfway. She realized she needed assistance, but before she asked, she examined herself in the tiny mirror for visible bruises.

"I need some help," she called out. She stepped into her shoes and trudged out of the dressing room dragging the cathedral train behind.

Missy zippered up the gown the rest of the way and directed Gianna to the three-sided mirror. Gianna's mother, Mrs. Kendall, and Jessica raved at how exquisite she looked in her dress.

"Honey, you look like a princess," Mom cried. She put her hand over her mouth. "Oh, and you remembered to bring your gloves."

Gianna felt her temperature rise. She glanced at Mrs. Kendall who gave her a reassuring smile.

"The gloves are classy Gianna and an appropriate choice for church," Missy said. "I know it's hot in here, so if you prefer, you can remove them."

"I'm fine, thank you. I want to make sure it all goes together ok," Gianna said. She took a deep breath. *No one else needs to know what happened.*

As Missy fitted the gown, she pulled out her tape measure. "I think the store in New York measured you wrong. I could've ordered your gown two sizes smaller."

"She's too skinny," Gianna's mother said, gesturing with her hands. "She eh' not eat."

"Mom, please."

"I'll tell you what, Gianna. I'm not going to take in too much yet, since you still have plenty of time before your wedding. I can do alterations up to a week before your big day."

Missy handed out the dresses for Gianna's mother, Mrs. Kendall, and Jessica to try on, then partially unzipped Gianna's gown, so she could change back into her clothes.

Gianna was relieved that the attention was off her, and no one had noticed her bruises. When she stepped back inside the dressing room, she took one last gaze at herself in the mirror and smiled. She imagined Danny waiting for her at the altar on their wedding day.

As she changed back into her street clothes, she heard Jessica's shrill voice. "I love it!"

Gianna opened her dressing room door and caught sight of Jessica twirling around in her ocean blue ball gown. "Oh, Jess! You look so pretty." It was the perfect color on her, and she was certain it would look fabulous on Tracy, too.

Gianna's mother and Mrs. Kendall were both wearing their floor length gowns for the first time, too. Mom wore platinum, and Mrs. Kendall wore a shimmering silver.

"Oh, Mom! Mrs. Kendall! You both look so lovely." Caught up in the moment, she briefly forgot about the drama in her life.

The drive home from the bridal shop was miserable. The sky rumbled and the rain hammered the truck's windshield. Gianna's happy mood reverted into a bundle of nerves. She flinched each time the sky lit up and the thunder crashed.

"Relax, honey, we're almost home," Mom said.

Gianna twirled her engagement ring. *Almost isn't soon enough. I wish this storm would end already.*

Mrs. Kendall pulled into the driveway. The front porch light was on, and the men were outside watching the storm. It was still pouring, and the wind threw buckets of rain across the porch. The lightning and thunder continued its performance.

Gianna, her mom, and Jessica contemplated their escape to the house. They opened the truck door and dashed toward the porch, splashing through the puddles, while Dr. Kendall made his way to the truck.

"Goodnight," they all said as they crossed paths.

When Gianna reached cover, she touched Danny's forearm and asked, "Were you out here all evening?"

"Well, no. We came outside for some fresh air after Austin the tuxedo man left."

Gianna raised her eyebrows. "O-k-a-y then." *You're nuts.* "Come inside," she said, grabbing his hand.

"Ok."

Danny followed her upstairs to her bedroom. As they stood outside her door, she took his hands and laced her fingers through his. "It's been a *long* day. I guess I'll find my teddy bear and hide in the closet until this storm blows through," she said, jokingly.

"There was once a time when I was your teddy bear," he said playfully.

"You still are."

He placed his hands on her shoulders and gently massaged them. "Did you have a nice evening out?"

"I did," she said, nodding. She lowered her voice and boldly added, "And, no one needed to know what happened. I'm ready to move forward and focus on our future together."

Danny smiled. "I'm glad it all worked out."

She wrapped her arms around him and nuzzled her face in his neck, breathing in the woodsy scent of his cologne. She showered him with kisses, wanting to feel the connection they once shared.

Danny reacted. He took her face in his hands and reclaimed her lips, devouring its softness, but Gianna pulled away.

"I can't, Danny. I can't. I'm sorry. It's too soon." She turned into her bedroom and closed the door.

Chapter 24

Dan returned to his bedroom and sat down on the edge of the bed. *Will it ever be the same again between us?* In a dazed exasperation, he shook his head. *What more can I do?* He breathed heavily. His head was too clouded, to unsure, too exhausted to think. He undressed, clicked off the light, and went to bed.

The ferocity of the storm eased to a quiet lull, but as he dropped into a dreamless sleep, another thunderstorm rolled in. Severe lightning flashed all around, and thunder rocked the house. The torrential downpour was like a heavy rain of judgment. In a matter of minutes, the powerful storm knocked out the electricity. In the middle of nature's light show, Dan woke out of a deep sleep by Gianna's terrifying screams.

"Stop, I don't want to die!"

Her cries repeated like a dominant chord. Her shrilling screams triggered his memory of the dramatic event that took place just over a week ago.

Dressed in pajama shorts and a muscle shirt, he jumped out of bed. He bolted up the staircase like the lightning that flashed through the windows, hoping he could calm her before she disturbed the entire household. But as he reached her bedroom door, her parents and brothers were right behind him.

Dan leaped to her bedside. She was still yelling and thrashing her arms about. "Baby, it's me. I'm here," he said, trying to calm her. He felt the tension in her body slowly release, but he could still feel her heart pounding against his chest.

Mr. Stefano crouched beside her bed and rubbed her back. "Bella, I've never seen you this afraid over a little storm," he said in a calm, but concerned voice.

Dan shook his head. *If only he knew the truth.*

Gianna lifted her head off Dan's chest. "I'm sorry. It was a horrible nightmare," she said in an unsteady voice.

Mark, Luke, and John stood in the doorway leaning against the wall, half-stunned and half-asleep.

Luke yawned. "It's just a stupid storm."

"Get over it, Gianna," John grumbled.

Mark sighed, then shuffled his way out of the room, followed by the twins.

"You ok, now?" Dan asked, wiping her tears.

"I think so."

Mrs. Stefano picked up Gianna's pillow, top sheet, and quilt off the floor. She tucked the pillow behind Gianna and blindly made up the bed using the lightning strikes that flashed through the curtains. Before she left the room, she kissed her daughter on her head, "Sweet dreams, honey."

Mr. Stefano stood up and yawned. "Good night, bella," then followed his wife back to their bed.

Gianna pulled the blankets up to her neck. "I'm ok. Thanks for not saying anything."

"Yeah, goodnight."

∞

Another flash of lightning lit up the room. Gianna pulled the covers over her head and waited for the thunderstorm to play itself out.

When she finally dozed off, an image of Chad attacked her. She woke up in a cold sweat, panting in terror. *It's just a bad dream…just a bad dream.*

She put her head back down on the pillow. When she closed her eyes again, Chad reappeared. He shouted at her, *'you're going to like this.'* Her heart pounded in fear. She kicked off the covers and vaulted out of bed. She pulled on her bathrobe and snuck downstairs to Danny's room. She climbed into his bed and snuggled next to his warm body.

∞

Dan woke up the instant felt her presence. He lifted his head from his pillow and whispered, "Babe, what's wrong?"

"I'm scared. When I close my eyes, all I see is Chad."

"Shh, you're safe here," he said.

He put his arm around her and kissed her cheek. At once, she was asleep, but now he wasn't. He lay there listening to her breathe. The thought of him being caught in bed with her prodded and poked, keeping sleep at arm's length. The scene came vividly to his mind. *I'm a dead man.*

He got out of bed and grabbed a pair of sweatpants from his suitcase. He pulled a blanket off the bed and settled into the recliner beside the window.

He inhaled deeply. *If she doesn't tell her parents the truth soon, this is going to get seriously ugly.*

In a few short hours, the bright morning sun greeted Dan as it peeked its way through the window slats. He glanced at the blinking clock. The power was back on.

He got up from the recliner and sat on the edge of the bed. He caressed Gianna's cheek. "Hey, wake-up."

He managed to get a groan out of her.

"Baby, wake-up before your parents figure out that you bunked in here with me."

She groaned again.

"Come on. I don't want to get my head kicked in by your father if he finds you here."

She slowly opened her eyes. When she realized where she was at, she sat up. "I have to get out of here!"

As she rose to her feet, she retracted her arms, bringing them close to her torso.

"You ok?"

"Yeah," she groaned. "I got up too fast."

He helped her to the door.

She listened for voices and slowly opened the door. She peeked in the hallway. "The coast is clear."

⊂₃₈⊃

Gianna tiptoed upstairs to the bathroom. As she grabbed the doorknob, her father opened his bedroom door, dressed in his overalls and t-shirt.

"Good morning, bella. That was quite a night you had. Is everything alright?" he asked warily.

"Yeah, sure, Daddy. You know how storms upset me." Without facing him, she stepped inside the bathroom, locked the door, and exhaled deeply.

Chapter 25

Dan sat on the front porch swing waiting for Gianna to finish getting ready for their Pre-Cana encounter with Father Anthony. The morning air was heavy and thick, unfit to breathe, but more bearable than facing Gianna's parents and pretending her nightmares weren't real.

Dan glanced at the time. *Matt should be here any minute.* He looked up from his phone when he heard the rumbling sound of a V8 Mustang backing into the driveway.

Matthew stepped out of the driver's seat and tossed Dan the keys. "Here you go."

"Thanks, bro."

"You know I don't even let Jessica drive this thing. Take care of my ride," Matthew said.

Dan laughed. "Don't worry. I'll be good." He patted Matthew's shoulder. "I really appreciate this. Gianna is in no condition to be riding on a motorcycle."

Matthew nodded. "Hey, whatever I can do to help." He glanced at the house. "How *is* my sister?"

Dan shook his head. "Last night she had nightmares. She has your parents believing it was the thunderstorms."

Matthew sighed. "I'm not surprised. Ever since she was a kid, she freaked out over storms."

"Bud, this was bad—I mean bad. She said every time she closed her eyes, she saw Chad—"

The front door opened, and Gianna stepped out. Dan's heart jumped in his throat. *Dang, I hope she didn't hear me.*

"Matt, what're you doing here?" she asked.

"Uh, I have some work to do on the tractor."

Gianna touched Dan's arm. "You ready to go?"

"Yeah. Matt's letting us use his car."

"Oh? And he trusts you?"

"Of course," Dan said, opening the door for her.

Gianna lowered herself into the passenger seat. "You know he doesn't even trust Jess with it."

Matt stuck his head inside the window and replied, "Because it's a man's car."

Gianna rolled her eyes at her brother. "In that case, you should give it to Danny," she said in a bitter tone.

Matthew's jaw dropped, clearly caught off guard by his sister's witty remark. "Ouch, that hurt, sis."

Dan laughed. "You set yourself up for that one."

"Yeah, yeah," Matthew said, his face bright red.

"Later, bro," Dan said, dropping into the driver seat. "Whoa, I'm not used to sitting on the ground."

"Just take it slow," Matthew said, nervously.

"If I wanted slow, I would have borrowed Doc's pick-up truck," he said, buckling his seatbelt. He glanced at Gianna and noticed her dazed expression. He caressed her arm. "Hey, I loved your wisecrack."

She gave him a tiny smile, then lowered her gaze.

"Baby, you ok?"

She peered up at him, her eyes pooling with tears. She asked, "Did my dad talk to you this morning?"

"No, I didn't see him. Why, was he supposed to?"

"No, but he stopped me before going into the bathroom this morning. He asked me if I was alright."

"Baby, you gave them quite a scare last night. Your family loves you. I think they deserve to know the truth."

"No. I don't want to talk about it."

Dan shook his head. "Fine!"

Fueled with frustration, he shifted the car into first gear and spun the tires out of the driveway.

⋘⋙

Father Anthony greeted Gianna and Danny at the church's parsonage house. "Good morning," he said. "Please, take a seat in the parlor while I gather up the educational packets."

"Thank you," Danny said.

Gianna and Danny sat together on the couch. The room had a fragrance of incense that reminded her of Sunday Mass. She glanced around the room. There were several chairs, books, and a television. She recalled the few times she had attended Bible study sessions there.

Father Anthony returned and sat in a chair across from them. "It's nice to see you both again," he said. "Let me quickly explain what Pre-Cana is about. As you know, many marriages today end in divorce. Pre-Cana teaches us about commitment and what the Church expects couples to follow as members of the faith."

Gianna and Danny nodded in acknowledgement of their obligations.

In length, Father Anthony discussed compatibility, conflict resolution, intimacy, and natural family planning. He then referred to his notes and directed his final question to Danny.

"Last November, you inquired about Gianna moving in with you for financial reasons. How is that working out for you both?"

Danny shifted in his seat and massaged the back of his neck. He cleared his throat and answered Father truthfully. "Well, uh, prior to moving in together, we discussed our vow to abstain from sexual relations, and we have been successful at avoiding the temptation."

Gianna peered up at Danny and noticed he had a glazed look of hopelessness in his eyes. Quickly, she looked away. All warmth drained from her body. She and Danny were so far from intimacy. Since Chad, their relationship had been so off balance that she didn't know if they'd ever make it down the aisle.

"Daniel, I'm pleased," Father Anthony replied. "Today's world has many negative influences, and it's comforting to hear of your determination to follow your faith." He looked at Gianna and said, "This concludes our session, unless you have any other issues you'd like to discuss."

A chill raced down her back. *Did he suspect a problem too?* Before she could muster up a *no*, she muttered his name. "Father..." She clutched Danny's hand for strength. "Something terrible has happened to me."

She kept her composure and told Father Anthony concisely what had happened. When she was through, she felt a sense of freedom.

Father Anthony's expression had softened with compassion. He reached for her hand and replied, "I am terribly sorry that you have endured such tribulation. Gianna, if there is one thing I have learned as a priest, terrible things do happen to good people. You may have asked yourself, *why me?* I can't answer that, but I can tell you that God gives us all free will, and that sometimes leads to temptation. Chad faced temptation and made a bad choice. And, he's going to have to answer to God for it through penance. It was fate that you were the person he trespassed with. God knows you are strong, have a loving family, and close friends that can see you through this. It was also fate that God sent an angel in the form of Daniel to protect you from the worst fate. Don't despair. God gave this test to both of you to see how resilient your love is for each other. It is up to you to work through this and make your love stronger."

Gianna nodded. Tears streamed down her face. What he was saying made sense, but she needed more time to sort through her feelings.

"Gianna, prayer is a powerful gift that the Lord has given us. Let us pray together now asking Him for strength, not only to heal your pain, but also to soften your heart, so one day you can forgive Chad for his transgressions against you. Let us pray for Chad that God can lead him to a path of righteousness."

As Father Anthony wrapped up their Pre-Cana session, he made one last comment to them.

"When a couple centers their relationship around God, their faith is strengthened, enabling them to work through their conflicts." He raised his hand over them. "Daniel and Gianna, you have God's grace within you. Use it, lean on it, and let it guide you as you journey through life together. God bless you both."

After their positive Pre-Cana session, Danny drove Gianna to a rustic restaurant for dinner. He pulled into the diner parking lot. "How 'bout a burger from here? We can eat at the picnic tables if you don't want to eat inside."

Gianna looked at the clapboard sign: The Chuck Wagon. She raised her eyebrows in disbelief. "O-k-a-y."

"What's that look? You never ate here before?"

"Mom always cooked a homemade meal."

"Your brother and I used to come here all the time. Friday nights were cruise nights. Matt still brings Jessica here in the Mustang."

Gianna shrugged. "If you say the food is good, I trust your judgment. You're the doctor."

"Well, I didn't say it was healthy, just tasty." He opened the car door. "C'mon."

They ordered and sat down at a picnic table outside the diner. When the server brought out their order, Gianna waited for him to taste his burger first.

Danny took a bite. "Scrumptious. Try it," he urged, watching her take a bite.

"Yum, you're right. These are delicious...and messy." She grabbed a napkin and wiped her greasy hands. "It beats the hotdogs from the street vendors in New York."

After splurging at the Chuck Wagon, Gianna and Danny took off in the Mustang toward the mountains, along the all-too-familiar curvy stretch of road. When they came to a huge, monumental rock, they turned onto a worn-out gravel road that led to Gray Wolf State Park.

Danny parked the car in the lot, and he and Gianna strolled through the pine trees until they reached a clearing. He crouched down and touched the grass.

"Amazing, even after all that rain last night, the ground is fairly dry." He spread out a blanket and plopped on the ground. "Sit with me."

Gianna sat beside him and rested her head on his shoulder. "I remember the last time we were here. It was our first real date, the day after the dance. You took me out on your motorcycle."

The memory thrilled her, but the idea of riding on his motorcycle that day had freaked her out.

"Yeah, that was a nice day," Danny said. He leaned forward and kissed her cheek. "And I managed not to kill us on my motorcycle."

"Well, that's a bonus," she said, laughing.

Danny pointed to the lake. "Look at that."

The golden sun bobbed on the lake. Its bright rays waved goodbye over the sparkling water as the night sky tiptoed its way in.

"It's so beautiful here," Gianna said.

"Just listen."

Other than the rhythmical sound of crickets chirping in the distance and an occasional croak from a frog, it was peaceful.

"I really miss this," she said.

"Do you regret moving to New York?"

Gianna fell silent for a moment, recalling the thoughts she had yesterday while at Buffalo Creek.

"The only regret I have is meeting Chad."

Danny nodded. "Me, too."

Gianna's stomach tightened thinking about Chad and spilling her dirty secret to Father Anthony. "I'm sorry I lost it at Pre-Cana today. I sounded like a blubbering idiot."

"No, no!" Danny said. His compassionate eyes locked on hers. "You did fine. I'm glad you told him."

Gianna pulled away. "But you don't understand—I'm not fine! I didn't want him to know, but I couldn't take it anymore." She covered her face and cried, "I *just* want to put this all behind me."

Danny reached for her hand. "Gianna, you can if you open your heart to your family. Let them help you."

"No!" Angry tears filled her eyes. "I'm not telling them! They'll just blame me for moving to the city."

She stood up and walked toward the lake. She plopped down on the bank and folded her arms across her chest.

Danny went after her. He crouched down beside her and touched her shoulder. "Babe, this was not your fault!"

"Yes, it is! I should've listened to my father and stayed here, but instead I tried to prove I was independent, and look where it got me. I'm damaged goods."

"And you believe that? Chad is the one who crossed the line here. I thought you understood that." He ran his hand through his hair. "Crackerjacks, Gianna! I give up." He turned his back and stared at the lake. Silence lingered over him like a thick fog.

Heat flushed through Gianna's body. *How can I make him understand?* She touched his shoulder and captured his attention with her tear-filled eyes. Her voice quivered as she spoke. "You have no idea what it's like to live half your life in anticipation and half in dread. I'm supposed to be happy planning *our* wedding, but when I close my eyes at night, Chad haunts my dreams."

"Baby, I know—"

"Don't tell me you know how I feel!" she shouted. She pointed her thumb to her chest and exploded. "I was the one threatened. I was the one assaulted. I was the one humiliated in front of my friends."

ॐ

Dan struggled to hide his tears. He closed his eyes and raised his clutched fist to his face. "Don't you think I share in your pain? Did you forget that I *witnessed* Chad sprawled all over you?"

His throat was raw, his heart under attack.

"Do you know how many times I asked myself *what if?* I can't bear the thought of Chad touching you, hurting you, or taking away..."

Sickened by the idea, he stood up and walked away not finishing his words. His heart was still bleeding, still wounded, still struggling to heal. He sat down on the blanket with his knees pulled to his chest and stared vacantly through the pine trees.

ॐ

Gianna stayed at the lake. She stared pointlessly at the water as she pondered the words that fell from his lips. It never occurred to her that he also endured such heartache. After a few minutes, she glanced over her shoulder at him. She realized if she didn't apologize, it would be like allowing Chad to destroy their love.

She jerked to her feet and hurried back to him. Dropping down beside him, she grabbed his hands. "Danny, I'm so sorry. I love you and don't want to lose you."

252

His gentle eyes embraced hers. "Whoa, slow down, baby. You're not going to lose me that easily. We'll get through this together. I promise."

The words, *together* and *promise*, were just what she needed to hear. She recalled what Father Anthony told them. '*And with God in the center of our lives, we'll be ok.*'

A hot tear rolled down her cheek. She reached up and stroked his cheek. She feather-touched his lips with hers, sending new spirals of excitement through her. She relived that tender moment of their first kiss on the dance floor.

Chapter 26

The next morning, the rooster crowed outside Gianna's bedroom window. She rubbed her eyes and glanced at the clock. *Five thirty.* She sat up in bed and gazed out the window. The sun was barely up. Her father's rooster perched himself on a fence post to display his colorful attire and sing his morning greeting.

"Ok, ok, Coo-Coo. I'm awake now, thank you very much," she grumbled. She dropped her head back on the pillow. "Why can't you let me sleep a little longer?"

She knew talking to a rooster was useless and asking to sleep longer was equally useless in this house. Her family always woke up early to do chores before Sunday Mass.

She kicked off the covers and rolled out of bed. As she shuffled past the window, she felt the intense mugginess in the air. The weather was not normal for May.

She grabbed her robe and headed down the hall to the bathroom to bathe. As she soaped up her body, she noticed the bruises on her arms and thighs were turning a greenish tinge. The pain in her thighs was now only a dull ache.

After her bath, she delved through her closet for something light and airy to wear. She discovered a super cute print dress that had black sheer sleeves. She slipped it on and admired herself in the mirror. The dress looked nice, and it was proper for church.

Satisfied with her appearance, she followed the delicious aroma of freshly baked apple cinnamon muffins downstairs. She wandered into the dining room where Luke and John were eating their breakfast.

"About time you woke up, sis," Luke stabbed.

Paying no attention to her brother, she sat at the far end of the table. A moment later, her mother walked in from the kitchen carrying a cup of coffee. She smiled, then kissed the top of her head.

"Aw, that dress looks pretty on you," Mom said.

Gianna glanced at her arms, then uttered, "Thanks."

"You seem a little off this morning. Sleep ok?"

"Actually, yeah." Gianna looked up and smiled. She was thinking about the pleasant dream she had of Danny but wouldn't dare mention it to anyone, not even to him.

"Well, you should've slept good," John snickered. "There was no thunderstorm to cry about."

Gianna ignored him, refusing to let his snide remarks spoil her morning.

Mom set down her coffee mug. "Do you always have to tease your sister?" Without waiting for an unkind reply, she said, "If you two are done eating, take your dishes to the sink and get ready for church. Remember you two are altar servers this morning."

"Yes, ma'am," the twins replied in harmony. They cleared their plates and left the room.

"Where's Danny?" Gianna asked.

"Helping Dad and Mark feed the stock." Mom sipped her coffee. "So, how'd Pre-Cana go yesterday? You two were gone all day. We didn't get a chance to talk."

"Fine."

"Fine? That's all?"

Gianna didn't want to get into it or let on that she and Dan had an argument. Thankfully, the conversation got sidetracked when the men walked in with their appetites.

An hour later, the Stefano family arrived at church. Gianna hadn't been there since Jessica and Matthew's wedding, which triggered fond memories. When she stepped inside the vestibule, a warm sense of belonging, a sense of peace enveloped her.

She chose a pew a few rows away from the lectern. She knelt and prayed. *Oh, God, so much has happened in the past week and a half. Forgive me for being so careless and for withholding the truth from my parents. Please heal my pain and strengthen my relationship with Danny. Also, help me to find it in my heart to forgive Chad for what he did. Thank you. Amen.*

During the Liturgy, Father Anthony read from the Gospel of Matthew, 11:28. "Come to me all you who labor and are burdened, and I will give you rest."

Goosebumps tickled Gianna's arms. The Gospel gave her reason to believe that everything was going to be ok. She reached for Danny's hand, and when she looked at him, he winked.

Father Anthony preached, "If you allow the love of Jesus to live within you, any obstacles you bear become meaningless. This is because Jesus himself will carry your cross to see you through."

After Mass, Gianna returned home, eager to change out of her dress. She dug through her suitcase, her closet, and dresser drawers for something proper to wear. She stumbled across her arctic blue, two-piece swimsuit. A moment of shame pulsed through her. *I never felt comfortable wearing that suit before, so I'm certainly not wearing it today.* She plopped on her bed with her swimsuit in hand and wept. *Why me?* She recalled Father Anthony's homily and wiped her tears. *Be courageous.*

Listening to her conscience, she tried on the suit. When she looked in the mirror, all she saw was her bruised torso and the greenish blotches that marked her arms, reminding her of Chad's power over her. *I'm a disgrace.*

An unexpected knock at the door rattled her nerves.

"Just a minute," she yelled, frantically searching for her bathrobe.

"Take your time. It's just me," Danny said.

Gianna threw on her bathrobe and opened her door. "I thought you were Mom," she said over her pounding heart. She grabbed his arm and pulled him inside. "I don't want her to see me." She tightened her bathrobe then folded her arms across her chest.

"What's wrong?" His curious eyes traveled from her face to her feet. He flashed his playful grin, and his eyes shimmered with desire. "You got anything on under that robe?"

"Stop! That's not funny," she scolded, tugging the strap on her robe tighter.

Danny's expression grew serious. "I'm sorry." He stepped backward and threw his hands up as if to surrender. "I was just kidding."

"I can't be seen in a swimsuit!"

"Let me see your bruises."

"No. I don't want you to look at me." She turned and sat on her bed. "I'll wear a big t-shirt over my swimsuit."

Danny shrugged his shoulders. "Ok." He sat down beside her. "Listen, I'm going to the store with your father for bagged ice and propane for the grill. But if you're not alright, I won't go."

"No, you go. I'm fine."

She gave him a once-over as he walked to the door. He was wearing a white t-shirt, black camouflage cargo shorts, and sneakers. He had sunglasses clipped on his shirt pocket and a cowboy hat on his head.

"You're going like that?" she asked.

Danny threw his hands in the air. "What?" It's the only swim trunks I have."

"Lose the hat, cowboy." She reached up and touched his shoulders. She slid her hands down his biceps and clasped his hands. She leaned in to kiss him, but all too quickly, pleasure left her. "Please, don't say anything to my father."

Danny sighed. "We'll be back as soon as we can."

Gianna returned to her closet and pulled out the biggest, oversized t-shirt she could find. She slipped it on over her swimsuit. The sleeves drooped past her elbows, and the shirt hung down to her knees. *Good enough.*

She went downstairs to the kitchen where her mother was slicing watermelon for a fruit salad.

"Need help, Mom?" she asked, popping a juicy watermelon chunk into her mouth.

"No, but thank you, honey. I'm managing quite well. You know, there's a warm breeze outside, better than being in a hot, stuffy kitchen. Why don't you go outside and relax?"

Gianna parted the vertical blinds on the slider door and saw John vacuuming the swimming pool and Luke setting up tables and chairs. "I see you put the twins to work."

"That was the only way I could channel their surplus of energy," Mom said, laughing.

"Where's Mark?"

"He went to the store, too."

"Oh. Well, I guess I'll go outside then."

Outside on the patio, Gianna parked herself on her favorite chaise lounge under a sun umbrella. While she applied her sunscreen, she noticed John had finished cleaning the pool, and Luke had all the tables and chairs set up. "What're you two going to do for fun now?" she asked, foolishly.

"I don't know, throw you in the pool," Luke said.

"Funny," Gianna said, faking a laugh. "Don't even think about it."

As she settled in her chair with a magazine, the backyard gate squeaked open, and Matthew and Jessica strolled in. They were dressed from head-to-toe like a day at the beach: brimmed hats, swimsuits, and flip-flops.

"Hey, bros!" Matthew shouted. "Looks like you started the party without us. Pool ready yet?"

"Yeah, you can go in now," John said, sprinting toward the house.

Matthew rubbed Jessica's back. "Going swimming with me, honey?"

"Not just yet."

"Ok." Matthew kissed her, then dived into the pool.

Jessica walked over to Gianna. "Well, look at you, chilling in the shade. How're you doing, sweetie?" she asked in her chipper voice.

Gianna peered up from her magazine. "Fine and dandy. Mom kicked me out of the kitchen."

"You're a lucky girl. Enjoy!" Jessica said. She turned and went inside the house.

Gianna lowered her gaze and mumbled under her breath, "Yeah, that's me, lucky."

"Hey, sis!" Luke shouted. "Jump in so we can play a game of volleyball." He punched a beach ball across the pool. "C'mon, the water's warm."

"No kidding. It's heated," she retorted. "Thanks, but I don't feel like swimming right now."

Luke climbed out of the pool and shouted to John. "Hey, let's make water balloons."

Gianna continued browsing her magazines, dreaming about the perfect wedding, while Luke and John started a water balloon fight amongst themselves. They circled around her quiet zone, starting a full-blown war.

"Hey, you two, quit it! I don't want to get wet."

Ignoring her, Luke and John continued playing. Luke launched a water balloon high in the air and misjudged the distance to John. The balloon dive-bombed her lap with a huge ice-cold splat, soaking her, along with all her reading materials.

"Blast you, little brats!" she yelled, leaping out of her chair. She wrung the excess water from her t-shirt and glared viciously at the twins. "I can't believe you little monsters!" She grabbed her towel from the table to dry off, then picked up her puddle-soaked magazines and carefully blotted the beads of water off the pages.

Luke and John laughed uncontrollably. Jumping around, they gave each other a high-five.

"You think this is hilarious?" she yelled.

"Hey, little bros. Games over," Matthew shouted from the deep end of the pool.

As Gianna placed her towel down on the lounge chair, someone's cold, rigid hands grabbed her waist and lifted her off the ground. Her body quivered with fear as the disturbing images of Chad attacked her mind. Overwhelmed with the traumatic recollection of the assault, she screamed hysterically. "No, stop! Don't touch me! Leave me alone!"

Disoriented from the present, she retaliated. She kicked and swung her arms frantically and desperately. For the briefest moment, she was free, but then someone grabbed her again. "Let me go! Please don't hurt me," she sobbed miserably.

"Baby, it's me," Danny said. He took hold of her arms and pulled her close, trying to console her. "It's me, Dan. I'm here now." His voice was gentle, yet powerful.

Gianna gasped. Through her tear-filled eyes, she recognized her surroundings. *What did I do?* John was sitting at the pool edge, soaking wet. Luke was on the patio with his hand to his bloody nose, and Matthew, Mark and Dad were standing around them.

"Gianna Rose Stefano!" Dad shouted. "What's a' matter with you?" His face was etched in disgust.

Gianna felt a tingling in her chest and a thickness in her throat. She broke away from Danny's arms and rushed inside the house to the guest suite.

Drenched from the water balloon fight, she peeled off her wet t-shirt and tossed it over the bathtub to dry. Chilled from the air conditioning, she scanned Danny's room for something dry to wear. His white, button-down shirt draped over the recliner. She grabbed it, put it on, then climbed into his bed to warm up.

She felt empty and drained thinking about the scuffle she had just had with the twins. *What's wrong with me?* Tired, she rested her head on Danny's pillow. The scent of his cologne that lingered on the linen pacified her.

❆

Outside, Dan crouched down beside Luke and handed him a towel. "Apply gentle pressure and lean forward so you don't gag on the blood."

"I'm ok. I deserved it," Luke said.

Mr. Stefano gave a brutal, unfavorable stare at his sons. "What happened here?"

The slider door squealed open, and Mrs. Stefano and Jessica hurried outside.

"Can someone tell me why Gianna just ran through my kitchen leaving wet footprints all over my wood floors?" Mrs. Stefano asked. When she noticed Luke's bloody nose, she freaked. "Luke! What happened?"

Matthew pointed fingers at the twins. "They were teasing Gianna. I was halfway across the pool when I heard her screaming."

"Sorry, it was our fault," John said, staring at the ground. "We tried to throw her in the pool."

"We were just having a little fun," Luke grumbled. He didn't sound the least bit sorry, despite being punched in the nose.

"I just about had enough of what you two consider having fun," Mr. Stefano thundered in anger. He shook his finger at the twins. "You two owe your sister an apology."

"Yes, sir," the twins replied. They tossed their wet towels on the chair and traipsed toward the slider door.

"Hold off, boys," Dan said. "There's something you need to hear."

He realized he couldn't cover for Gianna any longer. He looked at Matthew and Jessica for their consent to reveal her secret. When they both nodded, he lowered his head and rubbed the stress out of his eyes.

Once he captured Mr. and Mrs. Stefano's attention, he took a deep breath and said, "You may have noticed that Gianna has been a bit edgy since she came home." He swallowed hard. "The laceration on her forehead wasn't caused by a treadmill injury like she told you."

"Oh?" Mrs. Stefano said.

Mr. Stefano cast a troubled look toward his wife. He put his arm around her and waited for Dan to continue. Mark, Luke, and John stared blankly. Matthew and Jessica's expressions grew somber.

"Last week, Gianna was sexually assaulted," Dan said with tears stinging his eyes.

Mrs. Stefano slapped her hand over her mouth. Her eyes widened in shock. "Oh, my!" She sobbed inconsolably in disbelief. "No! No! Not my Gianna!" She broke away from her husband's arms. "I have to go to her."

"Mama, wait," Matthew said, encouraging her to sit back down. "Just listen to Dan."

She buried her face in her hands.

Wrath engulfed Mr. Stefano. "Who did this to her?"

"Her colleague, Chad Garrett," Dan said. The words left a sour taste in his mouth. "But I stopped him before—"

"What?" Mrs. Stefano asked, lifting her face from her hands. "You mean you were there?"

"Where'd this happen?" Mr. Stefano asked, his face glowering with rage.

"My...place. I heard her screaming and got there just before Chad..." Dan gave them the gist without going into private details. "She didn't mean to hurt you by keeping this from you. She swore me to secrecy."

"I know, son. I know," Mr. Stefano said. He shook his head. "That's my daughter, a stubborn, hot-blooded Italian. Shuts people out when she's hurting." He dropped his head and wiped a tear from his eye.

"How...bad was she hurt?" Mrs. Stefano asked, barely lifting her voice above a whisper.

"She suffered a minor concussion and bruising to her arms, thighs, and torso. She fought him long and hard."

"Where's this Chad now?" Mr. Stefano asked.

"In police custody."

Mr. Stefano stood up and paced back and forth on the patio. His nostrils flared viciously, and his face turned reddish purple. "Good thing he's in New York because if he was here, I'd castrate the filthy pig myself," he said, sweat pouring down his face.

"Vincenzo!" Mrs. Stefano's voice escalated. "Enough!" Her hands trembled in her lap as she cried.

Mr. Stefano sat down and held his wife. "I'm sorry Arianna, but this is our *bella ragazza*, not a stranger, and I'm feeling—"

"We need to talk to her," Mrs. Stefano said.

"Want me to go with you?" Dan asked. "Knowing your daughter, talking to her won't be easy."

"If you'd like, but just know that she comes down hard on the people she loves," Mrs. Stefano said.

"Yes, ma'am. You don't have to tell me."

◌⃝₷◌

Curled up in Danny's bed, Gianna heard a knock at the door. She suspected it was her parents searching for her. "What?" she answered.

"Bella, let's talk," Dad said. "May we come in?"

"There's nothing to talk about, Daddy."

"Babe, it's me," Danny said, slowly opening the door.

When the door opened, Gianna sat up in bed. She pulled her knees to her chest and looked away to hide her pain.

"Mind if I sit next to you?" Danny asked.

"No," she mumbled.

Gianna's parents sat down at the foot of the bed. Her mother reached for her father's hand, then looked at her. "Honey, your brothers are sorry for harassing you."

Gianna glared at her mother. "Whatever!" She looked away, still boiling inside.

Gianna's father cleared his throat. "Bella, we know about Chad."

She took a deep breath and looked at Danny. "You had to tell them, didn't you? How could you after I asked you not to?" She folded her arms across her chest.

"I had to, Gianna."

"I trusted you, and you betrayed me!"

"No, babe, Chad betrayed you," Danny said.

"Gianna, honey, you're our daughter," Mom said. "We love you and want to help you through this."

"Well, I'm fine. I'm over it now."

"But you're not," Danny said. He stroked her cheek with his finger. "No more denying the truth."

"Let us help you," Dad said.

Gianna couldn't bear to carry her cross any longer. She peered up at her parents. Her lips puckered and her voice broke. "I thought if I ignored it, it would go away. I blamed myself for not being more vigilant."

"What Chad did was not your fault. He violated your trust," Mom said.

Gianna grabbed a tissue from the end table and blotted her tears. A sense of peace came over her, and her grief lessened.

"Remember, bella," Dad said. "There's nothing that you can't talk to us about."

Gianna sniffled. "I know. There's one other thing you should know." She looked at Danny then shifted her gaze back to her parents. "I moved in with Danny."

"We know, bella," Dad said, his expression, serene.

She gulped. "You do?" She looked at Danny once again, waiting for him to fess up.

"Oh, honey, don't blame him," Mom said. "We knew from the return address on the mail you've sent us. We didn't question it because we trusted you were living according to our faith."

"I'm sorry. I couldn't find an affordable apartment."

"Bella ragazza...why you afraid to tell us?"

"I don't know, Daddy. I'm sorry," she said, lowering her gaze. "I'm really sorry about everything."

Gianna's parents stood up and retreated to the door.

"We'll leave you two to talk," Dad said, closing the door. Quickly, he re-opened it. With a smirk on his face, he asked, "Just one more thing, bella. Where'd you learn to throw a good right hook?"

The door closed. Danny looked at Gianna and cradled her face in his hands. "I'm sorry that your parents had to find out this way."

Gianna leaned into him and rested her head on his shoulder. "You were right. I thought I could hide the pain, and with time, get over it."

Danny gazed into her eyes. "It's love, not time that heals all wounds." He wrapped his arms around her. "I learned that, too. I've been working long hours at the hospital trying to drown out the pain of my parents' death." He took a deep breath. "Time didn't mend my broken heart, love did. God led me to you to fill the void."

Gianna touched his cheek with her hand. "I wish I knew how much you were hurting."

Danny laced his fingers through hers. "I know now that we're encircled by the love of God and our family, no matter how far apart we are."

Gianna nodded. "Amen to that."

"You know that you can extend your leave, right?"

"Y-e-a-h, but why?"

"It may be good for you to stay here with your parents until our wedding," he said.

There was a knock at the door.

Gianna sighed. "Who is it?"

"It's me, Jess. May I come in?"

Danny opened the door. He looked back at Gianna and said, "Think about it."

"But—"

"Just think about it," he said again. He gave her a wink then left.

Jessica stood in the doorway. "Can we talk?"

"Sure, why not? I have nothing else to hide."

Jessica grabbed the desk chair, dragged it over to the bedside, and sat down. "Don't blame Dan for telling your parents. I noticed the bruises on your arms the other day at the creek. When you took off, I pressed him to tell me what really happened. Do you realize I thought he was abusing you?"

Gianna gasped. "Oh, no! Danny would never...I didn't even think that it would look like that."

"Gianna, you're my best friend, and I love you like my sister. Please, talk to me," she begged.

Gianna reached for Jessica's hand. "I love you, too."

She lowered her gaze and fumbled nervously with her engagement ring. She looked up at Jessica and spilled her heart. "I'm so ashamed, Jess. I confess, I was attracted to Chad. I like the attention he gave me, especially with Danny working so many hours. Had I not been in love with Danny, I would have dated him."

She looked away again trying to hold back her tears. Revealing her true feelings for Chad scared her. "Only God knows what couldn't happened to me then."

"Gianna, you're only human. You didn't know Chad was a slithering snake. Dan is respectful, caring, and he loves you. You picked the right guy, so stop judging yourself."

"Thanks." Gianna grabbed another tissue and wiped her eyes again. "But I don't know what to do. Danny suggested I stay here until our wedding."

Jessica reached for Gianna's forearm. "I tend to agree with Dan. Stay here. I know a good counselor that you could see right away."

Gianna lowered her head. *Why is the right thing to do always the painful one?* She threw her hands out in frustration. "But I just started this job, and now this happens. The truth is, I don't want to be apart from Danny. Nine weeks is a long time."

"You make it sound like he's going to Timbuktu. You have your lifetime to be with him," Jessica said. "Your job will be there next year. Under these circumstances, they'll hold your position. Besides, how can you give yourself fully to Dan carrying this extra burden?"

Gianna squeezed her eyes shut. *I do need help.* A sense of peace came over her and her mood perked up. She hopped off the bed. "You know what, Jess? I'm feeling hopeful. Let's go outside and have ourselves a barbeque."

"Now that's the Gianna I miss and love so much."

Gianna pulled open the blinds and the slider door. Gathered around the patio were her family and friends.

"Surprise!" everyone yelled.

She placed her hand on her heart. "Oh, my goodness! I had no idea this was coming. This is so sweet, thank you, everyone!"

She never expected the Memorial Day barbecue to be her bridal shower. She looked around the yard and admired all the decorations. A handmade banner that read: Showers of Happiness, Gianna, hung on the back fence. Each chair had a cluster of white, helium-filled balloons tied to it. Attached to the patio canopy were blue and white streamers that fluttered in the breeze. *Aw, the blue matches the color of the bridesmaid dresses.*

Gianna looked down at herself. Caught up in the moment, she had forgotten that she was still wearing Danny's button-down shirt over her swimsuit. "Oh my! I must be a sight."

"You are, and you're beautiful," Danny said. He wrapped his arms around her and lifted her off the ground.

A comforting peace came over her as she clung to him. Looking at him through her tear-filled eyes, she said, "Thank you for helping me move forward with my life." She touched his mouth with her finger and parted his soft, moist lips. Craving to taste them once again, she kissed him slowly and passionately.

"You ok?" he whispered.

"Uh-huh."

Danny's beating heart against hers revived her. She recaptured his lips again, this time, more demanding.

"Uh-hum," her father said. "If all's good then—"

"Let's party!" Matthew shouted.

"You heard them," Danny said, twirling Gianna around. "Hey, aren't you hot wearing my shirt?"

"I am now. Ooh, that kiss!"

"I have the cure for that," he said smirking.

Gianna knew that quirky look and realized she put her foot in her mouth. "Oh, no, you wouldn't dare."

Danny picked her up and cradled her in his arms. He carried her over to the pool and jumped in, clothes and all. When their heads bobbed out of the water, he asked, "Cooled off now?"

"Oh, I'm going get you!" she said, tackling him in the water. "Two can play at this game."

"Ok, you win," he said.

Gianna kissed him again. Her mood lifted, and she felt more like her old, feisty self.

Jessica hollered, "Hey, Gianna, don't drown the groom!" She flagged her to come out. "We want to give you your gifts."

Gianna climbed out of the pool and peeled off her sopping wet shirt, revealing her swimsuit and her battle scars. Everyone knew the truth now, and that was ok. She wasn't going to allow Chad to ruin her special day.

Chapter 27

Toasty-warm underneath her blankets, Gianna drifted on dream clouds. *Hmm, this is heaven, Danny. I never want—*

A knock at the door yanked her out of her dream.

"Who is it?" she groaned.

"It's me," her mother called, opening the door. "Are you still sleeping?"

"I was." Gianna opened her sleepy eyes and peered at the clock on her nightstand. It was noon. "Sugar on bread! I can't believe I slept this late."

"It's ok, honey," Mom said. "You had an exciting day yesterday, and your body obviously needed the rest. I just wanted to tell you that I'm going into town."

"But Mom, do you know what day it is?"

"Yes, it's Monday."

Gianna ran her fingers through her hair. "Danny leaves early tomorrow. I wanted to spend the day with him."

Mom's eyes brightened with delight. "Oh, so you've decided to stay?"

She sensed elation in her mother's voice but didn't share the same enthusiasm. "Yeah, I suppose."

"I'm proud of you for being so strong," Mom said, patting Gianna's shoulder. "You made the right decision, you know."

"Did I?" Gianna twisted her mouth, making an unpleasant face. "These next few weeks better go quick."

"Oh, they will. Believe me, they will," Mom said.

Gianna climbed out of bed and walked to the door. "I'm going to take a shower."

"Honey?"

She turned around and raised her eyebrows questioningly. "Yeah?"

"The twins are at the Jenson's house for the day, and the guys are outside herding."

"Danny, too?"

"Yes, he was up at five, eager to help out."

"Oh."

Gianna poked through the kitchen pantry searching for something to eat. *Should I eat breakfast, brunch, or lunch?* Nothing appealed to her, but she was starving. She closed the pantry door empty handed and made her way to the refrigerator to peek inside. *Maybe there are frozen waffles in the freezer that I can toast.* When she opened the freezer door, her body shuddered from the chilly air. At that moment, a firm hand touched her shoulder. She jumped, whirled around, and kicked the freezer door closed. "Jumpin' Jehoshaphat, Danny!" she gasped. "You nearly gave me a heart attack!"

"I can give you CPR," he answered slyly.

Gianna closed her eyes, took a deep breath, and shoved the images of Chad out of her mind. She wasn't going to lose her sense of humor to Chad.

Danny took her trembling hands and pulled her close to him. "I'm sorry. I didn't mean to scare you."

"Mom said no one would be in the house."

"I came in and took a shower."

She nodded. "Please be patient with me."

"Babe, you know I will."

She buried her face in his chest and listened to his calming heartbeat. As she took a deep breath, she inhaled the woodsy scent of his cologne. *How am I going to get along after you leave tomorrow?* Being nestled in his loving arms settled her nerves. She looked up at him and smiled. "I'm Ok now."

"You sure?"

"Uh-huh," she said, looking up at him.

Suddenly, her stomach growled so blatantly loud, the people in the next town could hear it.

"A little hungry?" he asked with a chuckle. "If you don't mind burgers and hotdogs again, Mark's out back grilling some now."

"Ok," she said.

After lunch, Gianna and Danny trekked to the barn to saddle up the horses so they could take one last ride to Buffalo Creek.

Gianna touched Danny's forearm. "Are you sure you want to go? You've been riding all morning."

Danny wrapped his arm around her. "If you feel up to it, then I'll go with you," he said. "I don't mind being a cowboy a little longer. Besides, I know how much you miss your horse."

Gianna gave an appreciative smile. "Do you want to ride Mystery?" she asked, pointing to the black and white-flecked Appaloosa in the stall next to Gemma. "He's great on the trails."

Danny glanced inside Mystery's stall. "Buddy, looks like it's you and me."

Mystery bobbed his head up and down.

Gianna laughed. "I guess you have his approval."

Danny helped Gianna mount the horse, then the two of them rode off to Buffalo Creek. Together, they sat at her favorite thinking spot, reminiscing about the good old days.

Danny looked up at the trees. "Remember when we hung a rope on that tree branch and swung across the creek like Tarzan?"

Gianna laughed. "Yeah, and the first time I tried it, I was afraid to let go of the rope and got stuck hanging in the middle of the creek."

"Uh-huh." He chuckled.

"Yeah, Matt wanted to leave me there, but you felt sorry for me and waded through the creek to rescue me."

Danny faked a cough, and then his face turned red. "I really didn't feel sorry for you. I was just afraid of what might happen to me if I didn't. The licking I took after leaving you tied to the tree made a real impression."

"Thanks, and to think I thought you were my knight in shining armor."

"Hey, my armor might have been a little tarnished, but at least I didn't drop you in the water like Matt wanted me to do."

"You wouldn't have. Would you?"

With a devilish look in his eyes, he simpered, "The thought never crossed my mind. But hey, I don't think we treated you nearly as bad as John and Luke do now."

Gianna shook her head at the memory. "Oh, to be kids again." She wrapped her arm around his, resting her head on his shoulder. "I can't believe today is our last day together."

"I gather you decided to stay?"

"I want to go home with you, but..." her voice trailed off. Her heart was breaking at the thought of their separation.

"Come back with me then," he said.

"No, I can't. I need to get healthy again, but I can't in Manhattan."

Danny nodded his head. "Would you feel offended if I told you that I agree with you? I think you're making the right choice."

Gianna picked up a few stones and tossed them into the creek. "Why does everyone have to agree with me?"

"Because your family wants what's best for you."

Gianna cracked a tiny smile, then motioned him to stand up. "C'mon, let's get out of here."

Chapter 28

Gianna woke up to the irritating sound of her alarm and to the unsympathetic, blinding sun smiling at her. She slapped her alarm and grumbled, "Go away sun!" She wasn't feeling warm or cheery but chilly and gloomy. *Does it have to be Tuesday already?* She sighed. There was no stopping the inevitable.

After Gianna showered and dressed, she headed downstairs. The bitter, yet invitingly warm smell of coffee enticed her into the kitchen. Although she never acquired the taste for coffee, she always loved the aroma of a fresh cup brewing.

"Mom, I told you last night I'd make breakfast."

Gianna's mother stood at the counter buttering toast. "Nonsense, honey. I have it under control."

"I can help," Gianna said, walking to the stove to flip the sausage sizzling in the pan.

"I've got this, really. See if Daniel needs help packing," Mom said, scooting her along with her eyes.

Not about to object, Gianna said, "Thanks," and excused herself from the kitchen.

Gianna knocked on the guest suite door, but Danny didn't answer. *He can't still be sleeping, can he?* She opened the door and saw an empty, once-slept-in bed.

When the bathroom door opened, she shuffled back a step. Her eyes jumped on Danny, who was standing there only wearing a pair of jeans and a towel draped over his shoulders. She stood motionless, heart thumping, staring in awe. The thought of him leaving made her heart ache. She missed him already.

"I overslept," Danny said, as he towel-dried his hair. "Guess I took advantage of my last peaceful night in the country."

"Do you need any help packing?"

"No, I'm fine. Thank you for doing my laundry though. I really appreciate it."

"Any time," she mumbled. She lowered her head and stared at the floor.

"Hey, come here," he said with his arms open wide.

She looked up at him. With one forward motion, she was snug in his embrace. She felt protected, cradled against his warm bare chest. "I don't know how I'm going to get through these next few weeks without you," she said.

"You're going to concentrate on our wedding plans, and when you're feeling lonely—" He took her left hand and placed it on his heart. "Remember, I'm thinking of you, and I'm only a phone call away."

Danny kissed her. His lips journeyed down her neck to her shoulders. She savored the moment, not wanting it to end. But his kisses quickly became reckless, and his hands roamed from the small of her back to the soft lines of her waist and hips. Although she yearned to continue, she knew they needed to stop.

"Danny, please, we can't do this." She gently pulled away. "I'm sorry, but we have to wait."

It hurt her to have to reject him, especially since he was leaving shortly, but she knew they needed to save their gift for one other for their wedding night.

"I know. It's ok." Danny turned and tossed his towel into the hamper. He grabbed his shirt off the recliner and slipped it over his head. "Temptation's getting the best of me." He took a deep breath and went on packing his suitcase.

Gianna spotted his denim shirt hanging on the closet door. She reached for it and brought it to him.

"Oh, I almost forgot," he said, taking it from her.

"Can I have it?" she asked.

He shrugged his shoulders. "Sure, but why?" he asked, handing her back his shirt.

She held it against her heart. The lingering scent of his cologne on the collar soothed her. It was like having a piece of him with her. "It's a comfy shirt. I'd like to wear it as a nightshirt."

"What the hay, take it."

"Thanks."

There was a knock at the door, and Gianna's mother poked her head in. "Breakfast is ready, you two."

"Ok, Mom. We'll be right there."

During breakfast, Gianna listened to the grandfather clock ticking away the minutes, reminding her of Danny's impending departure. As time marched on, she was feeling emptier inside.

After breakfast, she snuggled with Danny on the porch swing while they waited for Dr. and Mrs. Kendall to arrive. There was a heaviness in her heart and an ache in her throat. She couldn't believe she wasn't going home with him. As they rocked back and forth, she gazed aimlessly at the row of evergreen bushes that lined the driveway. *Nine weeks is a long time to be separated.*

Her stomach twisted with anxiety. She worried that something bad could happen to him while they were apart. *How could I go on living without him?* She silently prayed, asking God to protect him in his travels.

When Dr. Kendall's truck pulled into the driveway, her heart sank. Reality hit her. Danny was leaving.

Danny patted her knee. "Time for me to go."

Gianna rose from the swing and followed him down the porch steps to the truck.

Danny tossed his bag into the back seat. He turned to Gianna and took her hands in his. His eyebrows drew together in an agonized expression. "Well, this is it."

"It's ok to cry," she whispered. She withdrew her hands from his and slid her hands up to his biceps to his shoulders. The feel of his muscular arms left her weak. She fought hard to stay strong. "See you in July."

Danny held her tight. "You take care of yourself, you hear?" A tear escaped his eye. "I love you."

Gianna held his face one last time, cherishing the feel of his stubble against her skin. "God be with you. Be safe." Between kisses, she breathed, "I love you, too."

Danny smothered her last words on his lips and whispered, "Bye." He reluctantly pulled away and climbed into the truck.

Gianna watched as the truck slowly drove away. She stood frozen in the driveway until it was no longer in her sight. Tears filled her eyes like puddles. She just stared pointlessly at the mountainside until a gentle hand tugged at her shoulder.

"Come with me, honey," Mom said, guiding her toward the paver sidewalk.

Gianna was in no mood to argue. "Ok," she said, accompanying her inside the house.

"I made some fresh lemonade. How 'bout you join me for a glass in the kitchen?" Mom asked.

"No, thanks."

Gianna immediately turned down the hallway toward the guest suite. She went inside and closed the door behind her. She dropped on the bed, grabbed his pillow, and prayed. *God, please keep him safe.*

There was a knock on the door.

Gianna answered, "Come in."

When the door opened, she hopped off the bed and wiped her tears. She pretended to straighten up the room.

"Are you ok?" Mom asked.

"I'm fine. I'm just cleaning up the room." Gianna wasn't in the mood to talk and just wanted to be alone.

"There are clean bed linens and towels in the closet," Mom said. "Would you like some help?"

"No, I got it." Gianna sat on the bed. "Mom, would you mind if I sleep down here? I hate sharing a bathroom with my brothers. They're such slobs. Not Mark, but Luke and John."

"If you'd like, but aren't you going to need this room when Tracy comes for the wedding?"

"I'm not sure yet. Tracy and Troy may stay at the resort. We're still working out the details."

"Well, if you want to sleep down here, pull your bed apart upstairs, too." Gianna's mother walked to the door. "Oh, and honey, before I forget, Dad and I have to go into town, but we should be back before the boys come home from school."

Gianna let out a long-winded sigh, "Ok."

The already fast-paced day was draining her.

"Honey, are you feeling alright?" she asked, stepping back into the room. "You look a little pale." She placed her hand on Gianna's forehead.

Gianna jerked her head back. "I'm fine, Mom!" She combed her fingers through her hair. "You know, I should be on that plane with Danny, but I can't ever go back to his home."

Gianna's mother put her arm around her. "What Chad did to you was a cruel and evil act. It won't be easy to forget. Do you understand that not every man is like that? You know Daniel would never hurt you. You can trust him."

Gianna sighed. "Yes, Mom. I'm not afraid of Danny. I just...I...need him here."

"Honey, sometimes you must be apart from the ones you love, but that doesn't mean you love them any less. In fact, sometimes it makes your love stronger."

"Arianna!" Gianna's father called. He poked his head in the doorway. "There you are. Time to go."

"I'm coming, Vin," she said. She gave Gianna a kiss on the cheek. "We'll be home soon."

As soon as Gianna's parents left, she frantically rushed to the front door to make sure they locked the dead bolt. She dashed through the house, checking all the other doors and windows, too. She was home alone for the first time in a long time, and she wanted to make sure that no one was going to get inside the house.

Now that she had secured the house, she darted upstairs and quickly changed the sheets on her bed. She moved all her clothes, plus all her wedding accessories downstairs to the guest suite, turning it into her haven. As she hung a few blouses in the closet, she eyed Danny's shirt that he had left behind. She removed it from the hanger and held it in her arms, trying to fill the void in her heart. The lingering scent of his cologne comforted her. She draped his shirt over her shoulders and collapsed on his bed. She closed her eyes and imagined herself embraced in his arms, then cried herself to sleep.

"Gianna? Where are you?"

The hollowed calling of her name roused her. She stirred in her sleep and became frightened when the bedroom door abruptly opened.

"There you are," Matthew said.

He stood in the doorway with his legs planted wide, sock foot. He wore mud up to his knees. He had grease smeared all over his shirt, face, and arms. His eyes were protruding, and his nostrils were flaring.

Gianna sat up and rubbed her eyes. "What do you want?" she asked sharply.

"Why'd you lock the house? Luke and John trekked all the way out to the far pasture through the mud and muck griping at me that they couldn't get into the house," he shouted. His face was beat red, and the vein in his neck was engorged.

"Mom and Dad went out, so I locked the house," she answered curtly, defending herself.

Matthew crossed his arms. "We never lock the house, Gianna! Now there is mud all over the front porch, and Luke and John's new sneakers need washing. Mom's going to have a cow."

Gianna stared at him dumbfounded. She was so used to living like Fort Knox. "Maybe I overreacted. I'm sorry, Matt. I'll clean it up."

Matthew dropped his arms to his sides. His tone mellowed. "You know what, never mind, I'll do it."

"No, it's my fault. I forgot where I was, and I was nervous about being alone."

"No really, Gianna. It was thoughtless of me to blow up like that. Don't give it another thought. I'm the one who should be sorry." He turned and left the room.

Gianna felt terrible. She was angry with herself for giving into fear. The least she could do was help her brother clean up the mud. She slipped her sandals on and went out to the front porch to help him.

"Matt, let me—"

She stopped talking when she realized he was on a phone call.

"Yeah, she's right here. Hang on," he said.

Gianna raised her eyebrows. "Who is it?"

"It's Dan," Matthew said, displaying his goofy grin.

Gianna smiled and grabbed the phone. "Hi, Danny!"

"Babe, I tried calling you, but—"

"My phone battery is dead. Sorry."

"I just wanted to tell you my plane landed."

"Thank you. You know how I worry."

"Yeah, I know." Danny spoke louder. "Hey, listen, it's noisy here. I'll call you when I get home."

"Ok, I love you."

"Love you, too," she said, smiling with contentment.

She ended the call and handed the phone back to her brother.

"Look at you," Matthew said. "Just one phone call from Dan gives you a smile from ear to ear."

Gianna felt her blood rush to her cheeks. "He makes me so happy. Thanks for giving me the call."

"No problem," Matt said, stuffing the phone in his back pocket. "Gianna, I'm sorry for snapping at you before. It was stupid of me."

"Matt, stop!" She raised her hand to silence him. "Just stop!" She pointed to herself. "I'm the one who's off track, and that's why I'm still here...to get healthy again."

"Ok, well, since you brought it up. Jess says she'll be here at eight tomorrow morning for your appointment."

Gianna nodded. "Thanks."

Chapter 29

Ugly gray tattered clouds welcomed Gianna Wednesday morning. She lay awake in bed, under the warm, cozy covers listening to the dreary rain pat tentatively on the windowpane. The icky, damp weather reflected her negative mood. She had no ambition to get out of bed, but today was her first counseling appointment. If she had a choice, she'd stay in her pajamas all day. She sat up in bed and rubbed the sleep out of her eyes. *Remember, one day at a time.*

She dug through her closet for something to wear. She picked through her dresser drawers then chose a pair of black leggings and a white tank top. After she dressed, she put Danny's denim shirt on over her outfit. The shirt still smelled like him, and she needed that comfort.

Jessica was on schedule picking Gianna up for her therapy appointment. During the twenty-minute drive to the behavioral health center, Gianna rode in silence, picking at her chipped nail polish. *How is therapy going to help me? Am I really going to forget what happened?*

When they arrived in the parking lot, Gianna's pulse raced. All sorts of questions that she was afraid to ask floated around in her head.

"Loosen up, Gianna. Everything's going to be ok."

Gianna tossed her head back against the car seat. "I never thought I'd be crazy to have to come here."

"Gianna, I work here. Let me assure you that you are not crazy, and all kinds of people with all kinds of problems seek counseling."

"Fine." she said, releasing her seatbelt.

Inside the building, Jessica directed Gianna to a small, quiet sitting area. There were only about a half dozen patients waiting. "Take a seat, and I'll be right back with your paperwork," Jessica said.

Gianna browsed the room carefully and chose a couch in the back corner away from everyone else. She picked up the first magazine she saw and pretended to read it. Intermittently, she peeked out from behind the pages and observed the people around her. She wondered what their problems were. In her eyes, they all seemed *normal.*

In the play area, there was a young mother with a toddler putting together a puzzle. In the front of the room was an elderly man who looked confused, and a few seats over from him, was a middle-aged couple who appeared peeved at one another. Across the room, a young man about her age with tattoo sleeves and a pierced eyebrow, sat alone. *Whoa! Last time I saw someone with so much body art, I was at the airport in New Jersey.*

She buried her nose back inside the magazine. *What exactly is normal anyway?*

"Here's the paperwork you need to fill out," Jessica said, handing her a clipboard.

"Thanks."

Gianna skimmed the paperwork and cowered at the number of questions asked. *It's going to take me an hour just to fill out this form.* First question: Why are you seeking help? She closed her eyes and took a deep breath. *I'm going to have to relive that Wednesday again on paper and again in the session. How many times do I have to talk about it?* To satisfy the first question, she wrote, sexual assault, and nothing more.

"Are you ok?" Jessica asked. "You look a little flush."

"It's just a lot of information."

"Take your time. Listen, I forgot to sign a report in my office. I'll be right back."

Gianna watched her best friend rush off through the heavy security door. *Why does it have a passcode? Are there that many irate patients here that would think about lashing out at the staff?* She looked around the room again at the people sitting there. They appeared calm and seemed friendly, but then again, so did Chad. She fidgeted in her chair. *Am I safe here?*

The reception door opened.

"Gianna?" A soft-spoken voice called out.

Gianna looked up and saw a middle-aged Asian woman standing there, scanning the waiting area. She raised her hand and smiled weakly. "I didn't finish the paperwork yet."

"That's ok. We'll go over it together in our session. I'm Dr. Jill Lin," she said, holding the door open for her.

Gianna pulled on a hangnail the entire walk down the long corridor to Dr. Lin's office. *What happens next? Where is Jessica?*

When Dr. Lin opened her office door, the aromatherapy candle and soft lighting drew Gianna inside.

"Please, Gianna, have a seat and make yourself at home. Would you like a bottle of water or a soda perhaps?"

"No, thank you."

Gianna sat down on the deep cushioned sofa. The atmosphere pleasantly surprised her. It was a lot friendlier and cozier than the clinic she went to in New York.

Dr. Lin sat down at her desk and browsed the paperwork that Gianna started to fill out. "Ok. I see you wrote here that you're seeking therapy for sexual assault. Before we talk about this any further, I'd like you to know that everything we discuss is confidential. Everything stays inside these walls. If you feel you need to bring a support person to our sessions, you may do so."

"Actually, I did come here with my sister-in-law, Jessica, who also works here, but I don't know where she went."

"Oh, yes. Jessica Stefano. I thought your last name and face looked familiar. I've seen you in her wedding photos on her desk."

At that moment, there was a knock at the door. Dr. Lin answered it. "Jessica, come in. We were just talking about you."

Jessica looked at Gianna. "I'm sorry I disappeared on you. I meant to introduce you to Doctor Lin, but I ran into some technical problems."

"Shall we begin?" Dr. Lin asked. "Gianna, can you talk to me about what happened that day? You can decide based on your comfort level."

"Yes," Gianna said, biting her lip.

Over the next hour, with Jessica's support, Gianna was able to retell her encounter with Chad.

"Thank you, Gianna. It was very courageous of you to talk about your situation," Dr. Lin said.

Gianna grabbed a tissue and wiped her tear-filled eyes. "The worst part is, I don't think I can ever go back to Danny's home. There's no way I will ever go into that kitchen again. Chad constantly pops up in my mind now. It'll be worse there. I just can't!"

"That's completely understandable," Dr. Lin said. "During our future sessions, I'm going to teach you some coping skills to overcome your fear, and some techniques to rebuild your self-esteem, so you can learn to trust yourself again."

Gianna nodded. "Thank you."

Chapter 30

Over the next few weeks, Gianna attended therapy independently, twice a week, on Tuesdays and Thursdays. She understood there were no guarantees to forget what happened, but she was hopeful knowing she had a supportive fiancé and a loving family by her side.

Danny called Gianna once, sometimes twice a day, just to hear her voice. 'You're never alone,' he promised her. The sound of his encouraging voice was all the reassurance she needed.

On days when she was troubled or wanted to be by herself, she rode Gemma to *Buffalo Creek*. There, she'd sit upon her favorite rock and talk privately to God. She even logged a journal of her daily thoughts, both good and bad.

Today was one of those troublesome days. She felt insecure about the way she handled herself when Danny revealed her secret to her parents. She felt guilty for blaming him, and the conversation haunted her.

She pulled her phone out of her pocket and dialed his number. The phone rang several times.

"Hey, babe," Danny answered.

Shocked to hear his voice, Gianna stuttered, "Do... you...have time to talk?"

"A few minutes. You ok?" he asked.

"Yeah, I'm at the creek. I started thinking...thinking about that day...I accused you of betraying me."

"Gianna."

"No, please, let me finish. I just wanted to say I'm sorry. You were right. My parents needed to know. I prayed for healing, and God answered me, but I didn't listen. He sent me you and my family, but I pushed you all away."

"Gianna, it's ok." Danny drew in a deep breath. "You don't have to apologize for your feelings. You weren't ready to talk about it," he said, his voice, tight with emotion.

"Are *you* ok?" she asked. "You sound stressed."

"I just miss you. I hate coming home at night and not finding you here napping on the couch with an open textbook on your chest."

Gianna laughed. "You're not making this any easier. I wish I were there."

"Soon, babe. You will be, soon. Listen, I have a meeting now with my boss. I'll call you tonight. I love you."

"I love you, too."

ᘓᘔ

The weeks flew by, and it was only a week and a half until the wedding. Dan had the day off. While he relaxed on his couch watching an old western movie, he decided to call Gianna. He glanced at the clock. It would be 10 a.m. in Sheridan. *She should be awake by now.* He dialed her cell phone, and it rang six times. *She can't still be sleeping.*

"Good morning, Daniel."

Caught off guard by the unexpected voice, Dan stuttered, "Oh...uh, hi Mom."

"Gianna forgot her phone and went to her final gown fitting," Mrs. Stefano said. "Wow, can you believe it's only ten days until the wedding?"

"Can't wait! It feels like an eternity," Dan said. "Um, how...*is* she doing? You know, Mom, she always says everything's fine."

"Oh, Daniel!" Mrs. Stefano's voice lilted. "She's doing fantastic! Thank you so much for encouraging her to stay here. She and I have done so much together. Oh, just yesterday, we made Italian pizzelle cookies, and every day she's been cooking with me, trying out new recipes." Mrs. Stefano laughed. "She even said to me this morning that she gained thirteen pounds since she's been home. Oh, but please don't tell her I told you."

"Believe me, I won't say a word, but I'm *so* glad to hear that. I begged her not to diet at all."

"Daniel, she looks great!" Mrs. Stefano assured him. "Listen, I'll tell her you called."

"Thanks, Mom. I'll see you soon."

When Dan hung up the phone, he reflected on their conversation. He was pleased to hear Gianna was doing well. He knew she still had a tough road ahead of her but was certain God would be there every step of the way.

The wedding was in three days. Gianna and her mother sat poolside, under a sun umbrella, enjoying the warm breeze that skipped off the water. They were reviewing the wedding checklist.

"Looks like all the RSVPs are back, honey," Mom said. "Tomorrow, I'll stop by the resort to give them the head count and the final payment."

"I can do that after therapy," Gianna said. "I have to pick up my wedding gown and go for a blood test for the marriage license."

"Thank you, honey. You'd be saving me a trip into town," Mom said. "Oh, can you stop by the florist, too? I have a check for Mr. Walters."

"No problem." Gianna held her pencil to her chin. "I don't know what I was thinking. If I only stayed here that weekend with Danny, all this follow-up stuff would have been dumped on you."

"Oh, please, Gianna. Planning your wedding together was one of our dreams, remember?" Her mother wiped a tear from her eye. "I love you so much, and I'd do anything for you."

Gianna had almost forgotten that dream. "And I love you, too, Mom," she said, hugging her.

Thursday morning came quickly. Gianna sat up in bed and stretched. Although she was exhausted from her late-night phone calls with Danny, the reality of him flying home tomorrow, gave her an instant drive. She bolted out of bed and got ready to start the day. It was her last day of therapy, and she had wedding errands to run afterward.

She dressed in a pink summer dress. She wore her hair down and even wore a little make-up. She was happier than ever on the inside and wanted to express her bliss on the outside.

At Gianna's therapy appointment, Dr. Lin welcomed her. "Today is your last session. Is there anything specific you'd like to discuss?"

Gianna shook her head. "I'm finally ready to move forward with my life. My fiancé' is flying in tomorrow, and we're getting married on Saturday. I feel like I have control over my emotions now."

Dr. Lin bobbed her head. She glanced at her notes. "Ok. I can certainly see you're smiling, and I can hear the joy in your voice, but Gianna, how do you think you'll cope when you return to New York? Let me just caution you. The emotional pain that you have endured *can* rear its ugly face in the future."

Gianna hesitated to answer. "I understand that, but I must deal with it. My life is in New York. You taught me relaxation and visualization techniques, and should I feel an anxiety attack, I'll have to implement them."

"Gianna, should you have a relapse and feel you can't handle things, please call me anytime," Dr. Lin said. She stood up and handed her a business card. "Here. A colleague of mine has a practice in North Bergen, New

Jersey. I don't know if that's too far from you but just in case you need to see someone." She shook Gianna's hand and said, "It was a pleasure working with you, and I wish you and your fiancé the best."

"Thank you, Doctor for *everything*."

The afternoon flew by. After stopping at Dr. Kendall's office for her blood test, and then dropping off the payment at the reception hall, Gianna had only two more errands to run. She drove several miles to the town square where both the tiny floral shop and bridal boutique were located.

She parked the car and strolled happily along the pebble stone sidewalk toward the floral shop. The heat of the sun beamed down on her head, but it felt good. She was freezing from the air-conditioned buildings.

The door chimed, welcoming Gianna inside the tiny floral shop. The sweet fragrance of flowers filled the air. The storeowner, Mr. Walters greeted her.

"Hello, Gianna. It's been some time."

"Good to see you again, sir."

"My wife will be right with you, dear. Please have a seat and help yourself to a cup of coffee."

Gianna sat down at a white wicker table next to a fishpond and became fixated on the goldfish swimming back and forth. While she waited, a young fascinating man entered the store. He walked up to the counter and spoke with Mr. Walters. Gianna tried hard not to laugh, but the young man didn't have a clue about buying flowers.

Mrs. Walters returned from the greenhouse and greeted Gianna. They shared some idle chitchat before getting down to business. Gianna reviewed the list of preordered flowers, confirmed the date and time, and made the final payment. As she left the store, Mr. and Mrs. Walters thanked her and wished her the best.

Outside the floral shop, Gianna checked her errand list. All she had left to do was pick up her gown. *Wow! Life is so exciting.* She was thrilled to be home in Montana and couldn't wait until Saturday. Aside from being apart from Danny, she really didn't miss New York at all.

She stepped off the pebble stone sidewalk to cross the parking lot when the thunderous roar of an old muscle car pulled up next to her.

"Hey, beautiful. Can you direct me to the hospital?" a deep voice called out from inside the rumbling car.

Gianna looked over her shoulder, but no one was behind her. He obviously was talking to her. A chill ran down her spine. This was déjà vu all over again, like the first day she met Chad – *Mr. Nice Guy.*

"Umm..." She scanned the parking lot trying to map out a route to the hospital in her head.

The man stuck his head out the window with his arm hanging down the side of the car. "Please, I must get to my mother. She's in critical condition," he said, his voice, urgent and desperate.

She gazed at his face and recognized him as the *fascinating* man that was in the floral shop. *Why didn't he ask them for directions?* Beads of sweat formed on her forehead. *How can I explain the best route?* She really needed to draw a map, which meant getting closer to his car, but that wasn't happening.

Gianna used her best New York accent and answered the man. "Uh, I'm not sure. I'm visiting from New York. Sorry." She stepped back onto the sidewalk.

The young man nodded his head as if he believed her. "Thanks anyway, beautiful. I'll check with the gas attendant down the road."

She watched him shift the car in gear, drop the clutch, and burn rubber out of the parking lot. As he raced off, she noticed his Wyoming license plate. She felt guilty for not trusting him. Perhaps he was harmless.

While Gianna ventured across the parking lot, she fretted about not helping the man out. She tried to justify her response and mumbled under her breath, "He should've had GPS." But if his story were true, the least she could do was say a prayer for his mother's recovery and his ability to reach her in time.

The second Gianna opened the door to the bridal boutique, she forgot about her encounter with flower boy.

"Hi, may I help you?" a teen with a mousy voice asked.

"Yes, I'm here to pick up my wedding gown."

"Oh, yeah. My sister said you'd be coming."

The teen walked over to the pick-up rack.

Gianna scratched her head. "Missy's not here today?"

"No. She had her baby girl this morning."

"Oh, that's exciting! Give her my best."

"I will. Well, here you are," the teen said, carefully handing her a white garment bag. "Your gown's pressed."

"Thank you very much," Gianna said, gently taking the gown in her arms.

"Good luck on Saturday."

Chapter 31

It had been a restless night for Gianna. She tossed and turned in bed. She rolled over and glimpsed at the alarm clock. *Ugh, it's three o'clock. Danny, Troy, and Tracy should be boarding their red-eye flight.*

Now Gianna was not only restless, but also wide-awake. She lay there, watching the digits on the clock change as the minutes passed.

"Hurry up, clock!" she scolded. She wanted it to be morning. She was gung-ho to get to the airport to welcome Danny and of course, Troy and Tracy, too.

At six thirty, her alarm buzzed. She groaned, then reached over and smacked the snooze button. *Ugh, just another ten minutes, and then I'll get up.*

"Gianna, honey?" Mom called.

Gianna stirred under her toasty-warm covers. When she felt a tap on her shoulder, she groaned.

"Are you ok? I thought you were going with your father and Joe to the airport."

"I am...in a minute," Gianna grumbled beneath her pillows.

"Honey, they already left."

Gianna shot up in bed, bright eyed and bushy tailed.

"What'd you say?"

Mom opened the blinds, letting in the intense sunlight.

Gianna squeezed her eyes shut. "What...what time is it?" she asked, squinting at the clock.

"Eight thirty," Mom answered.

"Sugar, honey, iced tea!" Gianna yelled, leaping out of bed. She slid across the hardwood floor toward the bathroom. "I overslept again! Why didn't Daddy wake me at six?"

"Your father tried twice, but you were sawing wood. He gave up. He had to leave."

Gianna stood in the bathroom doorway and rubbed her eyes. "I was up at three. Couldn't sleep. Think I finally zonked out around five."

"You obviously needed sleep. I'll leave you to get ready. Evelyn and I will be in the kitchen."

Gianna paced back and forth on the porch waiting anxiously for her father's Suburban to pull into the driveway.

"Honey, relax," Mom said.

"Relax? They're over an hour late."

"I just spoke to your father. They were delayed in baggage while customer service tried to locate Tracy's suitcase that had her gown in it."

"What?" Gianna covered her mouth. When she noticed her mother grinning, she asked, "What do you mean *relax?*" She put her hands on her hips. "This isn't funny, Mom."

"Calm down, Gianna. They found it. They're on their way home now," Mom said, laughing.

Gianna still didn't find humor in it. There was no way she could handle a huge airport blunder like that.

She sat on the porch swing just as she heard a slow-moving vehicle coming up the road. "I bet that's them now." Her body tingled all over. She rose to her feet and leaned over the porch railing. She peered through the bushes to see who was coming. "Oh, it's just Matt and Jessica."

"Relax, Gianna," Mom said.

As Matthew and Jessica climbed the porch steps, her father's Suburban pulled into the driveway. Gianna took off like a shot across the porch and down the steps. *At last, he's home.*

"Danny!" Gianna cried.

Danny nearly hopped out of the truck while it was still moving. He greeted her with open arms. "Oh, babe! I've missed you."

"Let me look at you." She reached up and caressed his face. He had shaved his beard, leaving behind a well-groomed mustache and goatee. "Wow, you even cut your tough hair!" She ran her fingers through his collar length hair.

"You don't like it?" he asked.

"I love it!"

Danny studied her face. "Oh, you look so pretty." He twirled her around and reclaimed her lips with a long, overdue kiss.

Lost in the moment, Gianna forgot about her guests. When her father cleared his throat, she awkwardly backed out of Danny's arms. She gave her father a bashful smile and said, "I'm sorry. Where's my manners?" She turned to Tracy and Troy and gave them a hug. "Welcome to Montana. This is my family."

Gianna's mother graciously welcomed the new guests. "It's so nice to meet you, both. Come in. Our house is your home."

Chapter 32

It was six o'clock Saturday morning when the sun shined its smiling face at Gianna. She sat up in bed, deliciously alive. *Thank you, Lord, for this glorious day.*

After she showered, she put on Danny's button-down shirt and a pair of shorts so it would be easier to change into her gown when it was time. She could not believe in a few short hours she would be getting her make-up and hair done.

The house was quiet without her rowdy brothers. Gianna didn't think anyone else was awake yet, until she moseyed into the kitchen and saw her mom making pancakes.

"Good morning, Mom," she said, giving her a hug.

"Good morning, honey. You're up early. Sleep well?"

Gianna nodded. Her heart was blissfully happy, fully alive. "I can't believe this day is finally here," she said, recalling the day she said goodbye to Danny. She realized Jess was right, time flew.

"Can I help you with anything, Mom?"

"I've got it," Mom said. "It's your wedding day! Let me have the honor of making your breakfast one last time, *Miss Stefano*. Besides, it's beautiful outside. Why don't you go for a morning swim? You have plenty of time before the stylists come to the house."

"Sounds tempting, I think I will. Please send Tracy and Jessica out when they wake up."

Gianna dipped her foot into the pool. The lukewarm water was heavenly. She dove right in and swam several laps before Tracy finally joined her.

"Good morning. Sleep well?" Gianna asked.

"I had trouble falling asleep at first because it was *too* dark and *too* quiet. But, let me tell you." Tracy tossed her wrist in the air. "Girlfriend, once I was out, I was out!"

"Good to hear. Yesterday was a long day for you. Hey, jump in before Mom serves us breakfast."

Gianna and Tracy swam for some time and then made themselves at home sitting at the patio table.

"This is paradise out here," Tracy said. "I could get used to this." Her head shifted in every direction taking in the scenic views. "The only dreadful thing is that rooster. Does he wake up the sun?"

Gianna nodded. "Yeah, Coo-Coo's loud."

Out of the corner of her eye, she caught a glimpse of her father in the pasture, filling water buckets. "The ranch is a lot of work, but Dad enjoys it. It keeps him young."

"I'll always be a city girl. You heard Troy last night. He wouldn't be happy here," Tracy said. "He thrives on his detective work amongst the city chaos."

Gianna quickly realized just how much she missed living on the ranch. "I love the wide-open space." Suddenly, a thought gnawed in her stomach. It wasn't wedding day nerves. It was her life in the city. "Tracy, I was, wondering, who took over my position at school?"

Gianna knew Tracy had a friend on the school board, and she'd have the scoop.

"Oh, Mr. Sterling brought in a substitute, someone new to the school. Rumor has it, she wasn't as good a teacher as you were," Tracy said. "I just happen to know Mr. Sterling is looking forward to your return in September."

"I don't know if I could go back," Gianna said, shifting in her chair. Her stomach churned again. "What about Chad? Where is he?" she asked, her words choking her.

Tracy reached across the table and took Gianna's hand. "What does it matter? Let it go."

Gianna took a deep breath. Her stomach was like a rock. Desperate and persistent, she pleaded, "Tracy, I need to know."

"Gianna, don't do this, not on your wedding day."

"Please, Tracy. Just tell me they didn't release him."

After a long pause, Tracy said, "No. The prosecutors indicted Chad on attempted rape charges." She sat back in her chair and folded her hands in her lap. "Troy has all the details about the case, but Gianna, just—let—it—go!"

Gianna lowered her head. Silently, she tried to absorb the facts but became distracted when her mother came outside with a tray of food, accompanied by Jessica.

"Breakfast is served," Mom said, setting the tray down on the table.

"Oh, Mom. This is too much."

"Nothing is too much for my daughter. Eat up, honey, you probably won't eat much later," she said. She leaned forward and kissed her cheek.

Gianna looked at Jessica. "It's about time you woke up, sleepy head."

"I've been up, out, and about already this morning," Jessica said, playfully sticking out her tongue. "I had a special errand to run."

Gianna raised her eyebrows. "Where'd you go?"

Jessica reached into her pocket and pulled out a small gift box. "This is for you," she said, handing it to her.

Gianna gasped, "What's this?"

"It's from Dan." Jessica smiled. "He forgot to leave it with me yesterday, so I picked it up this morning."

Gianna felt her entire body heat up as if she were on fire. She opened the tiny card that was attached and read it silently.

> *My sweet Gianna, you are the love of my life and my soon-to-be-wife. I love you always, Dan.*

"Aw," Gianna said with tears streaming down her cheeks. She opened the tiny box. "Oh, my!" She threw her hand over her mouth. Inside the box was a pair of heart-shaped diamond stud earrings and a matching necklace. "This is too much. I must call him."

"Actually, he's out jogging with Troy and Mark," Jessica said. She folded her arms across her chest. "Matt is home supervising Luke and John while they vacuum up spilled popcorn and chips from their movie night."

Gianna touched Jessica's forearm. "Sorry to hear about the mess." She looked at Tracy and tried to suppress a smile. "Well, anyway. I'll thank Danny later."

Too excited, she couldn't eat her pancakes. She placed the box into the pocket of her cover-up and carried it about for the rest of the morning, touching it when she thought about Danny.

By noon, Gianna, Jessica, and Tracy had their make-up and hair done, and were now upstairs putting on their gowns. There was a quiet knock at the bedroom door, and Gianna's mother stepped inside the room.

"For you, honey," she said, handing her a small box wrapped in gold foil.

"Mom? What is this?"

"This is a little something just for you."

Gianna carefully opened the box and gasped at its contents. As she removed the hand-cut crystal rosary beads with a golden cross, her mother explained their history.

"Honey, those rosary beads were given to me by my mother when I got married. Her godmother gave them to her for her First Holy Communion. Your Grandma told me that she prayed with that rosary every night to the Blessed Virgin for the safe return of your Grandpa, and her brother Giovanni during World War II. She told me that whenever she was worried, sad, or frightened, she would take those beads to the chapel where she was married and pray to Our Lady. God had answered her prayers. She gave them to me on my wedding day and I have used them throughout my life. I am now giving them to you, Gianna. Always remember, Our Lady will hear your prayers and guide you to Christ."

Through her tears, Gianna mumbled her thanks, and her mother quietly slipped out of the room.

After a few minutes, Jessica twirled around the room in her ocean blue tulle ball gown. The color was dazzling on her, especially with her green eyes and strawberry blonde hair.

"So, what do you think?" Jessica asked.

"Oh, you look amazing!" Gianna said.

Gianna helped Tracy zip up her gown. It was the same style as Jessica's but a slightly deeper shade of blue.

"Oh, Tracy! I love it on you!"

Tracy twirled around in front of the mirror. "Gianna, I must admit, working out with you all those weeks really paid off. Do you think Troy will like it?"

"Absolutely!"

"Gianna, let's get you in your gown before the photographers get here," Jessica said, while unzipping the garment bag.

"Ooh, girl, I can't wait to see it!" Tracy said.

Gianna stepped into her white satin ballgown, then poised gracefully in front of the mirror while Jessica arranged her cathedral waterfall train. "I feel like Cinderella."

"But we're not done yet," Jessica said, adjusting the dazzling rhinestone tiara and fingertip length veil. "Now you look like Cinderella."

Gianna imagined walking down the aisle and seeing her bridegroom in his white tuxedo for the first time. Every time she thought about Danny, she smiled. She never felt happier knowing that in just a couple of hours, they would become one.

"Now, for the finishing touch," Jessica said. She asked for the jewelry box from Gianna, who handed it to her. Jessica carefully placed the necklace on her, while Gianna put in her earrings. "Oh, Gianna, you are radiant! I am so happy for you. Dan is so wonderful, and you deserve him. I wish you so much love."

"Girlfriend, you look like a princess! You had shown me pictures in the magazine, but wow, your gown is even lovelier than I imagined," Tracy said.

"Thank you both," Gianna said, giving them a hug.

"Gianna, honey," Mom called from downstairs. "The photographers are here."

"Don't forget your flowers," Tracy said, handing her the bouquet of white roses and Baby's Breath.

"Thank you, Tracy. I think *now* we're ready to make our debut downstairs," Gianna said.

As Gianna walked carefully down each step, Tracy and Jessica followed behind, clutching her train. The photographers were flashing pictures left and right, while the video camera was rolling. A rush of anticipation flowed through her. She couldn't believe she was living this moment.

Her father stood at the bottom of the staircase watching her. "Oh, bella ragazza!" His eyes welled up with tears.

She smiled when she saw him. "You're looking mighty handsome yourself in your black tux," she said, choking on her tears. As she gave her father a hug, her mother walked in with Dr. and Mrs. Kendall. "Oh, Mom. You look so beautiful!"

Her mother was wearing the floor length chiffon gown she tried on at the bridal shop. The platinum color flattered her golden-brown hair and complimented her complexion.

"Mrs. Kendall, look at you, so elegant!" Gianna cried. Mrs. Kendall was wearing a shimmering silver, silk-crepe floor length gown with a matching shawl.

"Thank you, dear," Mrs. Kendall said, hugging her.

Everyone oohed and aahed over Gianna as she turned and twirled at their request. Her mother rushed over to Gianna and cried, "Honey, you look *so* beautiful!"

Mrs. Kendall turned to her husband and asked, "What do you say we go to the church, so we can check on Daniel?"

"Yeah, I guess we should give him our best wishes, and make sure he didn't forget how to breathe," Dr. Kendall said. "See you all in a little bit."

Meanwhile, the photographers took dozens of pictures of Gianna, her parents, Jessica, and Tracy.

The white limousine pulled into the driveway.

"Time to go, bella," Dad said.

Gianna daintily stepped outside onto the porch. She turned around and she glanced back inside the foyer. It just dawned on her that this was the last time she'd be there as Gianna Stefano. It brought tears to her eyes, but looking forward, she thought about the exciting life ahead of her.

Gianna's father escorted her down the porch steps to the driveway. As he helped her into the limo, he wiped a tear off her cheek. She carefully gathered up her train so not to get it stuck in the car door.

On the drive to the church, she stared out the window. In a solemn manner, she prayed.

God, you led me to Danny. Today, we will fulfill your will. I promise to be faithful and true, as Danny and I journey through life together. Amen.

"Gianna, you're so quiet. Are you nervous?" Jessica asked.

"Nope. I've never felt more certain about anything in my life."

When the limo pulled in front of the church, eagerness rushed through Gianna's body. She couldn't wait to see her bridegroom. The chauffeur opened the door and helped Tracy, Jessica, and Gianna's mother step out.

"Let me help you out, bella," Dad said, joyfully. He took her hand and helped her out of the limousine, careful not to drag her train across the dusty ground.

After Gianna pulled herself together, she looked up to find herself surrounded by photographers and videographers. She felt like a superstar inundated with the paparazzi. They made her nervous. She worried about tripping over her long gown, and that was not how she wanted to remember her special day.

Inside the church's vestibule, she waited with her father, Jessica, and Tracy, while the twins escorted their mother inside the church. A few minutes later, the hymn that was playing transformed into the wedding march.

"Ready, bella?" Dad asked.

"I'm ready, Daddy!" she said, taking a deep breath.

When her father lowered her veil, his smile faded away. She recognized that look and recalled the day she said goodbye to him at the airport when she moved to New York. "Come on, Daddy," she whispered. She took his hand and lined up behind Tracy and Jessica.

She watched Tracy and Jessica walk down the center aisle. She noticed the pretty mix of Stargazer lilies, pink carnations, and lavender daisies that decorated the altar so beautifully. She saw Father Anthony standing at the front of the altar, but she couldn't see Danny. All the guests were standing, leaning into the aisle with their heads turned, waiting for her to make her grand entrance.

As Gianna and her father began their walk, she remained calm. Halfway there, her eyes caught sight of Danny at the altar. He stood tall with his hands folded in front of him. Her heart throbbed, her mouth quivered, and her eyes welled up with tears. He looked so handsome. His deep brown hair and deep blue eyes contrasted perfectly with his pure white tuxedo. When she thought about their night together, she felt herself blush. She waited her whole life for this moment.

’ɔʒ⳹ʒℭ

Dan watched his lovely bride come forward. Gianna looked more beautiful and angelic than ever. Her eyes sparkled like the sequins on her gown. Her smile matched the liveliness in her pace. As their eyes met, he noticed her face blush with a rosy color. Suddenly, he realized that this was really happening. Today, he would leave his single life behind and now have a lifelong partner. He smiled at the thought of becoming one in every way. *I'm the luckiest man on earth.*

As Mr. Stefano escorted Gianna down the aisle, Dan noticed the empty expression on his face. He tried to imagine how difficult it was for a father to give away his only daughter. He reckoned that one day if God blessed him with a daughter, he'd have mixed feelings, too.

Mr. Stefano lifted Gianna's veil and kissed her.

321

"Ti amo, bella ragazza," he said softly to her. His voice quivered. He was crying a little, too.

"I love you, too, Daddy," she whispered.

When Gianna turned and faced the altar, Dan winked at her and took her hand in his.

ೞ

Father Anthony began the Nuptial Mass with an opening prayer followed by the Readings.

Jessica approached the altar and read from the Old Testament, Genesis 2:18-24. "'The Lord God said it is not good for the man to be alone. I will make a suitable partner for him...that is why a man leaves his father and mother and clings to his wife, and the two of them become one body...'"

Next, Troy approached the altar and read the Responsorial Psalm, Psalm 121:2. "'My help comes from the Lord, the maker of heaven and earth.'"

Tracy then read from the New Testament, 1 Corinthians 13:1-13. "'...Love is patient, love is kind. It is not jealous, love is not pompous, it is not inflated...'"

Father Anthony read from the Gospel of Matthew 19:3-6. "'...They are no longer two, but one flesh. Therefore, what God has joined together, no human being must separate...'"

He gestured to everyone to be seated. "Daniel and Gianna, the two of you had your own separate journeys through life in various places at various times. Your paths met, and you began to walk together, and that path led you to this day in this house of God. You are here because the Lord has brought you here. He put the spark of love in your hearts, a love that will burn a lifetime."

Gianna glanced at Danny and smiled. A tear rolled down her cheek. As Father Anthony continued his homily, Danny gently squeezed Gianna's hand and winked at her.

"Daniel and Gianna, I have had the pleasure of counseling you through Pre-Cana. I have learned that each of you has come into this relationship knowing different hardships. Daniel, the loss of your parents has affected you in many ways, and Gianna, moving to New York brought different hardships that have shaped you into the person you are. Although your separate journeys and experiences made you into the people you are in love with, it is now that you are joining each of those experiences, ideas, and feelings into one union.

"Gianna, as Daniel hurts, you will hurt. Daniel, as Gianna soars, you will share her success. But remember, it is important that you understand what you are promising today, because we know that not every road is straight. You're going to face sharp curves and barricades. You're going to need God's love and your love for each other to see you through. Never give up, Daniel and Gianna. As you continue together on this journey, the Lord will lead you and give you strength."

As Father Anthony completed his homily, Gianna reflected on what he said. She and Danny had already gone down one bumpy road and had already received God's grace and guidance.

"Daniel and Gianna, since it is your intention to enter into marriage, join your right hands, and declare your consent before God and his Church."

Danny took Gianna's hand in his. He gazed into her eyes and declared, "I, Daniel Joseph, take you, Gianna, to be my wife. I promise to be true to you in good times and in bad, in sickness and in health. I will love you and honor you all the days of my life."

Gianna's voice, soft, but clear, said, "I, Gianna Rose, take you, Daniel, to be my husband." Her voice weakened, and tears fell. "I promise to be true to you in good times and in bad, in sickness and in health." Choked up, her voice cracked, "I will love you and honor you all the days of my life."

Father Anthony raised his hands over them and blessed them. He announced, "What God has joined, man must not divide."

Chapter 33

A couple of hours later, Gianna and Danny, and their bridal party arrived at the Big Sky Manor and Resort. After cocktail hour, the newlyweds lined up outside the ballroom entrance waiting to make their first appearance as husband and wife.

Loud and clear, the DJ announced, "Let's all stand up and welcome for the first time in public, Doctor and Mrs. Daniel Christiansen!"

The guests whistled and applauded as Danny and Gianna made their grand entrance into the ballroom. They promenaded to the dance floor where they danced their first dance as a married couple. All eyes focused on them as they swayed back and forth to their favorite country love song. This time Gianna didn't mind being in the spotlight. She was proud to be shown off as Danny's bride. When their song ended, they shared a kiss.

When Gianna and Danny returned to their seats, the DJ invited Matthew up to the microphone to propose a toast.

Matthew raised his glass and spoke into the microphone. "I stand here tonight to toast my dear sister

Gianna and my best friend Dan. I've known both of you my whole life. I know the two of you were always meant to be together. Today, God has joined you as one. May faith, hope, and love fill your hearts and your lives forever. Congratulations, and God bless you both."

Matthew's speech left Gianna in tears. She gave her brother a hug. "Thank you, Matt. Those words mean so much to me, especially hearing them from you."

Next, the DJ announced for the father-of-the-bride to dance with his daughter.

Gianna reached for her father's hand. Together they stepped onto the dance floor and twirled around. She spoke softly in her father's ear, "Thank you, Daddy, for everything."

"Anything for my bella ragazza," he said.

"But you looked so sad walking me down the aisle."

"I'm going to miss you, bella, but I know Dan's going to take care of you. I trust him," he said.

"I know, Daddy, and I'll be ok." She leaned her head against his shoulder and whispered, "I love you, Daddy."

The night wore on, and it was time for the cake cutting ceremony. Gianna and Danny stood at their beautiful six-tier wedding cake. It was streamed with white roses cascading down the sides of each layer.

Together, they held hands and cut the first slice. When Danny raised his fork to feed her the first bite, he had this huge devilish grin on his face.

Gianna shook her head. "You'd better be nice."

Danny fed Gianna a forkful of cake, gracefully. Then it was her turn. She kept a straight face and lifted the fork from the plate. As she raised the fork to his lips, she smeared the cake all over his goatee just like the day she was decorating Christmas cookies. To her surprise, he showed no reaction.

Calm and casual, he said, "Two can play at this game." He reached for the plate, picked up a glob of frosting, and slopped it on her mouth.

Gianna licked her lips. She leaned into him and gave him a mushy kiss. The guests roared at the entertainment then applauded when they made amends.

After they tidied up, they strolled onto the dance floor for one last slow dance. Wrapped in each other's arms, they rocked back and forth.

"Well, that was exciting." Danny laughed.

"I know, I know. I asked for it," Gianna said. "I think I have cake crumbs down my dress."

"Ah, dessert for later," he said creatively. A mischievous look came into his eyes.

"Oh, stop," she said, playfully scolding him.

"I love you," he whispered. His gaze turned serious. His lips slowly descended to meet hers. His soft touch and sweet taste sent warm tremors through her body. Their kiss grew passionate, rousing her desire. She couldn't help but wonder what the night ahead was going to feel like.

The reception was nearing a close, and Gianna and Danny said their goodbyes to their guests.

"So, Gianna, what time is your flight tomorrow?" Jessica asked.

Gianna gave Jessica a dumbfounded look. "What're you talking about?"

"Oops," Jessica said. She looked at Danny. "I guess you didn't tell her yet."

"Tell me what?" Gianna asked.

Danny grinned and his eyes grew bright with enthusiasm. "I'm sorry, but we're not staying here for our honeymoon. I hope you don't mind, but I have airline tickets for us for tomorrow morning. We're going to Italy!"

"What? But I'm not packed."

"Yes, you are," he said, glancing at his mother-in-law.

"Yes, honey. I packed your suitcase for you," Mom said, smiling. "We were all in on Daniel's surprise."

"Oh, Mom! Thank you," Gianna said, giving her a hug. She then hugged Danny. "Thank you so much!"

She had never been to Italy before, but it was always her dream to see where her parents and grandparents once lived.

Meanwhile, her father and Matthew returned to the hall wheeling in Gianna and Danny's luggage.

Her dad grinned. "Well, sounds like the surprise is out. Sorry, bella, but I can't be your tour guide on this trip," he said, handing Danny his luggage.

Jessica took Gianna's bag from Mr. Stefano. "Gianna, come with me. I'll help you change out of your gown, so Mom can take it home with her."

"Ok, we'll be right back." Gianna followed Jessica out of the hall to a private room where she could change.

Jessica helped Gianna pull out a dozen hairpins before removing the tiara and veil. "Do you know how many times you're going to have to wash your hair to get all the hairspray out?"

"Yep. I remember from your wedding."

Jessica helped Gianna change into a pair of white denim shorts and a pink blouse. "Mom packed your ballet slippers and a pair of sneakers. Which do you want?" Jessica asked.

"Please, I'll take the ballet slippers. Where were these a few hours ago? My feet are killing me."

"I warned you," Jessica said.

Upon returning to the reception hall, Gianna and Jessica joined the family again. Danny was back, dressed in his signature black jeans, a dress shirt, and cowboy boots.

Gianna could not believe how fast he changed out of the tuxedo and into regular clothes. "You guys have it so easy. Look how long it took me to get out of that gown. You're done in minutes."

"That may be true, but you look so much prettier than me," Danny quipped. He drew a good laugh from the group.

Gianna's father glanced at his wife. "So, Stefano family, ready to go home?"

"Yes, I'm exhausted," Gianna said. Although the day was memorable, she was sad to see it end. Now, she just wanted to go home and sleep.

"Uh, bella, aren't you forgetting something?" her dad asked, grinning. "You are no longer a Stefano." He glanced at Danny. "Your room's waiting for you upstairs."

Gianna flinched at her father's comment. She bit her lip and caught herself glancing uneasily over her shoulder. It was nerve-racking enough thinking about the night ahead, let alone mentioning it in the presence of her parents.

"Oh, right, Daddy." When she spoke, her voice wavered. Her head pounded, and her face grew hot with embarrassment.

Gianna's mother took her hand. She smiled, then whispered in her ear. "It will be fine, honey. Daniel loves you."

Chapter 34

Dan carried Gianna over the threshold into their honeymoon suite. "I'm so lucky to have you," he said, setting her down on the king size bed.

"This is the happiest day of my life!" Joy bubbled in her voice. Eagerness shone in her eyes.

"Same here, baby." He sat next to her on the edge of the bed. He kissed her, slowly and thoughtfully. "Are you tired?"

"No, not since Italy appeared on our itinerary. I'll sleep on the plane tomorrow." A smile of appreciation touched her lips. "Oh, Danny! I always wanted to go there. For years, Dad talked about taking us there but between the cattle ranch and the expense."

"I know," Danny said. He pulled off his boots and leaned back against the pillow. "That's why I wanted to surprise you. I asked your father, and he was thrilled that I offered."

"But Danny." Gianna fiddled with her wedding band. "Between the beautiful diamond earrings and necklace, and now the trip, it's too much." Uncertainty flickered in her eyes.

"No, it's not. That's why I chose to work sixty hours a week, so we can share this special time together. I love you." He reached out and clutched her hand. "Lie next to me."

Gianna settled back into his arms. For the next half hour, they rambled on about the day's events.

"So, what did you think about Father Anthony's homily?" he asked.

She smiled. "It really hit home. His message to us was heartfelt. I am so grateful to be a part of a caring parish."

"Yeah, it was a beautiful ceremony. The reception was a lot of fun, too, especially the dramatic cake scene."

"That was good!" Gianna giggled. "You know, I am so glad we skipped the bouquet and garter toss. I would never put anyone through that."

Dan felt a tingling in his face. "I'm sorry, baby. I shouldn't have put you on the spot like that at Matt and Jessica's wedding."

Gianna held up her left hand and flashed her ring. "Oh, but that was well worth it. I have you," she said in a honeyed voice. She leaned over and kissed him.

"It was sweet of you to replace the bouquet and garter toss tradition with a dance honoring the longest married couples. Wow! Both sets of your grandparents married fifty years!"

"They married young, just like Joe and Evelyn."

"Yep. They married at eighteen," he said.

"Someday that'll be us, unless you trade me in."

Dan frowned. "I'd never trade you in. I love you." He gazed into her eyes and kissed her. As he eased away from their kiss, he mumbled, "I'm so glad those dating days are over."

"Me, too."

Dan was thrilled. He was finally married to his best friend, his soul mate, the love of his life. Still, he was nervous, his body tense. He wanted their first time to be special but feared a wrong move on his part could stir up an array of emotions in her.

He tucked a few strands of her hair behind her ear and then lightly kissed her neck. The faded scent of her sweet perfume mixed with hairspray, lingered on her skin. He breathed a trail of kisses from her neck to her cheek and then moved his mouth over hers. His tongue traced the soft fullness of her lips. He parted them and tasted her sweetness.

His hands began to roam her body. His fingers tingled as they skimmed her soft skin. The pleasure in his flesh was restless now. Carefully, he unbuttoned her blouse with his trembling fingers. With his other hand, he reached for hers, encouraging her to explore. He searched her eyes for approval.

"You ok?" he asked.

Her eyes were closed, and she had a painful expression on her face. "Gianna, look at me, baby—don't look at him," he said. "I promise not to hurt you."

Gianna slowly opened her eyes. A tear rolled down her cheek. She nodded then breathed, "I'm ok. I'm ok."

❦

Gianna focused on Danny's face, with tearful, yet urgent eyes. As he undressed her, she breathed more rapidly, and shivers rippled across her shoulders. She watched him pull off his shirt. He looked powerful, his chest broad and muscular, yet he moved with ease as he lowered himself onto her. She gasped as her bare skin met his for the first time. Her body craved his gentle touch. His masculine scent of sandalwood cologne and old spice deodorant kicked her hormones into high gear, and she hungered to taste his love.

As she clung to his warm body, she glided her fingers up and down the length of his back. She was ready for him now. She glided her hands along his lower back to his hips, gesturing to him to unfasten his jeans.

Now, when Gianna closed her eyes, she no longer had the horrific memory of Chad's brutal attack. She invited Danny in, giving herself freely to him. A deep feeling of peace entered her soul as their bodies melted together in harmony.

In the slow-cooling aftermath, Danny kissed her neck and whispered softly in her ear, "Thank you for trusting me."

Breathless, she replied, "Thank you for loving me."

Chapter 35

By noon, Gianna and Danny boarded their eleven-hour flight. They held hands and prayed silently for a safe trip. During the flight, they both napped intermittently.

When the flight attendant announced the plane's landing at *Abruzzo* International Airport, Danny rubbed her forearm. "Hey, wake up. You're our tour guide. At least you can speak Italian."

Gianna fidgeted in her seat, stretched, and then yawned. "At last, we made it," she said excitedly. She dug through her purse and found the notepad that her father had given her with her aunt and uncle's contact information and the hotel reservations. "What time is it anyway?"

"What time is it?" he asked. "I'm not even sure what day it is." He looked at his phone. "It's uh, 7 a.m., Monday."

"Ok. Let's get settled in the hotel first and then see what we want to do," she said.

"Whatever you say, you're the boss," he said.

Gianna and Danny checked into a five-star hotel and restaurant in the *Abruzzo* region. After settling in, they went out for a bite to eat and then went sightseeing at the Abruzzo National Park where they spotted mountain goats, deer, and roebuck.

Early that evening, she contacted her aunt and uncle and arranged a visit for the following day. She explained to Danny that her family lived in a little village in Monteferrante. The quaint village had a population of less than two hundred people.

The next day, Gianna and Danny arrived at her aunt and uncle's home. Danny parallel parked the rental car along the narrow alleyway.

Gianna glanced up at the cluster of tiny, stone cottages that were set in the green foothills. Her aunt and uncle's place looked just like the photos her father showed her. *This is it.* She recalled the last time she saw them. It was thirteen years ago when they visited her family in Montana. She remembered they had spoken broken English.

She looked at Danny and couldn't help but notice his hands gripping the steering wheel. She rubbed his shoulder to comfort him. "Hey, my family's your family. I promise you'll like them." She opened the car door and said, "C'mon."

Not saying a word, he nervously followed her to the front door, but before she could knock, the door opened, and Aunt Luciana welcomed them inside with hugs and kisses. Her Uncle Emilio and seven cousins greeted her and Danny.

Aunt Luciana squeezed her cheeks and cried, "Ciao, Gianna. And, this your bello, Daniel?"

"Si' Zia Luciana," Gianna said, introducing her *handsome* Danny to the family.

Gianna's family was so impressed that Danny was a doctor. Quickly, they bombarded him with medical questions. Uncle Emilio and two of the cousins showed him the house and their vegetable garden. They shared family albums along with lots of stories. Gianna and Danny joined her family for supper and stayed late into the evening.

Later, when Gianna and Danny arrived back at the hotel, they relaxed in bed recapping the day.

"You have a great family," he said. "And it wasn't that difficult understanding them either. I guess four years of Italian in high school was worth it."

"I'm so happy you had an enjoyable time. I was so afraid they would bore you."

The honeymoon days flew by. Gianna and Danny made the most out of each one by sticking to their itinerary. One day they visited a farm where they experienced direct contact with farm life, as they never had before. They went on a tour of grape picking and winemaking and learned about specialty food preserves. They even milked goats and made cheese together. Later in the week, they went horseback riding, hiking, and mountain biking.

During their last week in Italy, Gianna and Danny went fishing and canoeing, and then drove along the Tiber River. They spent a few days in Rome visiting St.

Peter's Square. One of the most stirring moments was visiting the Vatican and the Basilica. The celebration of the Mass enraptured them. Danny commented that although St. Patrick's in New York is beautiful, the Basilica is spectacular. Although they did not see the Pope, they were blessed by a Cardinal, who celebrated a special Mass for young couples. This delighted Gianna, thinking that God truly approved of their marriage.

On their very last day, they stopped at the *Fontana di Trevi*. Gianna handed a couple of coins to Danny and said, "Legend has it that whoever throws a coin in the fountain will return to Rome the following year."

Danny tossed the coins into the fountain and replied, "As long as I come back here with you." He swept her into his arms and kissed her. "We have a lot of great memories to bring home with us."

Later that afternoon, they returned to their hotel and enjoyed a fine, romantic dinner outside on the terrace.

Danny set down his glass. "Well, this is it. We leave tomorrow morning."

"Time sure went fast. I will cherish every moment we shared here," Gianna said.

While Danny was paying the check, a brief, fast-moving thunderstorm rolled in. Fortunately, they were able to dodge the heavy downpour and not get soaked.

After returning to their hotel room, Gianna plopped down on the bed while Danny relaxed in the armchair in front of the balcony window.

"We were lucky," he said as he watched the storm fade away. "We had fantastic weather the whole two weeks we were here."

Gianna nodded. "It was the perfect honeymoon."

She lay back on the bed and smiled. *God, you blessed me with Danny and this amazing honeymoon. Thank you.* She thought about having to leave Italy tomorrow and about beginning their new life together in New York as husband and wife.

She glanced at Danny and said, "If you could've told me twelve weeks ago that I would be smiling today, I wouldn't have believed you. Thank you."

"Come here, baby," he said.

With a springy bounce, she was beside him.

He pulled her onto his lap and wrapped his arms around her. He pointed out the window to a rainbow in the sky and whispered, "The rainbow is a reminder of God's promise that you won't have to walk through life's storms alone. When your heart is filled with uncertainty, remember that God is always faithful and true."

A note from the author...

To My Readers,

Thank you for reading, *Always Faithful and True*. As a self-published author, reaching exposure to interested readers relies on word-of-mouth. Please consider writing an honest review wherever you can. Any review, positive or negative, really helps readers determine if my book is worth their attention. Your opinion really makes a difference. Thank you.

Janet

Discussion Questions

1. At age twenty-four, Gianna was seeking her independence. Do you think her parents were too overprotective? Do you think they should've let her make her own decisions about her life? Why or why not?

2. What was your first impression of Gianna? Did your impression of Gianna change by the end of the story?

3. How did Gianna's character evolve from the beginning of the novel to the end? What events triggered her growth?

4. Both Gianna and Dan experienced hardships at various times in their lives, yet they never let go of their faith. Do you feel their healing process would've been the same without their religion?

5. Dan was sympathetic toward Gianna during her most vulnerable moments. Do you think the tragedy in his past attributed to his compassionate personality?

6. Was Gianna right to demand that Dan keep her secret from her parents? How might things have been different if Gianna was honest from the beginning?

7. How did Gianna's religious beliefs play a role in the choices she made?

8. Throughout the story, several characters were faced with making moral decisions. Choose one of those characters and determine if you would make the same decision they made. Why or why not?

9. At the end of the novel, Gianna seemed to have found peace in herself. How have other characters

helped Gianna come to terms with her feelings? Do you think she'll be emotionally stable to resume her life in New York?

10. The author emphasizes trust throughout the novel. Which characters and behavior prove this theme?

11. How does the novel's title, Always Faithful and True, connect with Gianna's life and the main theme?

12. How does the novel's subtitle, Psalm 118:5 apply to the story's theme?

13. How realistic was the characterization? Did you like them or hate them? Could you relate to any of them?

14. Did any scene in the book make you feel uncomfortable? If so, why did you feel this way?

15. Did the plot draw you in, or did you find the story to be a drag?

16. Did the story end the way you expected? Were you disappointed?

17. How did the book compare to other Christian romance novels?

18. Would you recommend the book to other readers?